D0773138

THE BIG TRAIL

By Max Brand

THE BIG TRAIL

ÆONIAN PRESS

MATTITUCK

W

211949

Library of Congress Cataloging in Publication Data

Faust, Frederick, 1892-1944.
  The big trail.

  I. Title.
PZ3.F2775Bf9   [PS3511.A87]   813'.5'2   76-41324
ISBN 0-88411-513-5

AEONIAN PRESS, INC.
Box 1200
Mattituck, New York 11952

Manufactured in the United States of America

1

THE BOSS was a hard man, and he was not at great pains to conceal his hardness. He had waited for a week to fill out his judgment upon the new hand, and now his mind was full.

After supper, he went into the bunk house and stood in the door.

"Fuller!" he called.

Tom Fuller leaned his head out of his bunk—he had turned in early—and lowered the magazine which he had been reading, while the vision of Indians, galloping riders, and rescued heroines slowly faded from his mind and was replaced by the solid image of Pete Stringham in the doorway.

"Here!" said Fuller.

The boss took a few long strides into the room.

"Fuller, you're a cow-puncher?"

"I'm a cowboy, I guess," said Fuller.

"Who made you a cow-puncher?" asked the boss.

There was silence.

"It's a sure thing that nature didn't intend you that way," said the boss. "Answer me one thing. Can you handle a rope?"

"Why, I've handled one considerable."

"Sure you have," said the boss, "but did you ever daub it onto a cow and make it fit where you wanted it to go?"

All hands were attentive, with broad grins.

Tom Fuller sat bolt upright, so suddenly that his head landed with a loud thump against the slats of the bunk above him. Then he swung his feet out onto the floor and sat there, wriggling his toes in his socks.

"What's the matter?" asked Tom Fuller.

"I'm askin' you," said the boss. "Who else should I ask? Did you ever daub a rope and make it fit where you wanted it?"

A broader grin passed around the circle, but their eyes dropped to the floor as the boy stared blankly around him. They were in no haste to meet his eye, no matter what their opinion of him might be.

"I dunno," said Fuller thoughtfully.

He raised his head and considered the question.

"I dunno as I've had much luck with a rope," he confessed.

"You know how to tail up a cow?" went on the boss.

"Why, I suppose so," said Fuller gently.

"Dash it! You suppose so, do you? What do the cows suppose?"

There was open laughter at this, and Tom Fuller flushed miserably. He stared down at his wiggling toes and sighed.

"What I mean to say is," said the boss, "did you ever tail a cow up without bustin' her tail?"

There was a loud roar of mirth. And again Tom blushed. Evidently, the taunt had struck home in a tender spot. He looked down at his big hands and muttered:

"The fact is—sometimes things happen that I don't intend!"

"The fact is, that you dunno what you can do and what you can't do!" declared the boss. "Take these!"

He scooped a greasy, well-thumbed pack of cards from the long kitchen table which stood in the center of the room. This pack he tamped solidly together, and then handed it to the boy.

"Tear it in two!" he commanded.

Without a word, Tom Fuller adjusted his grip a little

6

—and suddenly the pack was in two parts. The boss nodded grimly.

"You can do that, eh? But you can't get a rope onto a cow without havin' your hoss pulled flat and you knocked head over heels?"

Tom sighed again, nodding gently as he admitted the truth of this accusation.

"I could bulldog 'em better," he suggested in his mild way.

"You could bulldog 'em, could you? Now, look here, are we workin' on a ranch, or are we runnin' a circus? I ask you that, Fuller!"

The answer was so obvious that even Tom Fuller did not speak. He waited, a haunted look in his eyes.

"If you seen a heifer agin' the sky line, could you tell by the manner of her kickin' what kind of flies was at her?" inquired the boss.

Tom Fuller was silent.

"Can you handle a brandin' iron?"

The boy shook his head.

"When I sent you down to run the new wire on that southeast fence, last week, what happened afterward?"

"The cows busted through the next day," admitted the boy.

This frankness did not appease the boss.

"And they tramped down forty acres of good new wheat, and the old man'll give the dickens to who? To you? No, to me! To me! I'm likely to get the sack because I put a muttonhead on such a job. Cow-puncher? Say! You couldn't herd sheep!"

It was the most terrible condemnation to which a puncher could listen, and the boy hung his head.

"You couldn't herd sheep!" thundered Pete Stringham, raising his voice still higher. "Who ever told you that you could work cows, that's what I'd like to know?"

"Nobody ever told me," admitted the boy.

Again the circle smiled.

They were kindly enough, but it pleased them to watch the grilling of the new man. Not one of them but

7

had had extra work thrust upon his shoulders by the appalling inefficiency of the new hand. They watched, and they only partially swallowed their grins when the blank, tormented eye of the boy fell upon their faces.

"Who dropped the whiskey just last night, and busted it to bits, when everybody was hangin' his tongue out for a drop?" went on the boss.

"I did," sighed the boy.

Dark looks greeted him all around. This was too serious a matter for smiling.

"Who spilled the steak into the coffee pail and left us without any supper to speak of, at the camp?"

"I did," admitted Tom Fuller.

"Bah!" snorted the boss. "Who left the gate unlocked on the hoss corral, and let them mustangs go rampin' over the half of creation?"

"I did," said the boy.

"You did! You're darned right you did! And the rest of us toiled and cussed and wore our hosses out tryin' to get 'em back. And they's still one missin'! You been here seven days. Can you tell me seven things that you've managed to do for the ranch?"

Tom Fuller thought, desperately. His face suddenly flushed—for he blushed very easily—and his forehead knotted.

"I—" he hesitated. "I shot seven coyotes, and a couple of wolves, boss," he said at last.

"You shot some varmints," said the boss, more furious than ever. "Sure, this here has been kind of a huntin' trip, for you. This here has been kind of a pleasure outin' for you, and I say that you been out havin' your good time on a dude ranch, and gettin' paid for it! Is that right?"

Tom Fuller rubbed his big knuckles across his forehead.

"I was tryin' to recollect the pleasure, boss," he said slowly.

There was a brief roar of laughter at this. It ended soon. They were afraid to miss some of this man-baiting by covering it with their noise.

8

"You were tryin' to recollect it," sneered Pete Stringham, "and doggone my hide if I can recollect any pleasure that we've had out of you. If anybody can, let him speak up!"

He dropped his hands on his hips and glared around the circle, but no one spoke. If there were any heart which beat in sympathy with the persecuted new hand, its owner remained silent. It was not worthwhile to challenge Stringham on such a minor point. Jobs were none too plentiful on the range, at that season.

Stringham turned back on the persecuted man.

"I wanta know," he said, "what you gotta say for yourself?"

The boy was silent. He swallowed hard, and before his eyes there rose up the prospect of no work. It often had confronted him before, and he knew all the pangs of one meal a day, and that a scant one. It seemed to him that his famished stomach had hardly been filled by three huge meals a day out here on the ranch.

Suddenly he said: "I'll tell you what, Stringham. I ain't a very slick cowboy, I guess—"

"I guess you ain't," said the other.

"But suppose I was to stay on and work for my board?"

Stringham roared with indignation.

"You eat more'n three men," he said. "If you was to pay me fifty dollars a month, I wouldn't have the boardin' of you, and all the work that you done, it would take three men to undo it! And so they call you 'Honest Tom,' don't they?"

"I been called that at times," said the cow-puncher, fearful of taking too much for granted in this seemingly favorable turn of the conversation.

"They call you that, do they?" retorted Stringham. "Then I'll tell you somethin'. There's some that are honest because they're too dumb to be crooked! If that there shoe fits you, you put it on. You hear me?"

Honest Tom shrank, and blinked.

And this shrinking on his part put a false idea into the mind of the boss. Besides, he had been too much tormented by the new man during the past week, and it was hardly a wonder that his patience now snapped. He stood over Tom Fuller and shouted: "The way you've messed things up, I got a mind to soak you! I got a mind to put an eye on you, you sheep-walkin' Polack!"

"Oh," said Honest Tom.

And he stood up before Stringham.

He was not so tall, by inches. He looked rather sleek and fat about the shoulders, like a man who would quickly be out of wind, but the boss remembered certain details—the broken tail of a cow too forcibly heaved from the mud, the bulldogging of a full-grown maverick, and, just a moment before, the tearing across of that tightly compacted wad of cards.

Stringham stepped back more suddenly than he had stepped forward. There had been no challenge from the boy, but a faint light of pleasure had come up into his eyes, and the boss suddenly understood what it meant. He remembered, too, the seven dead coyotes, and the two dead wolves.

So, changing his mind, he roared with more violence than ever. "When the mornin' comes, I expect you to get out of here, y'understand? The only sign of you that I want to see around here is tracks headin' out!"

He turned on his heel and strode to the door. The other cow-punchers glanced keenly from one to the other. They had not missed the imminence of battle, and they had not missed the reason that the battle had not been fought. In spite of themselves, they depreciated the boss at that instant.

At the door the foreman turned, sneering:

"Cow-puncher? A blacksmith is all that you're fit to be!"

Then he was gone.

10

2

THAT HE WAS stupid, Honest Tom Fuller knew.

He had known it in school, where it was continually pointed out to him by the teachers in words not of one syllable. He knew it by the mockery of his classmates, too. But in the playing yard he had always been able to get back something of his own. The other youngsters might surpass him infinitely in the classroom, but when it came to the sports of the gravel-covered yard they were outmatched.

It never occurred to him to take pride in these physical accomplishments. It never occurred to him that they were of the slightest importance, even when other boys would sometimes draw him aside and say: "Look here, Tommie. I got a sack full of marbles, here. I'll give you half of 'em, and you show me how you can jump so far." Or: "Tommie, how d'you manage to hit so hard? You show me, will you? I'm gunna be your friend."

"There ain't any secret," Tom Fuller used to answer. "You just put your mind on getting there, you see."

"Yeah," would be the sneering answer, "the way that you get there in school, eh?"

To that taunt he never had a reply, for he was well aware of his deficiency.

And sometimes, looking around upon his fellows, he wondered at the brightness, the cleverness, the wonderful wit of all his peers. As for himself, he was always at the bottom of the class, in school, and after he left it.

He was willing to accept the superiority of the others without jealousy, but he could not well understand the bitterness with which they looked upon him. It seemed as though they hated him for his stupidity.

"Honest Tom, all beef and no brains!"

They used to taunt him with such words as these, and the sting of them had troubled him so often that there was a numb place somewhere in his heart—that place where cruel usage lodges!

Sometimes it seemed to him that, in the course of the years, the cloud in which he lived was lifting a little, and that he could look through it to a brighter future, where all things lay more clearly defined under a bluer sky, and under a more kindly sun. But the cloud never was quite gone.

He went to a doctor, once, and asked him if there was anything wrong with his head. The doctor was a very old and a very kind man, and he looked at the boy with the dim eyes of gentle wisdom.

"In our-lives there are turning points," he said to Tom. "One day the child turns into the boy. One day the boy turns into the youth. One day the youth turns into the man. I remember when I turned into a man. I'd fallen off a rafter in the barn. I was up hunting for pigeons' nests, high in the mow. I fell and gave myself a bad knock. And all at once I realized that I was not writhing around or groaning. I was simply lying there and accepting the pain, and setting my teeth against it. Well, I'd become a man. Do you understand?"

Tom could understand that, fairly well, and he said so.

"There's nothing wrong with your head," said the doctor. "On the contrary, it's a well-shaped head. It's big, and it's built in the right fashion. There's plenty above the ears, as they say, and plenty behind them, too! If you find that other people consider you dull, no matter. You're called 'Honest Tom,' I believe?"

"Some people have called me that."

"Then I can tell you this. There's no one in the world more wise than the honest man, because he's the only one who really exists, and really lives. Can you understand that?"

"No," said Tom. "I can't."

"Well, some day I think you will. And in the meantime, another day may come along when you'll wake up. You'll break through the mist. Do you understand what the mist is?"

"No," said Tom, "except that I don't know what other people know."

"Knowledge," said the doctor, "is simply a store of facts arranged together in systems. You have plenty of facts. Ten times as many as the average man. You have your compensations, because your eyes are clearer, your hearing is more sensitive, and your hands are stronger than those of your companions. And, after a time, it may be that a crisis will come in your life when suddenly you'll see the relation between all the facts with which your mind is now stored. And then you will have that brightness which you notice in other people."

"How shall I bring the time on?" said Tom with a bitter eagerness.

"That I can't tell," said the doctor. "That's in the hands of Providence, as I well may say. But, in the meantime, forget the things that you are without. Cling to what you are. Remain above all, honest. Then you are sure to lead a worthy life. If I were a prophet, my lad, sent down from heaven, I could not tell you a truer thing than that. Be honest, be kind, be brave, and the greatest minds in the world will find ways in which they can look up to you!"

A good deal of the speech slipped over the mind, or through the mind, of the boy, but there was so much directness about a part of it, that it could not fail to cling in his memory. So that he left the wise counselor with the vague hope that, one day, the fog would be blown from his mind and that he would find himself walking over the ridges of the world, and looking clearly down into the deepest shadows of the hollows.

This secret hope had warmed his heart in many a cold moment of despair, and it warmed him again, on

13

the morning when he left the ranch and rode to town. The sun was low in the east, but its heat already was beginning. The light shimmered upward from the rocks, or clung in the dew of the grass, and the songs of birds flashed here and there, driving loudly down the wind, and more suddenly snatched away into the background of murmurs and of music.

To these things, Tom Fuller listened with his head raised, and a little smile of joy upon his lips, though the sad look never quite left his eyes, for trouble and pain and self-distrust were too deeply imprinted in his soul. However, this outward world was more than a mere outwardness to him, and somehow it slipped through his eyes and through his ears and fed a starved self which never had food from human companionship. It seemed to Tom Fuller that the loftiest rock range was a gentle thing compared with the hardness of other men, and the ways of a wolf were simple and genuinely kind contrasted with the keen, cruel ways of wolfish man!

With this in his mind, he enjoyed himself without stint, as he passed through the countryside, always looking ahead, and never trusting himself to glance backward at the range where he had failed once more.

So many failures!

His life was paved with them. To every place he had known, and to the faces of all the men, and to the events of all his days, failure, failure and more failure, was hitched by association, so that he groaned inwardly. He could not look back. He could not look to the future with any confidence whatever. But he could let the landscape and the creatures of the landscape flow inward upon his mind and find a pure content in them.

The road swung over the brow of a hill and suddenly he halted his horse. For beneath him, in the hollow, he saw the town, with the shadowy half of the roofs still wet with dew, and the windows blazing, here and there in the morning light. Smoke rose from the chimneys and swayed out to the south, hardly able to climb. The whole town was surrounded by groves of trees, and the streets themselves were outlined by fine trees, as well. It made as pretty a picture as one could ask of a village, with the silver of the river flowing at its side, but it gave nothing but pain to the boy.

Here were men, again, blotting the landscape, as they blotted his life with their cruel sharpness of wit, more sharp than a cat's tooth!

And he wondered why it was that he had to cast in his lot with them, continually. Other creatures could survive in the wilderness; only men had to herd together, join hand to hand, work with the power of one another. In those human chains, he was always the misfitted link, and was cast out quickly.

However, he had learned to endure this pain. He drew in a deep breath and went on down the hill, and crossed the bridge, and entered the town.

He paused again at the head of the main street and looked at the signs. Carpenter, mason, store, coal and feed yard. He had tried all of these things, and he had failed in them all. He looked down at his big hands. Was there nothing that he could do?

Then he heard something like the tinkling of a bell. And he rode toward it as one in a dream.

The noise grew louder and louder, as he passed down the street, looking at one sign after another, feeling beforehand the emptiness, the hunger, which would beset him at noon—and then the tinkling as of a bell grew into a rhythmical chiming, and then a crashing, clangoring sound of hammers thundering upon a forge.

That noise ended.

Out from a doorway, carrying a wisp of the black forge smoke about his shoulders like some newly born spirit, ran a tall, wide-shouldered stripling, and behind him, in the door of the blacksmith shop, a big man, gray-haired, bare-armed, girt in a leather apron, roared oaths after him.

The boy turned, shook his fist at the big man, and then took to his heels as the blacksmith lurched a step after him.

15

Suddenly, Honest Tom remembered the last words of his last employer.

"Blacksmith!"

Well, if that was what he was fitted for, he would accept his fate. He would give up the shining open country. He had given it up many a time before, but those sacrifices had been in vain. Yet perhaps the bitterness of Pete Stringham had made him see the truth. His eye had been sharpened by malice until he was able to see to the central problem of his useless cow-puncher.

"Hullo!" said Tom.

The blacksmith glared at him.

"You want a helper? Is that one fired?" asked Tom.

The other glared again.

Then he beckoned with a grimy finger and, turning his back, he led the way into his shop. Tom swung down from the saddle and followed.

The thick-and-acrid odor of the coal smoke choked his lungs and made him cough.

"You're fat. You're too fat," said the blacksmith. "Can you hold that straight out by the handle?"

And he passed a fourteen-pound sledge to Tom. The boy took it by the end of the handle and held it straight out.

"Take off your coat," said the blacksmith. "Maybe you've come home!"

3

It was one thing to make a sudden muscular effort and hold out the heavy sledge hammer with one hand. It was still another to swing a fourteen-pound sledge hammer for the long hours which remained in that day.

But there was little respite.

Charlie Boston, which was the blacksmith's name, was forging some huge angle irons to use in the building of a bridge, and Charlie never gave under weight, either in his work or with his fists. Those irons he was barely commencing on, and he toiled at them without ceasing. It was a rush order, and could not be delayed. If it were executed in time, other orders were pouring in from the county supervisors. Therefore, Charlie Boston was ready to do his best, and he demanded the best from his new assistant.

When the great mass of iron, which Boston steadied with his huge tongs, was laid upon the forge, he turned it here and there, and gave the strokes of direction with an eight-pound sledge, which alone, in his capable hands, would do the work of an ordinary twelve or fourteen-pounder, but the instant that his smaller hammer had landed, he expected it to be followed with crushing force by the larger tool.

And this required labor almost without surcease.

When the iron cooled, it was thrust back into the fire, but then Tom Fuller had to work at the bellows. They were of the most antiquated pattern, old, ponderous,

17

working with a groan at every move, so that some huge animal seemed dying in agony in the shop, and furthermore, the bellows leaked mysteriously, so that the boy had to redouble his hand power on the lever. His master was too busy regarding the fire, stacking the coal so that it would produce the hottest flame next to the skin of the iron, frowning into the smoke, and beating it away with his great hands so that he could regard the metal more carefully.

Then out came the great lump of iron again, and there was more hammering, endlessly. The first moments were not so bad. The heat-softened mass yielded pleasantly under the tremendous strokes which Tom Fuller bestowed upon it, and all went well, so long as the sparks were spurting beneath the hammer face, but as soon as the metal darkened, then the work was doubly difficult. The hammer sprang back with a jar, and the hammer handle tore at the hands of Tom.

He had a fine coat of blisters in a single hour. Before noon, the blisters broke, the hammer handle became crimson. Still he gritted his teeth and said not a word.

For it seemed to him that there had truly been a prophecy in the words of Pete Stringham. He must have known. A blacksmith was what he was intended to be! Moreover, what else was there left for him to do? He had tried so many things, and he had failed in them all! So he sighed, and bent to his work, and taught his body a sway from shoulder to heel which eased the work, getting into a comfortable rhythm, only to have the terrible Boston roaring:

"Are you sleepin'? Faster! Faster! You're one of them that wants the fire to do all of his work for him! Faster, by gosh, or I'll keep you at it an hour when it's cold!"

He did not speak back.

There soon came a time when he could not answer, for fear lest the voice he spoke with should be a hopeless groan.

When noon came, the handle of the hammer was red,

18

but Boston appeared to see nothing of this. He led the way to his house.

"What sort of pay you want, kid?" asked Boston.

"I don't care," said Honest Tom. "I want a job. That's all."

"Is that worryin' you?" asked Boston. "Ain't the whole country full of work?"

"Sure it is," muttered Tom, "but not for me. I've been everything from a dry-goods clerk to a brick layer. I couldn't make a go of anything! Well, maybe I can learn to swing a hammer."

The other glanced keenly at him.

"You come on home and eat," said he.

He led the way to a surprisingly neat little house, with a wonderfully tidy little gray-haired woman in charge of it. She seemed appalled and astonished by the sooty appearance of her husband and she actually held up her hands at Tom's condition. However, he had a basin of hot water to wash his damaged and swelling hands. Suddenly she cried out: "Look, Charlie! Land alive, if the boy's hands ain't raw!"

"Bah!" said Charlie Boston. "Women and fools is always afraid of a coupla blisters. It's good for hardenin' the hands. If the kid had ever done enough honest work to keep warm, his hands wouldn't be so tender!"

"I never heard of such a thing," said Mrs. Boston, and with a great deal of skill she bandaged the raw places with rags and plaster. Still, his hands seemed to be on fire, and, after lunch, he went out on the back porch and lay flat on his back, aching, with waves of fatigue rushing into his brain. It seemed that he had lain there only a moment when the harsh voice of Charlie Boston roused him.

He had to start back for the inferno of the shop, and the first time he grasped the hammer, it seemed as though its weight were tearing the flesh from the bones of his hands. But he closed the fingers one by one, resolutely.

"It's this, or else to be a wandering bum!" said he.

19

And he thought of stolen rides on freight cars, of frozen nights in the fields, of crime, filth, and slow degradation. So he clung to his last hope in clinging to the handle of the sledge, and gradually the thing became endurable.

All that afternoon, his labor went on at what seemed an equal pace to him; if Charlie Boston slowed the rhythm, the boy did not notice. By five o'clock he was dizzy, almost staggering, when Mrs. Boston appeared with coffee, stewed prunes and bread. He ate a little, and drank greedily of the coffee until his brain cleared and gave him courage to continue. But longer than any month of his life was the period from this tea time to the close of the work. They labored until the forge fire cast more light in the shop than the sun; then the blacksmith reluctantly resigned his day's task.

"Where you going to live?" he asked. "The hotel?"

"I dunno," said Tom, his brain utterly numbed.

"You come home with me."

Tom went home with Charlie Boston. The bandages on his hads were sodden rags, and Mrs. Boston dressed them again, muttering fiercely. He ate a vast supper, but when it came to bedtime, and he was shown into a little white-painted room, he was barely able to take off his clothes, so stiff and sore were his fingers. His whole body ached for that matter.

He closed his eyes, and was called almost instantly, it seemed to him, for the beginning of the next day. At last he dragged himself to a sitting position and, looking down at his hands, wondered how he could use them even for dressing, let alone for seizing the ponderous hammer.

But that was only a beginning.

The first day was bad enough. The second day was terrible. The third day was a sword of fire that searched his very soul.

But then suddenly affairs began to improve a little. He felt, for his own part, that a sort of superhuman grace had been extended to him, partly because he had made a great effort, and partly because mercy had been taken upon him from above! But at any rate, he found it possible to keep at his work.

His powerful body, first of all, grew accustomed to that straining labor. At the end of the first week, he had nothing to think of except the pain of his raw hands. But even these were beginning to heal in places, and the healed parts were as tough as leather. There is an intricate mystery in the art of changing and adjusting grips, and of this art he became the master, for pain taught him the best ways. Yet the first ten days always appeared to Tom Fuller as a red mist, through which voices, faces, things, appeared dimly. And what was registered finally in his brain was a sense of exhaustion, a dull-red iron cooling on the anvil, and the tapping hammer of Charlie Boston, relentlessly showing the way, and insisting upon more speed.

But like one who has passed through the fire, after this his sufferings became more endurable. It was possible for him to stand at ease before the anvil. The fourteen-pound sledge was the merest toy in his hands. The least scruple of fat had been clawed from his body by the long agony through which he had passed, and the appearance of sleekness about his face and his shoulders was totally deceptive. But as the shoulder and the forearm of a tiger seem softly sleek, so did he appear, and the reality of both was much the same. From right to left, and from left to right, alternating his swing, he could whirl the great sledge and make it flash like a dancing sword. And, with that alternate beat, the blows would fall so fast that it seemed that two men were working at the forge. He cared not for the greatness of the work. His hands were hard, his body was accustomed to the sway and the beat of the thing, and he made this labor a trifle, a jest.

It did not seem to him that he was beating iron, but that he was hammering his own chance in the world into shape. He was securing himself from all disaster!

As soon as he was accustomed to things, he began to feel at home, and gratitude flowed out from his heart. On Sundays he used to work in the garden and the little or-

21

chard of Charlie Boston, while the young men of the town went by, laughing and talking to one another.

"He ain't a man; he's a hoss!" they would say.

Tom did not care, for Mrs. Boston approved of him.

"It's almost like havin' a son in the house," said she.

Charlie Boston would say nothing, but sometimes his cloudy brows descended and gathered above his eyes, and from those eyes out shot a spark that went to the very heart of the youngster.

At those times, he was vastly uneasy; he could not understand; but well he knew that in the mind of Charlie Boston some conclusion about his assistant already had been reached. Later on, he could find out what that conclusion was.

But, when it came, it was like a thunderbolt to Tom Fuller.

It was on a Sunday that word was brought that a man driving through town with a team of mustangs and a buckboard needed new shoes for his span. That was too profitable an order to be passed, week day or Sunday, and so Tom was ordered into his working clothes. Walking hurriedly down to the forge with his master, he saw before the locked doors of the shop the man with whom his destiny was to be so strangely entangled.

4

HE WAS a tall man of fifty or fifty-five, slenderly made, and the rough clothes which he wore looked totally out of place on him. A neat mustache, snowy white, gave a touch of refinement to his face, even when Tom Fuller saw him in the distance. And when the boy came closer, he was more assured that this was no ordinary traveler, no ordinary ranchman. He had the face of a student, topped by a great, pyramidal brow and sunken eyes of study. Those eyes were gently meditative, and the whole upper part of the face was suggestive of retired, unpractical thought. But the chin, and the aquiline nose, were made narrow and long and denied all the promise of the brow and eyes. If he were a man of thought, he was also a man of action, and the boy was sure of it at a glance, for he had something of a child's ability to read character. There was such dignity and personality in this man that his wrinkled linen duster fell from his shoulders like a robe of state.

He had attracted a great deal of attention, already. His mustangs were a most ordinary pair, and his buckboard was covered with dust. There was nothing about his turnout to take the eye of the village boys, but half a dozen of them were gathered about with a vaguely expectant air. Others were coming, and Sunday loungers were beginning to approach.

"Howd'ye?" said the blacksmith, as he came up and fitted his key into the big lock upon his doors.

"Well, I thank you," said the stranger.

And the boy stared at him. He had almost forgotten that "howd'ye" was a question, and not merely a casual greeting.

The doors opened. Tom Fuller began to unhitch the horses, and the stranger stood by, gently stroking his mustache, his manner as abstracted as though it never occurred to him to lend a hand to the business.

The mustangs were duly unhitched, but they were an unruly pair, newly broken, tough as nails, and wild as antelope. When the bellows groaned the first note of preparation, under the hand of Tom, the cream-colored mare jerked back with such force that she pulled the hitching ring fairly out of the wall. She whirled and started to bolt, but mere chance threw the swinging ring into the hands of Tom, and he swayed back with all his might. There was a heavy shock that snapped his body like the cracker on the end of a whip lash; then the mare toppled head over heels. Tom helped her up, and she stood trembling, and blinking, more than half stunned.

He tied her to a stronger place, and by a shorter rope, while the stranger approached in a leisurely way and examined the lead rope. Then he turned to look at the boy.

Tom, beginning at the bellows again, noted a peculiar, secret smile on the face of Charlie Boston, and he wondered at this. But he was accustomed to being bewildered by the sneers and the mockeries of men, and he accepted this as another mystery which he could not penetrate.

In the meantime, the forge fire began to hiss and the heavy fumes of coal smoke arose and clouded the sooty rafters. Tom, working the bellows with long, powerful strokes, looked upward, contentedly. He was glad to see the smoke, he was pleased even by the familiar look of the rafters, by the bulging faces of the hammers which leaned against the wall, and by all the evidences of the work with which he was growing acquainted. Far ahead of him lay the greater and profounder mysteries of

24

smithery. The welding of iron, the guiding of hammer blows in the forging of it to new shapes, the neat precision of Charlie Boston in roughing out with hammer strokes the most intricate patterns. And if he sighed a little as he thought of all that lay before him to be learned, he did not begrudge the years of effort. He was willing to be a blacksmith; there was no great ambition in Tom beyond the desire to live without too much humanly inflicted pain.

He looked down to his hands, and the leathered thickness of the skin was a comfort to him. He drew a great breath, and felt the pull of the muscles across his stomach and shoulders. He was fit. He never before had been half so strong, and it was a quiet delight to him.

Then the shoe was drawn out of the fire, the anvil work was beginning delicately, with quick, small blows. The boy, with knotted brow of attention and effort, did his best, and Charlie Boston lashed him mercilessly with his tongue.

"You ain't beating angle irons!" said he. "Neither are you tryin' to sink a ship! D'you wanta flatten the anvil or bash it into the ground? Ain't you got any feelin' in your hands? You handle a hammer like you had four feet, instead of two. I never seen such a man! What's in your head? Gimme that hammer and stand back and try to watch. You have eyes; try to see with 'em, will you?"

This brutal talk humbled the boy, but it did not crush him, since for weeks he had listened to a similar strain constantly pouring from the lips of his master. He stepped back obediently, while the idle circle of onlookers snickered.

And he stared around at them with another sigh.

Beside him, there was a tall fellow of eighteen, full of his new-found manhood, glorious in spurs and chaps, jingling with brilliant conchas. He stood with legs braced wide apart, conscious of himself, of his six brawny feet of height, of his wide shoulders, and of the increasing weight of his hands.

"Am I standin' in your light, kid?" said he to Tom.

"No, no," said Tom, in haste.

For he hated trouble, unless it were thrust upon him. And though the companions he had found on the ranch had learned the strength of his arm, he never had taken advantage of that strength. He was like a very sleepy bull terrier, smiling at battles, but leaving them to his dreams.

"You're standin' in mine, though, 'Lanky!" bellowed Charlie Boston. "Kid, grab him and throw him out, will you?"

"Let him try it!" said the new-made puncher.

"You better go home," said Tom to him, gently.

"Why, you Polack—" began the youngster.

Tom gathered him firmly in his arms. There seemed to be yards and yards of writhing, tugging, cursing humanity. He bore the burden forward. A wildly outthrust heel sank into the flank of the cream-colored mare, and she squealed with surprise and with pain.

The spur had cut her a little, and Tom saw a streak of red.

"You better be quiet," he said, and drew his burden closer to his breast.

All struggling ceased with one great gasp.

At the door he set the lad upon his feet, but found that he had to support him, while the other leaned over, drawing in groaning breaths.

"I hope you ain't hurt," said Tom. "You were in Charlie's light. Maybe you better go home?"

This he said seriously, as good advice, for the puncher was very pale. But all around them the children had gathered, chattering like magpies, chuckling, dancing with delight in mischief.

The tall youth, able to straighten at last, had now sufficient wind in his lungs to make other thoughts possible. He looked upon the impish faces of the boys, and suddenly he realized his disgrace. Far worse than death, to his young pride!

"You—you—" he yelled at Tom. "I'm gunna blow you inside out."

For he remembered that he was wearing a gun. He reached for it with a well-practiced motion.

26

Old hands will tell you that there is nothing more dangerous than a youngster on the range. He has not learned to settle into his saddle and his boots and accept his job as work. He is still in the red light of romance, and horses, and guns, and bright spurs, fill his mind, so that he is apt to spend endless hours of practice in snatching his revolver out according to the best Wild West model. He is always preparing for a bar-room fight, and because he is so well prepared, sooner or later he is fairly sure to have it. So this boy snatched out his Colt from the holster which was buckled low down on his thigh—the approved position, said the romances!—but as it flashed up, and as the children shrieked suddenly with fear, a long steel barrel flicked across his wrist, his fingers were numbed by the stroke, and his own gun fell into the dust while he found another weapon hanging from the right hand of Tom Fuller.

Tom leaned and, picking up the fallen weapon, handed it to the other.

"You better go home," he said in the same gentle voice.

And this time his advice was taken.

The tall boy started off with a downward head and with a shambling stride, but Tom ran after him, and touched his arm. The youth turned, his face white with grief and with shame, his eyes burning. He had been beaten, but there was still danger in him. He felt that his life was ruined, and, therefore, he was quite willing to throw it away.

"You?" he barked at Tom. "Whacha want?"

"Don't you feel bad," said Tom. "That was a trick my father taught me. Don't you feel bad, partner. I'd rather like to shake hands before you go!"

This he said with an eye so open, and so gentle, and a face of such perfect belief and good nature that the youngster was stunned. He had lived among the young bullies of the range, and had fought his way to an accepted place among them. He blinked, and then, overwhelmed by a philosophy which was not his own, he stretched out an uncertain hand.

"I've been a fool!" he muttered.

"No, no," said Tom. "I guess that things you can forget won't do you any harm!"

So his hand closed, gently, carefully, upon the hand of the other. He went back to the blacksmith shop to take up his work, and about him flocked the boys of the town. They had been laughing for a month at this stranger. They had been shying stones at him when he went down the street, and they had been winking at each other, shrugging their shoulders as he passed with his handsome, troubled, and unlighted face.

But now they had changed their minds. He was something more than the half-wit they had taken him for. He was, to their eyes, a great hero, and by the greatness of the fall of his last opponent he was just so much elevated and increased.

So they buzzed and murmured, and congratulated him, and admired him mightily, and turned up their shining faces toward him as flowers turn up to see the sun. But that atmosphere of joy was suddenly shattered at the door of the shop by the roar of Charlie Boston:

"Where'n heck have you been? On a pleasure trip? You been out takin' a Sunday walk and lookin' at the pretty girls? Come in here and work this here bellows!"

5

HE WENT back to the bellows, shamed, and, stealing a glance at the downward face of Boston, studying the fire in the forge, he was astonished to see on that face the same fierce smile of secret delight which he had noticed there before.

He began to dream about the possible solution of this mystery, but there was little time for dreaming, now. The shoes were turned out with all the rapidity of an expert, and soon their design had been burned into the hoofs of the horses, and the shoes remodeled, and the hoofs whittled down.

At last, the eight shoes were in the tempering tub. Nothing remained except to nail them on, and this business Tom himself could do as well as another. He delighted in taking a hoof under his knee, in sending in the long soft-iron nails with a few smart blows, and in clinching the ends of the nails against the buffing iron. In this work he had attained to such proficiency that the casual eye, looking in, might have taken him for a master workman in the craft.

He finished the cream-colored mare, in fact, almost as quickly as the master finished the other, and as he straightened up, panting, but proud of himself, he saw what shocked him far more than anything else that had happened upon this day. Both of those older men were looking at him. Upon each face there was the slightest of smiles, and in each smile it seemed to the boy that he could see the identical elements of amusement, knowledge that was secret, and, beyond this, a somewhat savage satisfaction.

It was, in short, the very smile which he had noted twice before on the lips of Charlie Boston. And now he shrugged his shoulders and gave up the struggle to understand. This was merely one of the many closed doors through which he might not pass!

"Will you tell me your name, young man?" said the stranger.

"Yes, sir," answered Tom. "I'm Thomas Fuller."

"Thomas," said the stranger, "I'm Oliver Champion. I'm very glad to know you."

"My hand is dirty," said Tom, scrubbing it vainly against the soot and the iron dust of his leather apron.

"I'm glad to shake it, though," said the other. "Now, Tom, will you tell me the name of your father, too?"

Tom parted his lips to obey, but a second thought made him close them again. He flushed.

"The name of your father?" said the other, quietly persistent, as though he thought that Tom had not heard him the first time.

"My father—he died a long while ago," said Tom faintly.

"Too bad," said Oliver Champion. "Your mother raised you, then, I guess?"

"No. I never seen her. She died. I was born. It was that way, you understand."

"I understand. That makes it hard on youngsters. Now, then, Tom, that trick with the gun, that you used just now—I've never seen such a thing done before!"

"It's not hard," said Tom. "It's quicker to get a gun from under your coat than it is to get it out of a side holster. You try it, Mr. Champion; you'll see how much quicker."

"I'll try it," said Champion gravely. "Of course, I'll try it. One needs to know such things, out in this country."

"No, sir," said Tom. "I guess you wouldn't need it."

"Because I'm too old for gun fighting?" asked Champion in his quiet manner. "Ah, I'm old enough, I'm old enough," he went on, "but the brand of whisky they drink in this part of the world sometimes steals away their sense of color. I've met fellows who couldn't tell whether my hair was black or white!"

He chuckled a little at this reminiscence, in such a satisfied manner that one would have thought that whatever danger of death he may have undergone in it was merely a stimulant to him.

"That's a true thing," said Charlie Boston. "The hills is full of them."

"Although newspapers say that the old West is dead," commented Oliver Champion.

"They say it! They say it!" said Charlie Boston. "Lemme tell you, Mr. Champion, that the old West ain't dead, and it ain't never gunna die, and I could tell you why, too!"

He said this with an air of the most profound knowledge, and he wagged a finger at the stranger until Champion said: "Why, that's a thing that I should like to know."

"Lemme tell you," said Charlie Boston, "that them that traveled out by pony trains and smoked pipes with the Injuns, and took Injun scalps, and white scalps, too —those folks thought that the old West was dead when the ox wagons begun to roll and squeak across the prairies; and them that traveled by ox teams, they thought that when mules come along, they killed the old days dead; and them that come by stagecoach sure seemed like a new day and the end of the old times, when they came along, and the mule skinners rolled their eyes and seen the coach go by in a cloud of dust. And then comes the railroad and everybody says that the East is sure let all through the West, and there ain't any more West at all."

As he paused here to take breath, Mr. Champion nodded encouragement and interest, and the blacksmith went on:

"They was a further step, when the automobiles came along. And they say that the automobiles are

31

gunna fill this land. But I say they ain't. Automobiles, and trains, and all the rest, they're gunna go only where people are, and where people've gone before 'em. But I can show you deserts where water ain't never gunna be brought, and mountains that ain't never gunna support no dude ranches, and rivers that'll never turn no power wheels. And that's what the West is! It's the country where they's room to breathe, room to think, room to step and hit nobody's corns but your own. That's what the West is, Mr. Champion, and that West ain't dead, and it never ain't gunna be dead, nor the time ain't ever gunna come when a few wild men don't ride out from that there desert, and over them hills! And I tell you, too, that the time'll never come when the West'll be safe for a fool!"

Mr. Champion laughed a little at this, but he agreed promptly: "It is true," he said, "that there are places which never will be crowded with people. And it is true that the wilderness brings out wild children. I've never looked at it in just that light before. I'm glad you said that to me."

"You're welcome," said the blacksmith. "My father said it to me. I just added automobiles, and finished the thing up. That speech it's been in our family for two generations, now, because my pa learned it from his old man. Only, he added railroads to the lingo. You see that it's been with us so long that we ought to know something about the idea!"

He laughed, and welcomed the laugh of the stranger.

Suddenly Champion turned on the boy again.

"Fuller? Fuller?" said he. "I've heard that name a good many times before. I've heard that name a good many times! Let me see. There was a Washington Fuller, or some such name—notorious gun fighter—I don't suppose that was your father?"

The boy was dumb.

"You mean the man that made Montana into his own backyard and throwed his broken bottles out the window and all over the State? Is that the one that you mean?" asked the blacksmith.

32

"That's the one," said Champion. "Washington Fuller. I'm not surprised that you're not his son. A good deal of a fellow was Washington Fuller, as I understand it."

"A good deal of a fellow!" echoed the blacksmith. "Why, I'll tell you for a fact. I've seen him!"

"You have?"

"I seen him. When he was in his palmy days just before his finish. That was when he was raisin' Cain around Toomah. I seen him come into a saloon, up there, and I seen him stand at the bar and order drinks for about a hundred people for an hour. There he stood, shakin' his long black hair back over his shoulders every time that he took a drink, and never lookin' behind him, as calm as you please—and twenty men in that crowd that would've give a lot to soak a knife into him, if they'd had a chance!"

"Why so?" asked Oliver Champion. "I have always understood that Washington Fuller was a very decent sort of a fellow."

"Nobody's decent to a yegg, and a sneak, and an ordinary, money-grubbin' houn'," said the blacksmith, "if they's a big enough price on his head!"

"Ah, that's true. He carried a price on his head, of course."

"Fifteen thousand dollars, the day he was killed!"

"Ah, that's a great deal."

"It sure is. He carried more'n ten thousand dollars for more'n five years, which is longer, and more, and further than anybody else ever toted that much gold around in the hair of his head."

He chuckled as he said it.

"Washington Fuller, he was just a large slice of trouble, I reckon," said the blacksmith, "and some folks say that he was the worst of all the murderin'—"

He stopped. A painful sound had come from Tom Fuller. And, as he uttered this murmur, he raised his hand to check the flow of the blacksmith's words.

"What's the matter, kid?" asked the blacksmith harshly, bending his darkest frown upon the boy.

"Why, I wanted to say—" began Tom, and paused again.

"You wanted to say what? Say it, then, if you ain't dumb!"

Oliver Champion, too, frowned suddenly on the boy, as though infuriated by this interruption of an amusing and instructive conversation. At this sudden focusing of attention upon him, young Tom Fuller grew tongue tied. Besides, it was hard for him to speak the thing which was at the end of his tongue.

At length he muttered: "Why, there was something in my mind," said Tom. "But it just jumped out ag'in."

"It must've been something tolerable light," said Charlie Boston, "to get as high as that head of yours!"

"I must go on," said Oliver Champion. "You've done a good job with the horses. You'll let me put a dollar or two extra on the bill and—"

"Stranger," said the blacksmith, "if you was a Creeshus, I wouldn't have no use for your spare change. I ain't a waiter that takes tips. But I'm mighty glad that you like my work."

"Speaking of Washington Fuller," said Oliver Champion, "I would like to know—"

"Don't!" cried Tom.

"Don't what?" roared his master.

"Don't talk about him. You got a world full of people to talk about, and why you gotta settle on him?"

"What's he to you?" bellowed Charlie Boston.

"He? My father," said the boy.

34

6

HE WAS leading out the two mustangs to back them into their places on either side of the buckboard's tongue, but now he halted a moment and faced Charlie Boston. He confronted the blacksmith with fear, for he felt certain that now he had lost another position. And it appeared that he was right.

Charlie Boston shouted out something inarticulate.

Then, as his speech became soluble into syllables, he was heard to cry: "Have I been keeping the blood of that man killer under my own roof? What's the matter with my eyes? And I seen Wash Fuller there in Toomah, standin' at the bar that day—What's the matter with my eyes, anyway? Why, the kid's a picture of him!"

"The picture of Washington Fuller?" asked the stranger.

"Why, sure, if his hair was a bit longer!"

"Well, well," said Oliver Champion. "It's a strange thing that I should have hit upon the name so quickly!"

"It is a strange thing," said the blacksmith. "Washington Fuller! Why, doggone me if it don't put a regular chill right into my old bones, Mr. Champion!"

Poor Tom began to tremble with excitement, with grief, and the beginning of indignation.

"Boston," he said sadly, "do you think that my father was the kind that would do a murder?"

The other roared: "Murder? No, it ain't murder—it's

35

gun fightin', ain't it? That's what it's called. A fine fair fight! Here I am, an honest man, stickin' to my work, never seein' a gun except for a coupla weeks of deer shootin' in the fall of the year—here I am, and a hound of a gun fightin' bully comes along—is that a fair fight? Why, he uses his guns pretty near to feed his face with them. He pretty near writes his name with 'em. He spends more money on that gun and buyin' it powder and lead to eat than he spends on his own ham and eggs! The only way that he can talk is with his gun. He says: 'Howdyedo,' and leaves you deader'n mud on the groun'! That's the kind of a man that your father was! Stand up and say no, if you dare!"

All this might have been endured, for the boy was fond of Charlie Boston, and accustomed to his rough talk, to a grain of real kindness which he thought he had discovered in him, to the gentle ways of Mrs. Boston, to the neat, white-painted bedroom, and above all, to the work in the shop. He was accustomed to all these things, and he felt sick at the thought of leaving them for anything else. He had felt that the future was settled, and that, at last, he stood upon bed rock.

Now, in a moment, the work was undone.

He went swiftly back in his mind over the stages—the appearance of the tall boy in the gay new dress of a cow-puncher—the quelling of him by a grasp of the arms—the jerk of his hand for a gun—

What else would he have done, except to conjure his own weapon out, as his father had taught him in the old days? What else but bring it out and tap the boy across his wrist? There was a quicker way, to be sure, and that was to strike with his fist and bring the youngster down, but he had learned almost to prefer his gun to his fist. The lunge of his arm he could not control, nor the iron hardness of his closed hand. It cracked a rib, or smashed a jaw, or opened up a cheek to the bone at a single stroke. It seemed half hammer, and half sword— so did men go down before it! Those blows never were forgiven, and he who was struck remained an enemy for

36

life. His way had left enough of these people behind him.

So, with malice banished from his mind, he had drawn that gun and tapped the boy on the wrist, unnerving his fingers. But the very kindness which was in his mind had betrayed him into mentioning his father, and from that had come about his downfall.

Still he had hoped to turn aside the storm with meekness, until he saw Charlie Boston raging toward him in one of his quick furies. He took a breath.

Then he made a quick little step to meet Boston, though he still kept the lead ropes in his left hand.

"I don't want to have no trouble, Boston," he said.

The blacksmith halted in mid-stride.

"Look at him!" he shouted to Oliver Champion. "Look at him! Kind of a peaceful sight, ain't he? Kind of a good thing to have around your house, ain't he? Look at him—ready to eat nails!"

Painfully the boy uncurved the taut fingers of his right hand. Painfully he removed his glance from the broad jaw of Boston.

"All right," said he. "I suppose you're through with me, Boston?"

"Through with you? I'll tell a man that I'm through with you! You can have your pay, now. Go jerk your blankets out of my house, and come back here. I'll pay you off. Leave the hosses be. I'll hitch them up. Not another lick of work do I want out of you!"

He went with a trailing step and a downward head back to the little white house, in its cloud of climbing vines. He went to his room and made up his pack with automatic hands, his teeth set, because of the ache in his heart.

When the pack was strapped hard, he went with it to the kitchen, and found Mrs. Boston rolling out biscuit dough, her hands pale with flour.

"Why, hello! And what does the pack mean, Tom?" she asked.

"I gotta go away," he said. "I gotta go away. He doesn't want me anymore!"

He looked at her with sorrowful eyes, hoping against hope that she would break out into her soft-voiced exclamations, and run protesting to her husband. For he knew that she was fond of him. As for the big blacksmith, he was such a cross-grained composition that it was hard to tell what he had in his mind, and he never had been sure of him as he was sure of Mrs. Boston.

However, though she first exclaimed and even threw out her hands to the boy, she caught them back to her again.

"Ah, well, poor Tom!" she said.

That was all.

Although she looked at him with tears in her eyes, there was no more than the exclamation of "Poor Tom!"

It seemed to show that, no matter what fondness she had for him, she knew that he was worthless material. She said it as one might have spoken, he felt, of a worthless dog—good for a house pet and good for nothing else!

Then he stretched out his hand and shook hers, and somehow he was out on the back porch and gone toward the little barn, glad to be away before she should have seen the moisture in his eyes. And yet, all the time, he was saying to himself that something was wrong—something which he could not understand.

Or did the whole world take a fierce pleasure in trampling upon him?

He saddled his veteran, tough-mouthed mustang in the corral, and mounted him, with the straps tied over his luggage. Then he went down the alley and into the street. Any way rather than the way past the blacksmith shop!

He had turned down the street, therefore, when a huge voice thundered behind him, and looking back, there was big Charlie Boston standing in the middle of the street, waving.

Gladly he jerked the head of the mustang around and jogged it back, for it occurred to him that Boston might have recovered his temper and realized that he was sending his willing assistant away for no real reason at all.

When he reached the front of the blacksmith shop, he found Oliver Champion in the act of climbing into his seat, holding the reins hard over the pair of mustangs. The blacksmith had a brow as black as ever, but his manner had changed from fury to cold distance which was even more disagreeable.

"Come here," said he to the boy. "You got your pay comin' to you. What you mean by ridin' off without it, eh?"

"I forgot about it," said poor Tom truthfully.

"You forgot about it!" boomed the blacksmith. "That's a likely thing, ain't it?"

He approached disdainfully to Oliver Champion.

"He says that he forgot about it! Well, what kind of pay are you gunna ask for?"

"I dunno," said Tom.

"Pay as a man, pay as a helper, or pay as a boy?"

"I dunno," said Tom, "you give me what's right."

"So's you can go hollerin' around the town, afterwards, sayin' that I robbed you?"

"Ah," said Tom, "I wouldn't go around behind your back. I've been happy here!"

He looked wistfully toward the dark mouth of the blacksmith shop, with the blue-white breath of the smoke curling out, and the sulphurous smell of it extending to where he sat on his horse.

"You been boarded and lodged," said Boston.

"Yes, that's true."

"Kept as good as me."

"That's a true thing. I never lived so clean and comfortable before."

"I reckon that you never did. That takes something off of the wages."

"I'm willing," said Tom. "I'm not counting on the money. You give me what you like."

"Well—we'll say thirty bucks." .

"That's enough," said Tom.

He looked straight into the eyes of Boston as he

39

spoke. It was not enough. A common hand on a ranch got more than that, and the labor he had performed in the shop was worth twice as much as that, surely. He wondered what other man—since other men were so absurdly weak in arm and hand—would take his place in the shop and strive to shower down the tremendous blows which Charlie Boston required!

But now he was turned off with hardly more than half pay, and he looked at his old master with a sigh. He was almost sorrier than all else that he should have to discover any actual meanness in the man.

Charlie Boston apparently did not see. He was busily counting the money.

"There's twenty-seven, seventy-five," said he. "You owed me two and a quarter for tobacco."

"All right," said Tom, with a twitch of his lips. "Good-by, Boston."

He held out his hand, and Boston, scowling, barely touched it.

"Try to go straight—you!" said Boston.

And with that last whip cut, Tom turned the head of the mustang up the street.

7

THE BRIDGE was not far away from the blacksmith shop of Bullhead, and as the mustang jogged up the slope toward it, he stumbled, and flung Tom forward a little. So, with a good chance to look behind him, the boy saw what surprised him as much as anything else

40

that had happened recently, for he observed Oliver Champion gathering the reins over the backs of his ponies and starting them at a brisk trot, while big Charlie Boston stood at the entrance to his shop, with one hand braced against the side of the door, and his head down.

He was not a man who ever dropped his head. No matter what the emergency, his shoulders were always squared to it, and his head was always high. And this made it the more strange to the boy, as he stared back for a moment, at the big blacksmith. It was more inexplicable to him, even, than the secret smiles which he had observed on the faces of both Oliver Champion and Charlie Boston. For, by the attitude of the blacksmith at this moment, one would have said that he had just received a crushing blow of some sort.

However, Tom had failed so many times to solve the little mysteries that came into his life that he would not devote too much of himself to the contemplation of this one. He shrugged it away from his bitter heart as well as he could and let the mustang jog on. He crossed the bridge, and the planks sounded loudly hollow beneath him, then the hoofs of the mustang were muffled in the thick white dust on the farther side. Another sound began again behind him, the rumbling of the light buckboard, and the rolling, small thunder made by the beating of eight shod feet.

The buckboard overtook him, and Oliver Champion slowed his team with a strong hand, until they were pulling the wagon with limp traces and taut reins. They began to walk, and then he let them put out their heads again, while they switched their tails violently from side to side, as horses will, to express their impatience with a master whose actions they cannot quite understand.

"You going this way, Fuller?" asked Oliver Champion.

"I dunno what way I'm goin'," said the boy. "I'm only headed this way."

"Taking the left-hand fork, up yonder?"

"Yes, that's the way that I figger on goin'."

"Then step in here with me, and we'll lead your

horse. This seat is more comfortable than a saddle, I suppose, and your weight won't be anything to these two brutes!"

Tom Fuller hesitated. Back in his mind there was an odd feeling that a state of collusion existed between the blacksmith and Champion; but such a pointed invitation he could not very well refuse. He thanked Champion, dismounted, and tied the mustang to the tail of the buckboard. Then he got into the seat beside the driver. He turned, there, and looking back he called: "Hài! Get up, bronc!"

The mouse-colored mustang lurched forward with the trotting horses, and they went on down the road.

"You've got that horse very well trained," said Champion. "He does what you tell him to do, and that's something not often seen with Western horses."

"No," answered the boy. "The fact is, that he trained me, more than I trained him. That's the hoss that taught me how to ride."

"He did? Is he a very old fellow?"

"He ain't very anything, except mean," said the boy. "But he's a champeen at that!"

"At bucking?"

"He's an all-round mean hoss," said Tom Fuller. "He'll kick with each hind foot, or with both of 'em together. When you're cinchin' him, he knows how to reach up and out with a hind foot and rip your feet out from under you. Then he'll try to maul you and jump on you while you're down. He'll play possum, and when you get into the mow to fill his manger, all at once, he'll climb into the manger after you. At strikin', he's mighty good—he's like a boxer. I've seen him lick a stallion by standin' up as pretty as you please and sluggin' him with straight-arm punches!"

He chuckled at the thought.

"He'll even butt you like a goat, if he can't do harm no other way, and one of his prime tricks is to edge you agin' a barbed wire so's it'll knife into your leg. I dunno how many pair of chaps that habit of his had cost me. And if he gets close to a wall, he'll pretend to stumble, and bash your legs to a pulp agin' the wall. You understand? He's a schemer.

"Biting is one of his main holds, too. Once I was up a tree for some apples, and that mustang, he come beneath and reared up, and got hold of one of my boots. He thought that he had the foot, too, and he jerked away, and the boot came off, and I nearly come off the branch that I was hanging by, too. If I had, it would have been the last of me. You should've seen the way he went racin' around that field and chewin' the boot, and finally he dropped it and begun to stamp on it, and when he got through, that good old boot, it looked like a dish rag, and not a mighty good dish rag, at that!"

He related these characteristics of his mustang in a quiet, rather hesistating voice, and kept his eye upon the face of his companion, as though he feared that the other might become greatly bored at any moment.

"What makes you keep him, if he's such a savage brute?" asked Oliver Champion.

The boy started, and then he raised his head and stared at the horizon with a frown of self-searching and of bewilderment.

"I dunno—I dunno—" he murmured.

"You must have some sort of reason," said Oliver Champion, and waited patiently.

And, as he waited, his quick, penetrating eye darted through and through the boy and searched him to the quick. A thousand speculations seemed to be flashing through the rapid mind of Champion, but of these the boy was aware only as he was aware of certain cloud shadows slipping softly over the distant foothills.

"You see," explained Tom at last, "a day's ride could be a pretty dull thing, if you didn't have something to keep your hands full. You—er—well, you don't get sleepy when you're riding that old moth-eaten bronc."

"I should think not. But one of these days, he'll be apt to eat you, won't he?"

"Nothin' would please him better than that!" said the boy.

He turned in the seat and swore fondly at the mouse-colored horse, and the mustang flattened his ears and tossed his head in response.

"He'd like to begin at my head," said Tom Fuller, "the way that a cat does with a mouse! Yep, he's a brute! He threw me every day for thirty days, I guess, before I learned how to handle him."

"If he threw you thirty times, did he never savage you?" persisted Champion.

"Sometimes he slung me clear over the corral fence, and sometimes he rolled me clear under it. But a few times he pretty near caught me. Once he came with his mouth wide open, and that mouth looked to me like the mouth of a shark. I seemed to get smaller, and that mouth seemed to get larger. He begun to look like a laughin' hippopotamus to me, when he come close, but I managed to jab the heel of a boot into his nose, and when he stopped to sneeze, I got away. That pretty near drove him crazy. He went a-rampin' and a-ragin' around that corral and tried to kick the clouds out of the sky and paw his way down to bed rock. When I walked around on the outside of that corral, he used to foller me around, like a tiger inside of a cage, watchin', and hopin' to feed on the spectators!"

Again the boy laughed.

"Is this savage of a horse tamed, now?"

"I don't know," said the boy.

"How did you master him, finally?"

"Well, it was a funny thing," drawled Tom Fuller, "but I guess that I've talked a lot too much about it, already."

"I'd like to hear the rest," said his companion.

"One day, that mustang bucked me off in a corral and I didn't quite get to the fence in time. But I dodged, and the hoss hit the fence ahead of me with a crash that shook it up a little. I said to myself that this was my chance. I took a dive at his forelegs and the first thing that he knew he was down—"

"You threw him down?" asked Champion.

"It's a trick," said the boy. "Not half so hard as bull-

44

doggin' a real hard maverick. But sometimes you might get stepped on a little, you understand?"

"I see," said Champion, biting his lip.

"Then I sat on his head for a while, and when I had my breath I got up. Well, he got up, too. There's a second when a hoss has just heaved himself up, before his legs are really well set. Well, just when that second came, I dived at his forelegs again, and down he went, and I suppose that hoss came up twenty times, and I put him down twenty times. I was all over blood, and he must have been pretty sore himself, because finally he just lay stretched out, and even when I stratched his stomach with the rowel of a spur, he didn't budge. He was dead out!"

He laughed at the memory.

"And since then you've been the boss?" asked Champion.

"Well, not always. He makes a fight of it, now and then, just to keep his appetite good, as you might say. But I dunno but he thinks that I'm really made of meat too tough for even him. I think that he'd rather eat plain rattlesnake flavored with sand than to try to digest me. But he still keeps up the bluff, and kicks at me, and snaps at me, and bucks pretty hard, and takes a shy close to a fence, now and then, and loves to play mountain sheep, and walk along the eyebrow of a cliff. But, just the same, I don't think he does any of those things serious. It's just a bluff with him, and he's always tryin' to show me that he's still got his self-respect!"

Oliver Champion laughed.

"He's not a pretty brute," said he.

"He ain't," agreed the boy at once, "but he'll come when he's called, and he'll run all day, and he'll get fat on prickly pears and Spanish bayonet. Sagebrush is his idea of a fine soft salad, and if he didn't get anything else, he'd just as soon eat the thorns off of an ocatilla."

Again Champion laughed.

"He's valuable, then?" said Champion. "He would serve about as well as a camel."

45

"Better," said the boy, "because a camel has to live off his hump, but Rusty, there, could live on his own mean thoughts. He's got enough of 'em to feed up himself and leave enough over for ten men."

"I'd rather like to buy a good tough horse like that," said the other.

"I couldn't part with him," said the boy.

"Then suppose I take you, too?" said Champion.

8

At this, the boy straightened. He looked with a flush of anger at his companion, who said, with a smile: "Hire you, I mean. Unless you are traveling toward another job just now?"

"Hire me?" echoed Tom Fuller.

"Yes, that's what I mean. Good pay, and work that would not be hard, I take it."

"Are you makin' a joke out of me?" asked Tom huskily.

"I am speaking to you," said Champion, "as seriously as ever your father could have spoken to you."

"There's nothin' that I could do," said Tom. "You seen me get fired!"

"What of that? There are other things in the world than handling horses and hammers in a blacksmith shop!"

"I've tried the most of 'em," said the boy. "I've been a baker even, for a month. I mean, I helped around,

46

and tended the fires. I did things like that. But I couldn't even be a baker."

"Neither could I, I'm sure," said Champion.

"You?" cried Tom. He looked at his companion with wide eyes, and then he nodded, assured.

"Why, you could do anything!" said he.

"Do you think so?" said the other, with rather a bitter intonation. "Well, I can't. But even if you have failed in other jobs, I think that you're the man for me."

"You got a ranch, I suppose," said Tom. "But I can't manage even that. I used to try plowing, but I was always running a crooked furrow. I used to try at riding herd. I couldn't do that. I'd get to thinking of something else, and the cows would make a break, the first thing that I knew. They seemed to know, somehow. I mean, that they seemed to know that I wasn't clever. They got more inside of my mind than I ever could inside of theirs! Hosses the same way!"

"You broke one hard horse," said his companion.

"You mean Rusty? Well, I happened to get my hands on Rusty."

He looked down at his hands and spread them palm upward, as though he was wondering at some special intelligence and capability concealed in them.

"Have you failed everywhere, Tom?" asked Champion.

"Well, yes. I always have."

"When the cream-colored mare, here on the near side, tried to break away, today in the shop, you handled her."

"Well, I got my hands onto the rope, you see. That was all. Of course, that length of rope gave me a leverage, and she wasn't expecting a hard jerk, just then."

"That may be, of course. At the same time, you handled the tall young fellow, a moment later."

"He was just a kid," said Tom.

"How old are you, Tom?"

"Me? Oh I'm twenty-one," said Tim. "I'm twenty-one years old and—"

He broke off with a sigh, and his retrospective eye seemed to be passing down the list of those years, which seemed to him so endlessly long.

"I've never done so good," said Tom.

"That kid, as you call him, was very quick with his gun," said Champion, "and I'll wager that if he'd got it out in time, he would have drilled a hole through you, my friend."

Tom considered. It was not his habit to make off-hand judgments of people or of events.

"He had a straight-lookin' eye," said Tom. "Yes, he can shoot a good deal. I mean, he could shoot a little."

"Could? Won't he be able to again?"

Tom frowned, for he felt that his imagination, or his intuition, or some buried sense which was in him, had caused him to speak too much upon this point.

"I mean to say that I don't know," confessed Tom, "but I reckon that he won't be very apt to reach for his gun, again. I would reckon, even," he said slowly, "that that boy, he won't ever reach for a gun again, if they's a man opposite him."

"What makes you think that?"

Tom started to speak, paused, and then went on hesitantly.

"You know the way that dogs are? If one licks another, then he's always the boss. He's always got the upper hand."

"But you won't always be around."

"Not that. I mean, sometimes, one beating is enough. The dog thinks that every other dog has got stronger jaws and quicker feet than him. This boy was young, d'you see? He hadn't hardened into himself."

"What do you mean by that, Tom?"

"Well, you take iron. When the fire has melted it down a bit, one hard smash will put the whole print of the hammer face into it. But when it's cold, it's able to break the hammer, before the hammer can hardly so much as dent it. Well, young boys, they're in the fire, or just out of it. They ain't been tempered yet. It's easy to knock sparks out of 'em. Those sparks, you might say,

48

would be likely to set the house on fire. That fellow might have set a house on fire, some day. But while they're hot, they're easily worked. And after they've been shaped, they gotta be tempered. That young feller, I'm afraid he was dumped into the ice water too quick. I reckon that he'll always be brittle."

Oliver Champion looked sharply and for a long moment at Tom, and then he squinted down the road.

"You never got on with any sort of work?" he said.

"Some say that I got no mind," sighed Tom. "Some say that what I got, I don't keep on my job. I guess they're right."

"You're not proud, Tom?"

"Oh, a man like you, you'd see right through me. You might as well know, before you've wasted a week's pay on me!"

"They call you 'Honest Tom'?"

"Sometimes I've been called that."

"Now, Fuller, I'll tell you what! Like a certain celebrated Greek, I've been looking through the world for an honest man. I've been looking for an honest man, with a strong pair of hands, with a fearless heart, and a familiarity with weapons. Do you understand?"

"Yes?" said Tom, rather bewildered by this explanation.

"And I think that I've found what I want! I don't quite agree with the opinions that other people have about you! I think I could use you, Tom!"

The boy shook his head.

"I never could do but one thing. I could swing the hammer for Charlie Boston, pretty well. But—I couldn't even hold down that job. I don't know why. I thought that I was doing pretty good!"

"Tom, did it ever occur to you that you might be thinking too much, instead of too little?"

"Thinking? Me?"

"Most people," explained Champion, "use their brains to tap away at big things and turn them into small things. Well, I think that you may have been doing exactly the opposite. You've been taking the little

49

things, and rolling them around with mystery, and making them greater and greater, until pretty soon, you're stumbling over your own imagination. The only thing that you don't appreciate may be your own talent."

"I don't just follow that," said Tom. "It—it sort of sounds to me like long division!"

The other laughed.

"What were you last paid a month?"

"Thirty, by Charlie Boston."

"I'll give you sixty."

"Sixty dollars a month?" said Tom, and turned sharply in the seat.

For those were the days when dollars had a meaning, and they were not scattered rashly. Sixty dollars raised one from the ranks.

"Sixty dollars, and find myself?" asked Tom humbly.

"Sixty dollars, and found. I'll pay all your expenses, and you'll live well."

"Sixty dollars and found," said Tom. "Why, I ain't worth—"

Champion interrupted with some show of irritation: "Do you refuse the place?"

"No!" said Tom.

"You don't know what it's to be about, as yet?"

"I'll take a chance on that!"

"Suppose I wanted to rob a bank?"

"Rob a bank!" laughed Tom. "I guess you wouldn't do that!"

He glanced at Champion and then quickly away, for, all at once, he was not half so sure of the virtue of his companion.

"Well," said Tom. "I've always kept the law."

"I hope that we'll be able to keep the law, still," said Champion dryly. "However, I might as well tell you what our task is."

"Yes?" said Tom Fuller, rather in dread after all of this preparation.

"I want to find this."

He took a fold of paper from his inside coat pocket,

and from the paper he sifted out a snapshot of mountains.

"Look at it!"

Tom took the picture and stared.

There was what appeared a pair of tall mountains in the foreground, one of them leaning outward at such an angle that it appeared as though it were about to topple over! And between the mountains a long valley began, heavily wooded, and ran straight down into the foreground, where a horse stood beside a storm-blasted stump of a great tree. The horse was the reason of the picture, no doubt. But at any rate, it was an indistinct picture, and not at all a success.

"You want to find that?" asked Tom.

"Yes. Ever see a place like that?"

"About ten thousand of 'em!" said Tom. "Except maybe that that mountain leans out in a sort of a dizzy way."

"We've got to find that place," said Champion. "And you're to help me."

"I'm not a very good eye for remembering things like that!"

"Then I'll do the looking after the mountains, and you do the looking after me."

"After you?"

"You understand, Tom? I'm not paying you something for nothing. But much as I want to find the place which is in this picture, just so much do other people want to keep me from it. And if they found me on the trail, they'd kill me, Tom, with as little compunction as you'd step on a poisonous spider! However, that is where you come in—with a gun in your hand, I have no doubt!"

9

To HAVE found a job was in itself enough, but to have a job at such a price as this was something to take away the breath of Tom Fuller. It made fair visions leap before his eyes—silver-mounted saddles, and blooded horses, and pearl-handled guns, and altogether, such magnificence that all eyes would gaze after him as he passed, and admiration would arise behind him as dust rises behind a wind.

He was half blinded by these dreams, so that he failed to put succinctly to himself any question concerning the other and darker half of his present position. He had been assured that the place meant danger, and sixty dollars a month is a poor salary—so is six thousand—if the hired man dies before he can use the money.

However, Tom was not as other men, and his fear had been so long that of starving, or being without employment, that he had lost all talent for fearing danger. A seasick man is never frightened by a storm. He is too busy with his equilibrium and a sense of nausea to care a whit about the danger of death. So it was with Tom Fuller. His mind was filled with fear of scorn, fear of mockery, fear of failure as he had failed before, and there was no room to worry about his personal safety. Suddenly, he was intrusted with a labor in which he could use the gifts with which nature had filled his hands.

The joy of that possessed him; songs formed in his

throat and dreams misted his eyes; and he fell into a profound silence.

Oliver Champion did not disturb his thoughts, for his own mind seemed occupied fully. The sun hung higher in the sky and then burned directly down upon them. It burned the wind out of the heavens; it burned the road to a white dust; it turned their hatbands into circles of fire, and soaked like scalding water through the backs and shoulders of their coats.

The mustangs jogged on endlessly. Where the reins flipped their backs and where the hip straps danced, appeared lines of white froth. Sweat streaked their bodies; then they were all sleek with water. The dust settled and whitened them; the sweat washed the dust away. But still they jogged on as wolves dogtrot without ceasing. Only, as the day grew older, their steps shortened until they were traveling not very much faster than a brisk walk. But the driver did not hurry them. The distances before them were so vast that one was not inspired to try to cross them at a burst, and the long road which toiled through the hills was to be nibbled at bit by bit, and so consumed by degrees.

Twice they saw, in the distance, little villages, half lost behind the heat waves which constantly washed upon from the surface of the earth; but they went on past the towns. They came to a creek, or rather, a little runlet of water, and here they stopped and, without a word of consultation, watered the horses, and dashed some water over the legs and the bellies of the mustangs. They allowed the pair to breathe, and when the labor of their flanks became less rapid, then they climbed again into their places.

"Look at Rusty," said Oliver Champion. "He hasn't turned a hair!"

"He's only been pulling himself along," said Tom.

"He's been eating all the dust, though," answered Champion. "That horse is solid iron."

The boy looked back and nodded. Rusty was iron, that was true; and perhaps there would be a need for his durable strength before long.

53

The sun wore lower down into the west, and as its strength abated, and the sky was less pale with heat, Tom began to find questions rising into his mind. Far before them he saw a little town, like a figure of smoke among the hills, and they were doubtless to stop there for the night; it would be almost dusk before they reached it.

"Suppose that some of the people that are after you should come along, how would I know them, Mr. Champion?"

"What people?" asked the other.

And he turned to the boy a face wan with dust, and with circles of weariness beneath his eyes.

"Why, I mean people who are apt to make trouble for you. You were saying something about them. If you could tell me what they look like—"

"They might be old, and they might be young," said Champion. "They might be negroes, Mexicans, whites. I don't know. We might have no trouble at all, as we cruise about, but, on the other hand, we might find it any moment. A man might shoot at us from behind that cactus; or a dozen scoundrels might charge down on us when we get through that gap—I don't know who they'll be. I can't suggest any one to you except—"

He paused, and then, shaking his head, he added: "There's no use telling you about him, because he'll never appear. He'll keep behind the smoke!"

He said this with a new note in his voice—a quiet, metallic murmur, as it were; and the boy knew that Champion was speaking of some great enemy.

They talked no more as the day wore on, and they came into the town at dusk. It was a village at a junction of two lines of railroads, and the roundhouses and other railroad buildings made a great heap in the center of the town. There was an eternal taint of coal smoke in the air, and always the sense of grinding wheels, somewhere in the distance, and of engines panting strongly and too fast for human lungs to imitate. On the outskirts of the yards, the town houses began. There was a crooked Main Street and a disordered lot of short alleys. It was a place of fifteen hundred inhabitants, say. The railroad supported its life, and not the naked brown hills around. As they drove in, they passed under a big sign—"Orangeville." Beneath the large letters of the name appeared a legend: "For homes and home lovers."

They went on, hunting for the hotel. Presently they had to slow the mustangs to a walk, so pitted and rutted was the street; it was like rowing through a choppy sea in a small boat. It was as ugly a town as well could be. There were no gardens, and there were no trees.

"Orangeville! Orangeville!" said Oliver Champion. "That's the trouble with these people. There's too much imagination; there's no sense of proportion. That's the trouble, I tell you! Orangeville! For homes and home lovers! Bah!"

He seemed almost childishly violent, and the boy was startled. Then he remembered the fatigue and the heat of that day's journey. Champion had driven every inch of the way, and he was struck with a pang of remorse. He really should have offered to take the reins.

"There's not a blade of grass in the place, is there?" asked Oliver Champion.

"They's been so much coal smoke over the town, that the rain couldn't get through," suggested the boy. "Maybe they been trying for oranges instead of for grass."

He laughed a little. It was easy for his spirits to rise, now. So they turned into the main street, and saw the hotel sign on the left, a little distance before them.

"Looks like hard beds and bad food to me." said Oliver Champion. "Well, I gotta take this, and a lot more!"

He said it through his teeth, but it was apparent that he was very tired, and that his patience had worn thin.

"Is that a crowd of fool cowpunchers celebrating?" he asked a moment later, as a cavalcade rounded a corner before them.

"It ain't that, said Tom Fuller. "They're going too slow. They're going as slow as bad news, I'd say!"

The riders came closer, and presently it was seen that

55

they were grouped around a central figure of a man whose horse was led on a lariat hooked over the pommel of another saddle, and that the central form, furthermore, had bright new handcuffs holding his wrists together.

"Ah ha!" said Champion. "A sheriff's posse—and it looks as though they've actually caught their man! That's an unusual thing, isn't it? I thought that sheriffs in this part of the world were chiefly employed in galloping wildly and bravely across the hills and galloping wildly and bravely back again! But here, by Jove, something has been caught! I'll wager that the fellow was drunk!"

He seemed to take a great deal of pleasure in sneering at the rest of the world, at this moment, and the boy made no reply. The cavalcade, at the same time, began to go past them, and they could see the prisoner very clearly, in spite of the dimness of the light. He was the very type of a criminal, with a pale, broad-jawed face, little eyes, bright as the eyes of a pig with greed, and a shower of greasy black hair cascading over his forehead and seeming to thrust into his very eyes.

He was a man of some note. People were running out onto their front porches and letting the screen doors slam behind them, while they stared after the captive, and a murmur ran up and down the street. His importance was reflected in the attitude of his captors.

They tried to be free and easy, and casual, and careless, but every man of them rode a little straighter than usual, and squared his shoulders, and stole glances from the corner of his eye to collect admiration like a deacon collecting contributions for the church.

"A low-looking ruffian," said Oliver Champion, as the procession went by.

At that moment, the captive jerked his head to the side and stared fixedly at Champion. It seemed as though he had heard the remark—though that would have been impossible at such a distance—and now he glared back with a wild malice, until his horse had carried him past.

"Not drunk, I guess," said Tom Fuller. "But crazy, I suppose. He looked like he knew you and wanted to cut your throat, didn't he?"

Champion did not answer at once.

Then Tom glanced sharply at him, and saw that he was frowning, and that the fingers of one hand were working nervously.

"He does know me," said Champion. "And what's more to the point, I know him!"

He pulled up the team in front of the hotel, at this point, and gave the reins to the boy as he climbed quickly out of the buckboard. "You put up the team," he directed, "and I'll get the rooms."

Tom obeyed the orders.

He had to wait a moment at the barn behind the hotel before the stable boy came back from the street.

"Who've they got, there?" asked Tom.

"Why, they've got Cressy—that's what they've got."

"Who's Cressy?"

"Him? Bud Cressy? Why, that's the murderer and the stick-up man!"

Tom Fuller bit his lip in bewilderment. How had Bud Cressy known Champion, and how had Champion known him?

10

BUT NO MATTER how odd might have seemed the recognition which had passed between Cressy and Champion, the boy determined that he would take no notice. It was not his problem to solve the relations between Champion and other people. His task was more precise—he was simply to guard the safety of his employer.

So he tried to push the problem out of his mind, and he went back to the hotel after he had watched the team and Rusty put up. Two rooms had been taken by Champion, in the rear corner of the second floor of the hotel. They were small, wretchedly furnished, with thin grass mats on the floor, and a section of paper taking the place of a broken windowpane.

"But they're away from the rest of the house," said Champion. "That's what counts about 'em! They're away from the rest and—I hope you sleep light?"

"I sleep pretty light."

"Fix your mind on my room. Then you'll waken if you hear a sound in it."

They went down to supper and ate a large meal. But Champion was nodding before he finished his coffee. He rose with a great yawn, and fairly fumbled his way out of the room, like one walking in his sleep. Tom went behind him, and Champion yawned again as he said good night.

"I'm going to sleep—the first good sleep in a year! The first sleep with both eyes closed—"

He disappeared into his room and presently the boy heard Champion fling himself heavily into his bed.

The man was plainly exhausted and, standing at his own window, Tom looked out over the roofs of Orangeville, and saw the dark cloud of the coal smoke from the yards climbing the sky and making the stars disappear, or fade; and he listened to the restless panting of a locomotive which was busily sorting cars on the side tracks to make up a train. There was something of the tone of a manufacturing center, with all this noise and the confusion and the smell of soot in the air. But the thoughts of the boy were with Champion.

That man was haunted with fear, Tom now knew. For a year, according to his own words, he had not really slept himself out; and perhaps as a sort of last and desperate move, he had clutched at Tom for safety—a mere straw which would go down with the first whirl of the water!

Very insufficient Tom seemed to himself, and yet he felt that he was a little happier now than he had been for a long time. He was happier than he had been in the employ of Charlie Boston, for life was not only busy, but he himself was respected. In a sense, Champion actually looked up to him and his skill with weapons, and the strength of his hands. Then Tom turned back to his bed and undressed, shaved by a smoky light in a cracked mirror, took a cold sponge bath, and lay down to sleep. He had only to straighten himself and draw a single long breath before slumber fell over him; there were no nerves in Tom Fuller!

He took into his mind one last thought—which was to keep alert to any sounds which came from the room of Champion, and it seemed to him that he had barely fallen to sleep when such a sound reached his mind, and waked him suddenly.

He was halfway to the door, gun in hand, before he was thoroughly roused. Then he looked about him, blinking, and saw a smear of gray sky at the top of his window, and black roofs pricking up above the sill. It was the earliest dawn, and yet he was confident that the light had not wakened him. Something had sounded in the room of his employer.

He scanned the door, anxiously. There was no glimmer of light around it, and no eye of light blinking through the keyhole. This reassured him, but still he went closer and leaned his head by the door jamb. Then he was aware of a murmur of voices in Champion's room. He could not break up the flow of sound and distinguish the meaning of the words, but he waited, uncertain what to do. If there was a noise in that room, he was to enter. That had been agreed. But surely this sounded like a quiet, private conversation! ·

However, his first orders had not been changed. He found the knob, turned it softly, and let the door fall open of its own weight. Silence followed, and then the faint fluttering of a piece of paper. No voices spoke, and the chamber was a deep well of blackness into which he could not see at all. Shapes seemed to move vaguely within that blackness, but he guessed that the forms were only in his own eye.

Then he heard a gasping voice which he guessed came from Champion:

"Tom! Tom Fuller!"

"Here!" said Tom, with caution.

"Thank Heaven!" said Champion. "It's all right, Bud. There's nothing to fear."

Two forms drew closer to Tom, in the doorway. Instinctively, he raised the muzzle of the Colt which he was carrying.

"Who's this bird?" asked a muttering voice.

"A friend of mine. Perfectly safe."

"What's he know?"

"Nothing."

"Does he know you?"

"He saw you today; that's all."

"I'm gonna beat it out of here," said the voice of the

stranger in answer. "You couldn't spare another hundred?"

"No. I've told you that."

"You've told me, well enough. Telling don't make it so, though."

"I've told you the truth, Cressy."

"Darn it, you could leave that name out!"

"He's safe, I tell you."

"What's safe for you might be poison to me. They got a price on me, now. Darn 'em, they'd as soon shoot me down as to shoot a pig that had broke into a field of wheat. Well, I'm gunna leave. I need a hoss, though. You see a good hoss there in the barn, old son?"

"I didn't go into the barn."

"The kid did, then? Fuller, did you see a good hoss in that barn? A hoss that could pack a hundred and eighty pounds for a hard run?"

"There's a big roan gelding," said Tom. "He'd cost you a good deal, I think."

"Would he?" chuckled Cressy hoarsely. "Maybe I could borrow him, though!"

It sent a tingle through the blood of Tom. He had been raised to look upon the violence of his own father as a pardonable thing. His father had killed many a man; his list was long, in fact. And yet he never had stolen so much as a crust of bread, let alone a horse. It was the last crime, the unpardonable act. The whole West had been raised in that creed, and yet Bud Cressy proposed to steal a horse this night!

Somewhere down the main hall of the hotel, a door squeaked, and thereafter, they heard other small sounds.

"They're after me," said Bud Cressy calmly. "You better get me out of this, partner!"

Champion fumbled in the dark until he found the arm of Tom Fuller, and into that mass of rubbery sinew and muscle he dug his fingers.

"Tom, get him out of this!" he exclaimed.

"How can I?" said Tom.

61

"You got a rope?" demanded Cressy.

"No."

"No rope? What kind of a puncher are you, then? Well, you got a blanket on your bed. You can lower me down on that, I guess."

"I can do that."

"Get out of my room!" said Champion nervously. And he pushed them before him.

"Might leave your hands covered with tar, though, old-timer!" reminded Bud Cressy. "Now, kid, step lively!"

Yet there was a drawling lack of haste in his voice.

The door closed softly, and Champion turned the key in the lock. In the meantime, Tom had snatched a blanket from his bed, and Cressy caught it from him and gave it a twist which brought it into a more narrow compass. Then he slipped through the window and caught hold of the blanket.

"Can you hold my weight?" asked Cressy.

"Yes. Easy."

"So long, kid. I'll have the roan in two minutes."

He slid down the blanket as he spoke, and at the same time, a heavy hand fell upon Tom's door. Once and twice the noise was repeated, and then the weight disappeared from the blanket.

"Yes?" said Tom.

"Open up this here door, stranger."

"What for?" asked Tom, snatching up the blanket and peering out the window.

He saw that Cressy had succeeded in dropping safely from the end of the blanket to the ground, and now he was slinking down the side of the building.

"Open up the door pronto," commanded a voice which was suddenly harsh, "or I'll bust it down!"

"I'm comin'," said Tom.

He tossed the blanket back on the bed and went to the door, unlocked it, and opened it wide.

Suddenly, three or four strong shafts of light blazed against his eyes as lanterns were quickly unhooded, and he saw behind the lights stern, eager faces, and the gleam of weapons. Quickly, they shouldered past him into the room.

"Jack, try the room of that other gent—that Champion."

"Jack" and a few others went to do as they were ordered. In the middle of Tom's room, the man of authority paused and swept a band of light around the walls, and beneath the bed. Her jerked open a closet door, and examined the contents of that, also. Then, with a scowl, he walked straight up to Tom.

"Who's been in here with you, tonight?"

"No one," said Tom, blinking.

He was frightened, not by the man, but by the law which the man stood for, and by the gleaming of the star on the breast of the stranger.

"No one?" said the other savagely. "You're lyin'! Come out with the truth!"

The door to Champion's room opened.

"Nobody in here, sheriff," said the searcher.

"Look here!" called another who stood by the window, lantern in hand. "Here's a chunk of red flannel stuck on a splinter, and Cressy was dressed in a red flannel shirt!"

11

THE HEART of Tom dropped like a stone when he heard this announcement. It threw the others of the group into confusion. The sheriff, shouting to two of his men to remain and guard Tom, dashed off in front of the rest, and though he was by no means young, yet he led them all out of the hotel.

The two captors of Tom were furious because they had been detailed to this ignoble business. They looked bitterly on him, in contempt of his pale face and his big, staring eyes, while they listened, far off, to the sound of the pursuit. There were money and glory, yonder, and they were held here helpless. They could only gnash their teeth and curse their luck, and the boy.

Tom made no answer to them. In the first place, he had a great sense of guilt. In the second, he could not see that his employer was much involved in the affair, and thought it was better to let the blame rest entirely upon his head.

Guns crackled behind the hotel, a horse squealed as though in pain, and then there was a vaster outroar of voices, and more gunshots mingled with the sound.

The guns ceased. The shouting continued. A score of men seemed to be shouting at the top of their lungs, demanding something from some one.

"Hosses!" said one of Tom's guardians. "They're yellin' for hosses, and that means that the skunk is in the saddle."

"They'll never catch him then. Maybe—"

"Aye, if we'd had our crack at him. We had to stay here and take care of this kid, instead. You know what's gunna happen to you?" said the man to Tom.

"No," said Tom, blinking, "I don't."

"He's pretty near scared to death, ain't he?" sneered the second guard.

"He ain't gunna have time to die of a scare," said the other. "They're pretty apt to string him up to a tree, ain't they?"

"Yes, I suppose they are."

"Hang me?" echoed Tom. "Would they do that?"

A leer of tremendous, cruel satisfaction appeared upon the faces of the two.

"They're a hard crowd to deal with, the crowd here in Orangeville. They like nothin' better than the hangin'

64

of a skunk, now and then, and I dunno but that you'd
fit into the bill, all right! Who are you, kid?"

"My name is Tom Fuller."

"Tom Fuller, here comes the sheriff. Maybe he'll be
able to save your neck for you and get you into the jail,
and maybe he won't."

The sheriff returned and came into the room with a
pale face and compressed lips. When he spoke, it was as
though the words bubbled and burst up out of him with
an explosive force of their own.

He went straight up to Tom and glared into his eyes.

"You helped Cressy out of that window," said he.

Lies came hard to Tom, for it was not an accident
that he had been nicknamed "Honest."

However, he managed to shake his head and say,
"No."

"You lie!" declared the sheriff. "You helped Cressy
get loose!"

Tom was silent, beginning to wonder. And the keen
faces of the other men as they surrounded him, panting
from their run, looked to him like the faces of dogs,
eager to tear a prey.

Here the door opened from the adjoining room and
Champion, fully dressed, came in. He seemed ready for
the road. His duster was already on and his hat was in
his hand.

"We'd better leave this madhouse, Tom," he said.

Then he came closer and appeared surprised to find
the youngster in the hands of the sheriff's men.

"What does this mean?" asked Champion, with au-
thoritative dignity.

The sheriff whirled on him in a fury.

"It means that that scoundrel Cressy is loose again. It
means that the pair of you helped him to get away!"

Champion's face was a study. He looked straight into
the sheriff's face, and then the smallest and the coldest
of sneers formed gradually on his lips. He turned away.

"Who's in authority here?" said he.

The sheriff seemed to go half mad with fury. He

shouted: "I'm in authority. I'm in enough authority to throw the pair of you into jail, and by heck, I think that I'll do it, too!"

"What are you?" asked Champion.

Here, in a moment, he had fixed all eyes upon himself. The others stood back a little, and their glances passed between Champion and the sheriff, as though to see who might win the struggle. The sheriff had numbers and all authority with him, but he did not seem to have a road before him that was by any means clear.

"I'm the sheriff of this county," said he.

"It appears," said Champion, "that I've mistaken you."

"It appears that you have. But it don't appear yet that I've mistaken you! I accuse the pair of you of passin' Cressy out of the window, there!"

"Cressy?" said Champion, and he frowned a little, not indignantly, but as one striving to place a name.

"Why, you can't bluff me! I ain't such a fool!" said the angry sheriff.

He went on: "The scoundrel is loose again. He's dropped Pete Myers with a bullet through his right shoulder. I dunno that poor Pete's arm will ever be worth anything again. And Sammy Strand is gunna be in bed with another bullet through his neck. A mighty lucky thing for him that an artery or the backbone or something wasn't touched! That's what Cressy done in this here one night—and it was you that got him clean away. I'll bet that you got him out of the jail, too! You passed in the tools to him!"

"I begin to understand," said Champion, with a wonderful calmness. "I am accused of helping a criminal to escape from jail. And then—"

He shrugged his shoulders.

"I helped him to escape and brought him here to my room in the hotel. Is that the idea, sheriff?"

The sheriff blushed. Certainly, this suggestion seemed most unlikely.

"He was here. We traced him here—to these here

rooms. I dunno why he should come here. That's between him and you!"

"By gad, Tom," broke out Champion, as though suddenly inspired. "Suppose the fellow slipped in through this room while you were asleep?"

Tom Fuller said nothing; his mind was still blank, and the chill of the shadow of the law was still cast upon his very soul.

"The pair of you'll rest pretty easy in the jail," said the sheriff. He whirled on the two who had guarded Tom.

"What did this kid say or do while you had him here?"

"He didn't do nothin'. He froze in his tracks. Plain scared to death!"

The sheriff grinned faintly.

"If my young friend," said Champion, with his usual calm, "had thought that there was actually a serious charge against him, do you think these two could have held him?"

The sheriff glanced sharply at Tom. But there was very little impressive in the appearance of that young man.

"I reckon they could have held two brace like him," said the sheriff.

"Throw those two in a corner, Tom," directed Champion.

The two who were guarding that youngster freshened their grips upon his arms, but Tom, flexing his muscles felt their fingers spring wide. A single shrug, and their hands fell away as rain from an oiled surface. Guard number one, recoiling a little, sprang at him with a hoarse shout. But Tom picked up the second fellow by the nape of the neck and the seat of the trousers and fairly flung him at his charging friend.

They went down with a yell and a crash, rolled half stunned, and only slowly picked themselves up again.

At this, the ill nature of the posse dissolved. They might well have been more irritated than ever by this

67

sight, but instead, they burst into a roar of laughter. The sheriff struggling with a native grimness for a moment, finally joined in with the loudest shout of all.

He said to young Tom Fuller, still chuckling: "And they said that you were frozen stiff, kid, did they? You couldn't move out of your tracks?"

He laughed again.

"I guess you're all right, the two of you," said he. He looked again at Champion, with an additional respect.

"I might've knowed that you were straight enough," said he. "But I couldn't be sure. Cressy has made me trouble enough before, and it looks as though he'll make trouble enough again. I suppose that he sneaked out through your rooms after he'd helped himself to some ready cash that he found in the pockets of some of the gents in the hotel. Boys, get out of here! We're on a cold trail!"

He led the way from the room; the two discomfited guards followed, their heads hanging, and their eyes bewildered, as though they could not quite make out what had happened here.

In another moment, the boy was left alone with Oliver Champion. There were no lighted lamps in the room now. And the gray of the morning light came coldly through the window, so that it illuminated merely the outline and the suggestion of Champion's features. But of one thing the boy was sure. Champion, in this half light, was smiling, and there was something wolfish in his pleasure.

Then he came a little closer, and his voice, lower and controlled, barely reached the ears of Tom.

"You want to know what Cressy was doing in my room. You'll never know. It's the beginning of a lot of things that you'll never understand. But in the meantime, the thing for you to do is to concentrate on the future, and realize that you haven't any eyes and you haven't any ears except when I tell you to see and to hear. Do you follow that?"

Tom nodded. He would have been glad, just then, of more light upon the face of the speaker, but he could

68

use his own intuition and guess at many unpleasant truths. And among them was this unhappy fact—that between the murderer and ruffian Cressy and his employer there existed a close intimacy.

12

"OUR NEXT STEP is to move and move fast," said Champion.

"That may make them follow," said Tom.

"It's better to be followed than to be lodged in jail," said Champion. "And that's where we're apt to wind up."

They gathered their belongings at once and went down to the ground floor, taking the narrow, steep, rear stairs of the hotel. Champion left on the clerk's desk an envelope containing money sufficient to pay their bill, then they went on to the side entrance of the hotel and out into the alley which ran back to the stable.

Down this they started, and passed a lighted window inside of which they saw two men seated at a table. One was the sheriff, a cup of coffee at his lips, and the other, facing him, was a round, rosy-faced fellow who smiled as he talked.

The sight of this couple seemed to affect Champion powerfully. He stopped, and clutched the arm of Tom, leaning his whole weight on the boy, as though he had just received a staggering blow. For a moment he stared through the window, and then gasped hoarsely: "There he is! Tom, put a bullet through that smiling scoundrel's head!"

Tom, amazed, did not stir.

"Do you hear?" groaned Champion. "He's on our heels already. He'll have the sheriff baying after us in another moment. Do you hear me? Shoot, I say!"

"That's murder!" said Tom slowly. "How can I harm a man that's never harmed me?"

The hand of Champion trembled violently on the shoulder of the boy.

"You young simpleton!" said he. "You've come to the wishing gate, and you don't know it! There'll never be another chance like this. There he is—in the palm of your hand—now, now!"

As he spoke the fat man, still smiling, rose from the table, and Tom was so far persuaded that he actually drew out a Colt.

"Shoot!" groaned Champion.

But the fat man stepped back from view as the sheriff rose in turn. And the bullet remained unfired.

"I couldn't do it," Tom managed to say.

Champion drew in a breath which was like a moan.

"Go on, and go fast!" he commanded. "They'll be going up to have a look at our rooms, now, and when they find we're not there, they'll look for us in the stable, next. Hurry, Tom. The horses—"

His voice failed him, but they ran forward together.

There was a single lantern burning just inside the door of the barn, but the stableman was not there. Undoubtedly, he had run to the hotel to find out the result of all the excitement. The entire town of Orangeville was up. Lights shone in the windows; doors slammed, screens jingled here and there; and rapid voices went up and down the streets.

In the stable, they worked with frantic speed.

If any spur was needed for Tom, he received it from the terse remark of his companion as they entered the stable:

"If they catch us, it means a necktie party!"

70

That was more than enough. He fairly jerked the pair of mustangs into their harness, flung the saddle upon Rusty, and, leading the horses out, found that Champion already had drawn the buckboard out from the wagon shed.

It took interminable seconds to back the unruly horses into their places on either side of the tongue. Then the stiff new breast straps refused the buckles; and the cream-colored mare began to kick as the traces were about to be fastened.

"The supreme young fiend," groaned Champion. "I wish her throat were cut—"

But Tom ended the kicking by a rough trick which he had learned long before. A lifting punch in the ribs jarred a grunt out of the mare, and before she had recovered from the surprise of meeting a man who struck with the force of a kicking horse, her traces were fastened.

The stableman came out, at this juncture, carrying a lantern with him.

"Hello!" said he. "Who's here? Who's pullin' out?"

There was a suppressed oath from Champion as the man raised a lantern above his head and the light fell strongly upon them.

"Making an early start, ain't you? You've got a bill to pay for these hosses, strangers! I hope you ain't forgettin' that!"

Champion, grinding his teeth, jerked a five-dollar gold piece from a vest pocket and tossed it to the stableman.

"This here is too much," said the stableman. "I'll get you change in a minute."

"Darn the change," said Champion. "Get out of here, Tom!"

Rusty had been fastened behind the wagon, again; Tom in the driver's seat slackened the reins, and the mustangs stepped out.

"What you got on your minds?" asked the stableman. "Now look here, you ain't—"

71

His voice stopped. The lantern was lowered to the ground and presently the stableman disappeared toward the hotel with flying legs.

"Seven thousand fiends are giving me bad luck!" said Champion. "Whip up the horses! Let 'em run—"

He snatched the whip from its holder and laid it with a hearty smack on the back of each mustang.

The result was a furious burst of running. They went down the rough surface of the alley with the buckboard leaping like a galloping horse behind the rushing pair of broncos. They swung out of the passage with a furious skid that kicked up a great cloud of dust, and behind that dust they whirled on down the street. Voices wakened behind them, pealing forth like trumpets. And Tom told himself grimly that they had not ten minutes grace. There were plenty of saddled horses standing before the hotel, and on these mounts, the breakneck riders of the range would soon overtake them. So he pulled the two from a gallop to a trot.

"Go on!" shouted Champion. "Faster! Don't pull up!"

He swung the whip, and the mustangs began to scamper, but Tom held them down with a mighty pull that made the footboards groan beneath him.

"We can't outrun saddle hosses with this outfit," said he, and as the pair slowed to a jog, he turned them into the mouth of the first alley to his right.

Plainly, they heard the rushing of horses down the street, and the clamor of excited voices. The people of Orangeville had missed one prey on this night, and they would fight hard before they relinquished a second. But, in the meantime, the boy was not even trotting the horses. He dared not allow the rattling buckboard to make so much noise until he had bent around two corners. Then he let the stamping pair back into a fast trot once more.

It was still between dark and dawn. The windows of the houses facing east glimmered like deep water with the morning light, but outlines were still dim and uncertain. However, they made an object which could not fail

72

of recognition. A buckboard with a led horse could hardly be missed! And though noisy horsemen seemed to be flowing through all the streets of the town, yet no one headed for them! Tom could not understand it, unless it were that the Cressy alarm already had brought the majority of the men near the hotel. The resources of Orangeville were pooled already, and that was why new men did not appear, saddling their horses and cantering out into the street.

Behind them, a bell began to beat from the steeple of a church, and its rapid clangor washed in waves through the dim air of the morning. An alarm bell, no doubt, which could call men to pray or to fight, according to the manner in which it was rung. Its beating now had the very pulse of danger in it. It hurried and made faint Tom's breathing.

They turned from a bending lane onto a broad street.

"Halloo!" yelled a voice behind them, and Tom saw a rider cutting for them like mad.

He knew there was only one thing to do, and he did it. Handing the reins to Champion, he picked up a rifle from the floor of the buckboard and put a shot whizzing just above the head of the stranger.

The latter jerked flat on the back of his horse, with a cry like a frightened cat, and pulled his horse aside, darting from view into the mouth of a side street.

"They're after us now," said Champion. "Boy, if it comes to the worst, we would cut the cream-colored mare out of the harness and I could ride her! We could make better tracks, that way!"

"You couldn't stand it," said Tom. "It'd wear you out in a few hours. And you'd wear out the mare. We gotta carry on the way that we've started."

He was surprised and rather flattered that the older man accepted this advice without further hesitation. And now the swiftly trotting team turned a gradual bend of the road, drawing out from Orangeville, and they saw before them the long embankment of the railroad. They drifted closer, and saw that the shadowy arm of a bar was stretched across the way. Champion

73

started up from his seat, with the last of his patience and his courage, as it seemed, exhausted by the stroke of ill-luck.

"Turn back, turn the buckboard, Tom!" he exclaimed.

"We can't turn back," said the boy. "They'll be out after us as thick as hornets, in another five minutes. That last fellow has gone to get help and I reckon that he won't have to go far."

"But the road's barred!" exclaimed Champion. "Are you blind, boy, not to see that?"

"Then we've gotta go through the bars," said Tom resolutely.

He pulled up the team, and leaped to the ground.

It was a long balance pole, weighted at the butt end and raised and lowered by a mechanical device. The lodge of the keeper of the crossing was near by, and he might be persuaded to open the way for them, but they had no time to waste on persuasion. A small iron key projected near the balance point, and turning this, the weight was released, the shadow rod soared.

"Drive through!" Tom called to Champion. "Drive through, and turn to the left down the far side of the embankment. We gotta chance, that way!"

For he knew, as he looked at the gray stretch of the road that ran before them, that they could not proceed far in this direction without being overtaken. The buckboard passed through, and throwing his weight upon the bar, Tom brought it down to the horizontal again, and with a turn of the key lodged it in its proper position.

The rails were already humming with the approaching train, as he ran across the grade, but a louder noise of hammering hoofs rolled behind him from the town. He looked back, and saw twenty riders scooting out of Orangeville onto the highway.

13

But Champion, with grimly set face, already had heard that noise and understood it. He had the horses moving as Tom went in with a leap over the tailboard of the wagon. They were galloping as Tom swung onto the seat. With a great clattering, they rushed forward, the wheels threatening to smash every instant on the larger stones of the grading which had rolled down to the side of the right of way. Furthermore, they were traveling on a steep slope, and were in danger of caroming from the impact of a rock and crashing into the stout railroad fence.

But Tom, grasping the reins, sent the mustangs into a wilder gallop. He had in mind a spot not far in advance where the right of way widened and a cluster of poplars stood. With that point gained, there might be enough of the trees to shelter them.

When he got to the place, therefore, he pulled up the team sharply, and swung the buckboard in behind the trees. These made but a paltry shelter against any searching eye, and their only hope must be that the posse would not think of scanning the railroad line itself too closely. The pursuers might be interested in pushing on down the highway.

He looked at Champion and saw him, with locked jaws and desperate eyes, climb down to the ground and take a rifle with him. Tom made no comment on this foolish act. But it seemed to him that the actions of this night had revealed Champion as a man not at home in violent physical danger. He did not doubt the essential courage and the strong mind of this man; but he was acting, now, in a strange environment. And Tom was puzzled and alarmed. It was almost as though a child were intrusted to his care and his responsibility!

They had not waited ten seconds before the flood of riders reached the railroad crossing. Half a dozen revolver shots brought the keeper as by magic; the bars swayed up, and the riders poured through. But they did not go straight on. Instead, they gathered about the keeper, obviously demanding what he had seen or heard of a buckboard and three horses.

There they milled back and forth for a time, and they were still hesitant when the throbbing of the rails grew louder and from the east the tall front of a locomotive came swiftly into view around the bend. It came across the road. It thundered on, and whipped past the two fugitives. Scores of faces looked out at them from the windows. Arms pointed and gesticulated. And every pointing hand was to Tom like a pointing gun.

How simple a matter, then, for the engineer to stop the train, and then for a score of the passengers to sweep back down the tracks?

But the train did not stop. It whirled away with undiminished speed, sucking up a trailing flag of dust and flying cinders in its rear. Then it was gone, and the group of riders at the crossing looked after it. Tom could see every face turned in his direction.

Surely they would see something, now, beyond the interstices of the poplars!

But no; in another moment they were drifting down the highway, at a trot and then at a hard gallop. Only three or four, as though giving up what they felt to be a wild-goose chase, turned back toward Orangeville. But the rest of the posse streamed on, drawing out in length as the slower horses fell behind, until they were lost in their own dust.

In the meantime, the sun rose, making the front windows of the keeper's house appear like so many squares of living fire. The keeper himself retired; smoke began to float above his roof, and now Champion climbed back into the buckboard.

"Are we out of danger?" he asked eagerly.

"I dunno," said Tom. "It depends on where that train stops and sends back word of what it saw."

"The train wouldn't be suspicious," said Champion. "What does it matter if there are some people on a right of way?"

"A buckboard?" queried Tom, with a smile. "And a pile of armed men at the last crossing, and us pulled in behind the trees, and the mustangs all shining with sweat? Most of all, there was you with a rifle in your hand, lookin' back through the poplars!"

"I've played the part of a child and a fool," he admitted tersely. "I'm deuced sorry for it. The next time we're in a pinch, you'll find that I come through it in better style. But some things have happened tonight to upset me. Every nerve was jumping. However, you've proved the stuff you're made of, Tom. From now on, I know what I have beside me! Charlie Boston was right!"

"Right about what?" asked the boy, bewildered by this remark, for certainly it seemed impossible that Charlie Boston should have made any complimentary remark about him on the very day when he was discharged from Boston's service.

"Drive on! Drive on!" said Champion testily. "There's no point in staying here until the posse comes back down the road and spots us!"

So Tom drove on, but he had not failed to add another item of mystery to his strange story.

For three miles they bumped and jarred and grated over the big stone of the embankment, until they came to a level crossing, without a gate, without a keeper, and through this gap they passed out upon the worst sort of an ungraded, unworked country road. It was one of those relics of the earliest days, when trails were laid out as much by the leisure of wandering cattle on their way to and from water and pasturage as to the fore-

77

thought of man. This road passed into the sea of hills, dipping, twisting, winding without excuse for many of its bends.

There seemed no reason for the very existence of the road, for that matter. It journeyed on for hours, without passing so much as a single house, or another road turning off from it. The surface of it, also, was made of big stones which had rolled down from the slopes of the hills on either hand and made it a difficult process to get through without breaking a wheel.

"Where will this thing take us?" asked Champion, irritated at last by the long silence.

"It'll take us out of the way, and I guess that's what we want!" suggested the boy.

"Aye. It will do that," said Champion, "and perhaps it'll take us far enough away to give us a fair chance of starving!"

"If you're hungry," said Tom, growing more and more patient as his companion developed uneasiness, "we can stop and bag something."

"Waste an hour hunting?"

"Just as you please, then. We'll keep joggin' on, Mr. Champion."

"You can drop the title!" said he.

"Drop what, sir?"

"You needn't 'sir' and 'mister' me, Tom. I'm not as old as your grandfather!"

Tom fell silent, since there seemed no way to please this hot-tempered man. But, in a way, he guessed the cause of the other's impatience. He was displeased with himself and the side of his character which he had shown to Tom, and, therefore, he could not speak easily in the presence of the boy.

Again they made an all-day trip, except for a few moments when they paused to let the mustangs eat a ration of oats, and twice to water them at streams which crossed the way.

They were leaving the hills now, and marching up into bigger country, and the mustangs rarely got out of

78

a walk. The grades were too steep and the way constantly too broken.

Suddenly Champion said: "Tom!"

"Yes, sir."

"Tom, you were a little surprised, this morning?"

"What by?"

"By the order I gave you to shoot that fat fellow who sat with the sheriff behind the window. Is that correct?"

"Yes," admitted Tom. "I never was brung up to shoot at a man that was lookin' another way."

After a moment of thought, Champion went on:

"What did you think of that fellow, Tom?"

"I thought he looked pretty cheerful and good-natured."

"He does," said Champion, half to himself. "He is, too."

Then he said more openly: "You know what makes a great many people happy and good-natured, Tom?"

"No, sir. Just being born that way, I suppose."

"Some of them. They're the lucky ones. But a good many people, Tom, are happy and good-natured, because they use all the force of their minds and of their hands to please themselves!"

Tom nodded, prying into the remote corners of this thought.

"Your smiling man isn't always your generous or your big-hearted man."

"No, perhaps not. I recollect a judge in my home town, now that you speak about it. He was always smiling and joking, but they say that he sure did love to soak on the heavy sentences."

"Now, then," said Champion, "if you suppose that that judge had all his cruelty and his meanness multiplied by a hundred, you'd begin to arrive at some idea of the cruelty in the mind of that same smiling fellow whose face you liked so very well!"

Tom was silent, wondering.

Then a note of profound emotion came into the voice of Champion, as he added:

79

"Tom, I've been my share about this world. I've known mean men, and hard men, and treacherous men, and cunning rascals, and bloodthirsty brutes. But you don't need to travel very far, if you have a chance to sit down and study that smiling fellow. Because he combines every horrible quality that a man could have—except cowardice and weakness. Everything else is in him!"

Tom hesitated, remembering the bright eyes, and the flashing smile, and the ruddy health in the cheeks of the man.

"You're sure of that, sir?" he asked.

"Sure?" said Champion. "Sure of him? He's the one thing in the world of which I am sure. I've spent my last twenty years studying him, and that's why I'm here in a buckboard driving my thousands of miles through the West, lad, and with a shadow haunting me all the way!"

He grew silent again, and Tom ventured to ask at last: "What's his name?"

"His name is the handiest name that he can pick up. His real name nobody knows. For that matter, what name has the fiend himself got? It changes in every country. And it's the same with him."

He paused again, laughing a little at his own comparison, but the laughter came through his teeth.

14

THE SUN had sunk far enough in the West to make them worry about the oncoming of dark, and Tom suggested that they should prepare to spend that night in the woods, which were now beginning to clothe the sides of the mountains. For the hills were behind them, and real mountains were in front.

But Champion declared that they should force their way on in the hope of finding a house of some sort. For, as he pointed out, they probably had a great distance before them to travel and it would be useless for him to make a point of camping out every night. The weight of the utensils, and the other articles, and the food supply, would slow down their progress perceptibly, and they must go in light marching order. As for remaining in that order, but simply roughing it as they went, and lying down by the road, he had not the constitution to stand such a life.

"Ah," said Tom, "but if we keep on stayin' where other people are, that smiling gent you say is so terrible is liable to find you again, as he found you out before!"

Champion made a wide gesture, looking up.

"Tom," said he, "if I were a bird, I couldn't fly so high in that sky that he wouldn't follow me and find me. If I were a fish, the sea's not deep enough to cover me from him. If I could walk into one of these rocky mountainsides as though it were free air, he'd manage a way to come after me."

"Are you sure to go down, then?" asked Tom, amazed and alarmed by this point of view and the fatalistic manner of his companion.

"I? Oh, I'm done for," said Champion, almost carelessly, as though this were a question which he had been able to answer a long time before. "But my hope is that I may be able to pull him down with me! Of course, there may be a better chance, later on. I may have somebody beside me, different from you, and I may see him through a window again."

He stopped short and then muttered for a moment to himself.

"I should have tried my hand then, myself," said he. "I should not have trusted to you. But the fact is that I was shaking. My hand was shaking at the sight of him and my heart was shaking in my body. However," he went on, "I might meet him again with the odds all on my side. One never can tell. One gets the thousandth chance, now and again. I must wait for that!"

It bewildered Tom more than ever. "You're trying to get somewhere, do something, before he arrives. Is that it?" he asked.

"Yes. That's it, Tom. I'm trying to find the hidden place. And, having found it, I'm going to try to dodge my way into it. Let me have five minutes there, and I don't much care what happens afterwards. I'll have laid his work in ruins. His life work!"

He drew in his breath as though the thought were a delicious potion to him.

But such total savagery made the brain of Tom spin. Vaguely, he could fumble at the story which lay behind this, and what the thing was which Champion was striving to reach, and how he could destroy it in a moment —as if with a word, or the mere sight of his face! He fumbled at the story, but failed to guess a probability, and resigned the puzzle. And now the team jogged around the brow of a hill, where the trail almost disappeared, and the grass grew long among the rocks. First, they saw a wisp of a white smoke, then a growing column of it against the dark trees of the mountainside, and next they were aware of a small log cabin laid away among the big boulders, and behind the cabin there was a mine mouth with a windlass above it, and a length of rope, and a big bucket.

"Somebody's sinkin' a shaft," said the boy. "That's as good a place as any to put up for the night, I suppose."

"If the man is willing to take us in," said Champion. "It's hardly likely that he'll have room."

The boy stared at him.

"Why," said he, "what would he do? Turn us out? What sort of a gent would he be to do that? Not in this man's country, I guess!"

"True, true, true," said Champion. "I forget that this is the West. We'll try him, at any rate."

The sound of their wheels on the rocks, and the clicking of the hoofs of the horses, brought into the doorway of the cabin a man of middle size, with a fat paunch, and a face covered with grizzled beard. He had a skillet in his hand, and this he waved toward them. He did not wait for them to draw up at the door, but shouted from a distance: "Get your hosses yonder under the shed, strangers. I got a morsel of hay there. Hurry up! I got some fixings here that's worth any man's time!"

"Ah, yes," said Champion. "This is the West, after all!"

And he sighed a little, and looked about him with wide eyes, as though he were seeing the countryside for the first time, but the boy could guess that it was not the mountains, and the rocks, and the trees, which were in the mind of his companion.

They put up the horses in the shed. It was the rose-gold time of the early evening when they came to the door of the cabin again and entered.

All within was misted over with drifting smoke, and the scent of frying meat filled the air. The miner was clouded by the steam of cookery before his stove.

"If you wanta wash up," he called, without turning from his frying pan, "you'll find a hunk of soap on that

83

shelf by the door, and a piece of something that maybe will pass for a towel. Hurry up, old sons. This here is venison steak you're gunna break into, pronto!"

They hurried, at that happy tidings; they found the runlet of water near the door, washed, dried their hands and faces, and came back armed with enormous appetites. Their blankets they threw down in a corner, and Tom made himself busy preparing the homemade table with three places while Champion looked around the room.

It was a solidly built cabin, made of heavy logs, and the chinks stopped with moss and mud. Each corner served as a definite room. One was the kitchen. One was heaped with powder, drills, hammers, and other tools and provisions of the miner's trade. In another appeared a collection of rusted traps, together with some hides on stretchers. And the fourth corner was occupied by a bed of evergreen boughs on which the blankets of the sour dough were laid out.

Presently they all sat down at the table and ate in a great silence, broken by murmurs of appreciation, now and then, for the deer was newly killed, wonderfully tender, and present in quantity. Coffee and corn bread completed the menu, but it was enough!

Over their coffee they lingered, the miner puffing at a pipe, his big, rough elbows on the edge of the table, and his tired, contented eyes watching the faces of his guests.

"You heading for somewhere?" he asked, finally.

Champion took some papers from his pocket, and in the handful appeared a sack of cigarette tobacco with which he began to make a smoke. The photograph of the mountains, too, was spilled on the surface of the table.

"We're aiming to get across to Porterville," said he.

"Porterville!" said the miner. Then he chuckled. "You couldn't be aimed much worse," said he.

"No?"

"Didn't you ask down there in Orangeville?"

"We asked. I thought we were directed to this road."

"Why, they lied to you. You should've kept on the main road north, and switched off of that two turnings beyond the one that heads into this. Doggone careless of the gent that give you the directions. Have some more coffee?"

"I've had enough."

"That a picture of your home country?" asked the miner, as he glanced down at the photograph.

"Picture that a friend of mine sent, a while back."

"That so? Friend of yours?" murmured the miner.

He took up the photograph, and studied it with some appearance of interest.

"Looks sort of familiar," said he.

"Familiar?" said Champion in a matter-of-fact voice.

"Yes. Where is it?"

"Why, I don't know! He sent it to me. He'd simply taken a snapshot while he was wandering about, I suppose. That hill looks as though it would fall down. I suppose that caught his eye."

"Aye. Likely it did," said the prospector.

"Where would you locate it?" asked Champion, still casual.

It appeared to Tom that a faint shadow passed over the face of their host. However, he nodded as he continued to examine the photograph.

"I could tell you, I guess. That's north of the Comanche Desert. Right on the edge of the hills."

"Comanche Desert? That's rather far south, for such trees as those!"

"You take," said the miner, "where the wind hits off of the desert and rises along the face of the mountains, it always lets down a bit of rain. And that's the layout there. Trees? It grows trees aplenty, some part of that country down there!"

"You're fairly sure of that?"

"As sure as I am that I'm sitting here."

"Recognize that leaning mountain?"

"Sure I do. You go down from here to Freshwater. It's about a hundred and fifty mile, I suppose. You go down from there, and you find it. Lemme see. They call

85

that the Leanin' Hoss, that mountain there. You take a good look at it and you'll see why. Like a hoss leanin' into his collar and startin' a mighty heavy load. This back here, this makes his hind quarters. And there's his shoulders, and his neck. You can see where he's stretchin' out his head! Not really much like a hoss. Like a hoss you'd see through a fog, maybe."

"Well," said Champion. "Isn't there a pass ahead of us, here, where we could break through to Porterville?"

"Porterville? Why, sure there is! You could push right on up the valley. It'll be rough goin', but you don't seem to mind that, and you're travelin' light—"

He glanced at their packs in the corner of the room.

"You could make it through," he concluded. "There ain't any snow, except a few drifts under the trees where they got south shadows layin' over 'em most of the days. You could make it through all right!"

"We'll try."

"You'll come out through the other side of the pass only about eighteen miles from Porterville."

He began to describe the course in detail, but Tom ceased to follow the talk. He was too busy in his own mind dwelling upon the marvel of this discovery which they had made. Perhaps the goal of their expedition was not far off—that place where the man of the smiles was to be smashed and then utterly ruined.

15

WHILE CHAMPION, in rather a helpless fashion, worked over the beds and finally got them in some order, Tom helped to clean up the tin dishes. Then all three turned in, and almost the moment that the light was out they were asleep, as only men can sleep who have been working hard in the open air all day. In another moment the night had ended, and they looked up with aching eyes and buzzing brains at the beginning of the dawn.

The miner, Rankin he had given as a name, was up before them, cheerful and shouting at the briskness of the chilly mountain air. They soon followed, crawling miserably from their blankets. And then they set about the cold work of the morning wash and shave, and after that, blue-nosed with the freshness of the air, they cooked breakfast. It is the breakfast coffee that unlocks the door and opens a pleasanter world in such circumstances.

When they had finished, before starting on the hard day's journey through the pass, Champion tried to pay his host for their entertainment, but the latter's face darkened.

"I ain't running a hotel," said Mr. Rankin. "You're welcome to what you've had."

They thanked him, the boy in confusion because of Champion's mistake; and, seeing his red face, Rankin remarked with a faint grin in a lower voice: "It's all right, kid. He doesn't know this neck of the woods."

They left that hospitable cabin and went to the west, up the valley, the mustangs perfectly refreshed, and pricking their ears at the work which rose before them, but as soon as they had passed around the shoulder of a hill which blocked their view of Rankin's place, Champion suggested a halt.

"The hosses ain't winded yet," said Tom, surprised.

"But I'm winded," said the older man. "You just slide back there to the top of that hill and look down at the cabin, and if you see Rankin making a break, let me know, will you?"

Bewildered, Tom looked earnestly at the other, but found no sign of his meaning. Champion was filling a pipe, tamping down the tobacco with his lean fingers and paying no regard to the effect which his words might have had on the boy.

So Tom Fuller went back and crawled among the summit rocks of the hill until he found a secure place from which he could spy on all the lower valley. It was a dark day on the mountains, with heavy clouds brushing over the mountains' shoulders and wetting the evergreen woods. All looked dreary enough except for a bright streak on the eastern horizon which, as Tom could guess, meant fair weather and bright skies over the foothills. As for the cabin itself, no sign of Rankin showed about it, and he surmised that the miner was working on the breakfast dishes. But in another moment Rankin appeared at the door of the horse shed with a saddled horse—a lump-headed mustang. He mounted, and the pony took out his kinks with a brisk bit of pitching which Rankin sat out with perfect ease.

Then, with the wild little beast well under control, he headed down the valley rapidly. Once, as the trail narrowed below the house, Rankin turned sharply about in the saddle and, it seemed to the boy, looked straight up into his eyes. He flattened himself lower, and when the boy looked again, Rankin was out of sight around the next hill.

He came back to report what he had seen.

"Nothing at all, sir," said he. "Except that Rankin has gone sashayin' down the valley on a hoss."

"Is that nothing at all?" queried Champion, and Tom saw that the other was smiling in a very odd manner at him.

"I don't make anything out of it," said Tom.

"Why should Rankin be heading down the valley?"

"Well—hunting, perhaps."

"Did he have his rifle with him?"

"I didn't notice. It might have been in his saddle holster."

"If he were out hunting, wouldn't that rifle be across the horn of his saddle?"

Tom shook his head. "Maybe," he admitted.

"Would he take a horse at all if he were hunting?"

"I don't know," said Tom. "Maybe."

"Why should he? This valley must be full of game. There's nothing to disturb it or work it up, except Rankin himself."

"Aye, that's true enough."

"Well, then?"

"He might be going to town."

"Yes," said Champion, "he might be going to town. How long would it take him to get there?"

"I suppose about four hours. He could go four times as fast on a hoss as we went bumpin' over those rocks with the buckboard."

"Four hours to get there, eh? I think you're right. Perhaps even in three hours! Now, then, it's a strange thing that he didn't tell us he was going to town today."

"He didn't say anything about it," said Tom, nodding.

"Why would he go to town?"

"For powder—provisions, something like that."

"But the house was full of stuff."

"Yes, it was."

"We even had apple jam on the flapjacks this morning."

"Yes," said Tom, "he seemed to have everything that he needs."

"But perhaps he could have used a little ready cash, eh?"

"Why, I suppose anybody could always use that."

'D'you understand me now?"

"No, I dunno that I do."

"There's ready cash in plenty for the man who captures me, Tom! Now, does that make it clear?"

"Cash for you?"

"From Plank! From Henry Plank!"

"Who is he?"

"Why, the brown-faced fellow, the one with the smile that you liked so much. That's the man. Did you see the face of Mr. Rankin when he looked at the snapshot?"

"He got a little dark," nodded Tom.

"He was thinking very hard, Tom. Thoughts such as he was having were enough to darken the face of any man, I should say! Do you see what was going through his head?"

"No, I can't say that I've got any idea about it all."

"He was thinking in this manner: Here are two wanderers, traveling light, as he noted, and headed for they hardly know where. Fifty miles off their road because they haven't asked the way. Why haven't they asked the way? Because they were afraid to stop and take the answers. These suspicious fellows show me a photograph of a country which I recognize. I even recognize the mountains in it! They pretend that they show me the snapshot by accident, but really they had planned the whole thing out. They wanted information. Well, I gave them a lie, and now I'll send them out on a false trail and while they're on it, wandering around in the rocks, I'll slip into town and find out about them. They have the look of being worth a bit of money! A thousand dollars to a penny! That was how his mind reacted, Tom!"

The boy looked at him in wonder. It seemed to him that the entire argument and all the deductions were based upon the merest shadows.

"And there's Rankin galloping as hard as his pony

will take him, down the valley!" said Champion. "Is that proof enough for you?"

Tom started.

"That's proof enough," said he. "I suppose that's proof enough. What would we do, then? You think that there's no way through this valley?"

"I think that everything he told us was a lie and the reverse of the truth. We'll go back to the cabin first, and have a bit of a look around there."

Back to the cabin they went, and as Tom entered first, he found what they wanted lying crumpled on the floor, just before the door. It consisted of a large-sized poster which carried the picture of a man with the shaven head and the striped suit of a convict, and beneath the picture was inscribed the legend in large black print:

ONE THOUSAND DOLLARS
REWARD!

Beneath it, in smaller type:

For the capture, or for information leading directly or indirectly to the capture, of O. C. Franchard, bank robber, recently escaped—

"He dropped this here," said Tom. "Does that mean anything?"

He turned and confronted the gleaming eyes of Champion.

"You're not blind," said Champion. "Use your eyes, boy, and perhaps you'll be able to make the thing out better. Who is the man that's wanted?"

"A man called Franchard, a bank robber!"

Champion laughed softly.

"Look at me again, Tom," said he. "I'm O. C. Franchard. I'm Oliver Champion Franchard. And what took you so long to recognize that fellow Rankin saw at a glance."

"But—bank robber!" exclaimed Tom.

91

"The Farmers' & Merchants' Bank in Buffalo," said Franchard. "Is that job too old for you to remember it? Yes, of course it is! But that's the job that I went to prison for!"

"But you're not the man in this picture!" said Tom insistently. "You—you might be his older brother, though!"

"Look at the date of that poster," said Champion. "It's five years old, my lad. I kept young in the prison. I had a good deal of hope when I was there. But for five years I've been wandering around the world—and that work has aged me. I'm Oliver Champion Franchard. You can be sure of that. And the reward isn't a thousand dollars, any longer. It's five thousand, Tom. There's a pocket full of money for you, if you want to make an easy little fortune. Fame, too! Young boy of twenty-one captures celebrated bank robber, five years out of prison! Why, you'd become a celebrity in no time, Tom, and you could marry the girl you want—pick her up as you pleased!"

He painted this picture in a dry and drawling voice, while Tom's ideas fell about his head like a house of cards. He looked at the bright eyes and at the faintly sneering smile on Franchard, and knew that the man had told him the truth.

"I'd never be a traitor," said Tom slowly. "I guess I'd never take blood money."

"You wouldn't. I knew that, or I never would have talked outright like this. Now do you see what this means, Tom? Do you see the link that we've found by the grace of fortune?"

"I don't," said Tom, shaking his head.

"Well, then, I do. It means that we've found the road to Henry Plank!"

16

At this, Tom fairly threw up his hands.

"I'm not clever," he admitted. "It's hard for me to see things quick. I don't see how you mean that you've found the road to Plank!"

"To Plank's house—to Plank's house!" cried Champion. "Oh, that's what I want a thousand times more than Plank himself! I want to get to Plank's house, and there I can do my work."

He had brought himself to a high state of excitement—so much so that suddenly he dropped into a chair and gripped the edge of the table, as though he had grown dizzy.

Tom, alarmed at the white, working face of his companion, stood back from the door, as though to let in more light and air upon the other.

"The drift of feathers shows what way the wind blows," said Franchard. "You remember the shadow on Rankin's face when he saw the picture—the shadow of knowledge—the shadow of knowledge! Ignorance has a bright, empty eye. But knowledge is dark. It makes wrinkles and seams. Knowledge and pain, they work on the face in the same manner. Now then, Tom, listen to me. If I cannot prove the case to you, I'm wrong, and we're following a wild chase!"

"I'll listen," said Tom, still overawed.

"Do more than listen. Sit down here where I can watch your face."

Tom obeyed and took a stool on the farther side of the table.

"He sees the photograph. He recognizes the country. Why? Because he knows Plank, perhaps. He knows Plank's country. There may be half a dozen, scattered here and there, who know Plank's secret. At any rate, join that with this other thing—this poster on the floor. Why did he have that? Who could have expected that I would escape from Sing Sing and come West? When, as a matter of fact, I didn't come West for years. I've been following other trails all over the world!

"But Plank, who was here all the time—he was afraid that I might come here. And so he gave some of these posters to a few men who he thought might be of use. He scattered them here and there. 'Watch for this man!' said Plank. 'Where the law gives a thousand, I'll give ten thousand!' Do you follow my logic?"

Tom, listening with all his might, began to perspire.

"You mean that the posters wouldn't likely have been set up out here?"

"Who should expect me around here?" said the other. "I'd never spent a day in the West in my life. There was no reason to search for me here. No, Plank must have secured some prints of these and distributed them. There was fear in him, and when Plank's afraid, he'd pay with diamonds. He has them to pay with!"

This last he said in a softened voice, with a snarl in it that reminded Tom not for the first time of the snarl of a great, cornered cat.

"Plank scatters these about, and to Rankin among others. Rankin sees me, remembers the poster, plans to get that money for himself."

"He might have murdered us both while we were sleeping," said the boy. "He could have done that, if he'd wanted to get the money—he could have called it fighting, afterward!"

"Twice," said the older man, "a shadow leaned over us in the night, and twice I woke up, and twice the shadow went away."

"You didn't call me?" said Tom in horror.

"I wasn't quite sure. It was like the passing of a hand over my face, while I was asleep. When I woke up, I wasn't sure. The cabin was as dark as pitch, and I only had a sense of something withdrawing. I was half asleep, still; but now I know what had happened. He came twice and stood over us and wondered if he couldn't handle the two of us. But then he changed his mind. He would be striking in the dark. And perhaps he had an idea of the strength that's in your hands, Tom. That was probably what stopped him. But when the morning came, he sent us off up the valley to try a pass that can't be made. We were to waste hours in it, and when we finally gave up and turned back, he and a dozen other men would be lined up in the valley! We would have been corked up tighter than water in a bottle. It would have been prison for me again, if they caught me alive; it would have been prison for you, too!"

"Prison for me?" cried Tom. "What have I done?"

An expression of remorse came into the face of Franchard.

"You'll curse me for this, Tom. But the fact is that you'll be wanted for willfully and knowingly assisting a man wanted by the law—outlawed from the help of all other men. Do you know that?"

"What harm have I done to them, then?" said Tom. "If they send people to prison for that, I'm willing to go!"

The other nodded cheerfully at him.

"Strike hard enough and I always can get a spark out of you, Tom! But some day I may break my hand trying you!"

He laughed a little at that.

"You see how we narrow down the case?" said Franchard. "If it had not been for knowing about Plank, Rankin would never have had the old poster—five years old, as you see. And, having the poster, he knew about me. Very well, then, if we want to find the way to

95

Plank's house, all that we have to do is to get our hands upon Rankin and force him to tell us the way to Plank's place."

"Hold on," said Tom. "He's gone to town, according to you, to get a whole posse of men to come back here and to hunt us. Well, then, how can Rankin be caught by the two of us—"

He paused suddenly.

"And one of the two not much good?" said the other, smiling a little.

"I didn't say that," said Tom, flushing.

- "Ah, my lad," replied Franchard, "I have no false pride. Here I am, a rather old, feeble convict, escaped into the world and trying to down a great man. I have fairly clever wits, very weak hands, and not the strongest nerves in the world. But I have found a man who gives me what I lack. Between us, Tom, we are going to cut our way through mountains, and bridge valleys!"

To this speech, Tom replied with a wide stare. He never before had heard a man speak so frankly. This was a laying of the cards face up, and suddenly he felt that Oliver Champion Franchard would be very apt to accomplish what he decided to accomplish. And if he, Tom Fuller, were a tool in the hands of such a man, he would be apt to cut even as deeply into the rock as the other desired.

"Now, then," said Franchard briskly, "we come to the crux of this little matter. You understand that I have against me not only the criminal brain of my old friend Henry Plank—"

"Criminal?" said Tom.

"Yes, criminal. He helped me to rob the bank in Buffalo. As for the details of that, we haven't time to go into them. Besides, they can't matter to you, except that Henry Plank was the master mind, and I was his assistant. And you may as well know, furthermore, that the assistant went into prison for the offense—and that he went there willingly! But aside from that the point is that Plank can fight me and trace me and overreach me with a mind like my own, except that it is perhaps

96

stronger. And, at the same time, we have against us the strong hand of the law, which commands all the sheriffs and their deputies, and the militia, and the thousand and one forces which they can muster."

Tom drew a breath.

"While I floated about the world, unseen by the eye of the great Henry Plank, all was easy enough. I rarely had great adventures, and if suspicion came down on me, it was always comparatively simple to cover my trail and leave the spot of danger behind me. But now you see that affairs are very different. Plank knows that I am working, as it were, in his own yard. He is going to try desperately to keep me from reaching his house. Think of the good fortune and the cleverness of that scoundrel! The greatest criminal in the world, nevertheless, he is able to buttress and support himself with the very law which he had defied and broken a thousand times. He knows that I am here. With his own brains he will direct the law, and show it where to find me and how to act against me. On the other hand, he has undoubtedly established a hundred underground ways of his own, through which he can strike at me. How and when those blows will be delivered, I don't know. But against all those resources of theirs we have two things— my wits, and your instinct, Tom. And where my wits fail your instinct may pull us through. And where your instinct fails, my wit may serve us. That—and the fact that we are a moving base, and where we are today we will not be tomorrow. These things may serve us until I've found the place and delivered my blow!"

Tom, amazed by the ready sweep of the man's imagination, merely sat blinking.

"I dunno what you'll do," he said at last, "unless you carry along dynamite with us, and blow up something when you get to the place that you want!"

"Dynamite?" said the other with a soft and bitter laugh. "Nitroglycerin can only disrupt a house, blow it timber from timber and stone from stone. It can only turn the glass windows to powder and pile up the furniture like matchwood, scatter the roof in flying bits, and

97

crush and dissolve every living body within the four walls of the building."

Tom listened, overawed by the terrible picture.

"Listen to me," said his companion, lifting a finger, and making his voice gentler, as though he were instructing a child. "I have the miseries of twenty years to repay. I have twenty years of shame and neglect and silence and despair to return. Do you think that it can be repaid with death only? Why, my dear boy, death is a mercy! To death all life is flowing, and what is more benign than to render death suddenly and mercifully, and to cut off this wretched life of ours with a single stroke, without warning, without throwing a shadow of what is to come on those who are to be destroyed? Do you think that I would do such an act of grace to this supreme fiend among men? Do you think that I would destroy him before he had an opportunity to know that I was dealing him the blow? No, no, no!"

He paused and turned his raised hand into a fist.

"I am going to let him see me, and see me at my work. I am going to make him sit by, wrung with agony, unable to halt me, while I pour his life full of poison and let him live!"

This final speech drew him out of his chair, and left him beside the table, tall and trembling, very white, and his eyes blazing with an unnatural light.

"If you had done what I told you to do, and had killed him with a bullet from your revolver the other night, all my own hopes would have been destroyed. When I reflected on that, I afterward saw that you were actually an instrument put into my hand by fate! I felt, when I saw it afterward, that you and I were appointed to run him down and to deal justice to him on this earth!"

17

VERY MUCH as one is disturbed by the actual sight of madness, was Tom Fuller impressed by this outbreak. He did not answer a word to the peculiar words of his companion. He could see that there was some inspiration, much distortion, and a world of venom in what Franchard had said, but for his own part, he did not know what to say.

He could safely say that Franchard was not a good man. The law was pursuing him and the law had reason for its pursuit. Nevertheless, thickly shadowed across his mind, he guessed at a vastly greater wickedness in the person of Henry Plank, that genially smiling and brown-faced man at whom he had looked through the hotel window. And in spite of himself, Tom felt an enthusiasm rising within his heart, and a desire to attempt this very act which Franchard had planned, this baiting of the whole herd of the bulls of the law and the cunning wits of Henry Plank. The desire of the impossible, the strongest of all desires, began to burn up in him. The fanatic enthusiasm of the lost cause possessed him.

Perhaps it was because he expected this, or because he saw the light rising in the boy's eyes, that Franchard made his strategic pause. But now, suddenly, he held out his hand.

"Tell me, Tom," said he, "are we one mind and one spirit to do this job?"

The answer came with instinctive quickness from the boy.

"Yes," he said, "I'll try to do my share. I'll be your man to the finish!"

Instantly Franchard relapsed into the most matter-of-fact quiet.

"We'd better get out of here, then," said he. "We don't know when they'll return."

He replaced the crumpled poster on the floor, exactly as he had left it, and then looked about to destroy any signs of their return, even kneeling on the floor to sweep up some ashes which he had dropped from his pipe.

Then they left the house.

It was beginning to rain. The clouds had closed above the mountains, shutting out the summits, and leaving truncated slopes which appeared more vast than ever, and turned the place into a valley of giants. They took their places in the buckboard.

"Where's the last place you see that a buckboard could go around here, Tom?" asked Oliver Franchard.

Tom looked about him, and saw an almost precipitous slope of rocks, with tufts of brush breaking it, and then a growth of lodgepole pines, closely shouldering against one another.

"There," said Tom. "It don't look likely, and I guess that it ain't possible!"

"We'll try it, however," said the older man, "because we must get where we can see and not be seen!"

With that they drove toward the place, keeping the buckboard on a route where the wheels were almost always upon rocks, leaving no trace behind them.

On closer examination the slope was not half so difficult as it had seemed from a distance, a fact that mountain climbers all learn in their earliest lessons. Still, they both had to get out of the wagon and urge the horses forward with a whip, zigzagging back and forth until they reached the trees. Through a breach in the ranks of these they entered the little grove and there found some shelter until the skies opened and the rain came down in great torrents. Then the water flooded down through the branches, and there was no comfort to be had.

Franchard began to turn blue and his teeth to chatter, so Tom made a shelter for him in the bed of the wagon. Blankets beneath him gave him a comfortable couch, and a slicker above him was an improvised tent under which, presently, he fell asleep. Tom remained on foot, wandering ceaselessly back and forth among the trees, petting and talking to the streaming horses, then employing himself to rub them down, to keep up some flow of blood in them.

From time to time he peered out from among the trees and looked down into the valley. All there was removed to a strange distance, for the spume of the heavily falling rain was blown up by the clouds, and drifts of water mist, like fog, blew up and down the place. The hut itself, which the miner lived in, now appeared clearly, and again was removed behind a great veil. In the brighter moments, Tom could see the whole valley floor bright with running water, and he nodded at this, satisfied that the last tracks of the buckboard surely would be washed out.

Long hours went by. Sometimes he looked beneath the slicker in the wagon, to make sure that it was securely protecting his companion, and always to find that the other still slept, his lips slightly parted, his eyes hollow and dark with fatigue. He could realize now more clearly than ever that Franchard had hardly the strength of a stripling. All his force was in his mind, and that mind alone was opposed to the gigantic forces which he was challenging.

Suddenly the boy began to pity Franchard; and in the same instant he was filled with a great respect which was almost reverence.

The day wore on. The rain, instead of ceasing or growing thin, now was carried on a stronger wind, whipping home with such force that the drops stung the face and hands of Tom, and snipped off all of the half dead or insecure twigs of the pines. There were flurries of snow, too, which sometimes turned the valley to gray, only to have it washed black again by the next downpour of the rain. It was a miserable day, and yet there was a latent excitement beneath it. He was hardly in a hurry to have it grow old, because, before the end of it, he could guess that something of importance would happen, and that that thing might involve both him and Franchard and sweep them away to ruin.

It was not until the middle of the afternoon that Franchard wakened and came from beneath the slicker, his teeth chattering until he had run up and down for a time, beating his hands together to grow warm, and eventually he came to a stand beside Tom.

"You're holding out?" he asked. And then as though the question answered itself, he went on: "We'll have a sight of them in a short time, I think."

"Look!" said Tom.

For at that moment, like figures conjured by a magician's words, he saw forms riding around the next bend of the valley. In their slickers they looked like twelve knights-errant in armor kept shining by the torrents of the rain. And, like in armor, they went slowly, heavily, until they came to the cabin.

"Twelve men! Twelve men!" exclaimed Franchard. "I told you that they'd come. Twelve black demons walking through the night," he went on, muttering to himself; "twelve black ghosts in the rain. Look well, Henry Plank! Don't let the rain be a smoke in your eyes. Here we are, in touch of your guns. Here we are! Find us, find us, if you can!"

And he began to laugh, almost hysterically, and to shake his fist at the party.

The twelve were in the cabin for the better part of an hour, to eat and have coffee, no doubt, and then they came out, remounted, and pushed up the valley at a brisker pace.

"Another hour or so to make sure that we are not in the throat of the pass, lodged among the rocks like small fish in the teeth of a shark," said Franchard, "and then they'll come back again, with rain in the face to reward them! No, they'll have the dollars of Henry Plank to warm up their blood! He never begrudges money in his own cause. He's liberal in that behalf!"

They had to wait for two more hours, and the sunset time had come, showing a red crack in the western grayness of the sky, before the twelve black knights came back. They paused only a few moments at the cabin—perhaps only for coffee. Then they went on once more at a steady jog, like men who resigned themselves to the bitter night of rain and darkness and slippery trail that lay before them.

"Look in the rear, the man on the gray horse—or white, perhaps. That's Henry Plank," said Franchard. "I know him as clearly as if we had him three feet away from us!"

The boy looked, with such a shudder as he would have felt in looking on the fiend himself, and it seemed to him that he, also, could have known this for a man of importance by something massive in his bearing and carriage, and the leaning of his head against the wind. It would take a great human storm, surely to affect him!

Around the next hill shoulder they disappeared.

"And now?" said Tom.

"Only eleven men went down the valley," said Franchard. "The twelfth man remained in the hut, and that man is Rankin, of course. We'll wait a little longer. Then we'll leave the horses tethered here and go down and call on him. Hospitable fellow, that Rankin, and no doubt that he'll be glad to see us again!"

They waited until the darkness was thick. The rain still came down in pencil strokes of solid gray, glimmering in the night; and then they secured the heads of the horses and climbed down the slope, finding it difficult and slippery enough.

When they were in the bottom of the valley they could see the light from the cabin, glimmering small as the flame of a candle through the wet air, and then, from high behind them, a horse whinnied!

"It's Rusty, the rascal! He's feeling lonely without me!" said Tom.

103

"Oh, confound him!" said Franchard. "Will Rankin hear?"

It was hard to suspect that he would, for the rain crashed about them with ceaseless violence, and the wind howled across the canyon like a wolf, now and again.

They drew closer and closer to the outline of the cabin. The mustang from the lodgepole pines whinnied again, and this time there was a sudden burst of light before them. They had not realized that they were so close to the cabin, until the door opened just in their faces, and let out the lantern and fire light. Rankin stood there, his vast shadow falling into the rain and the dark, and quivering there.

Then he closed the door.

"Did he see us?" whispered Franchard in the ear of the boy.

"He didn't. We'll try the lock."

"Aye, aye! And walk in on him! Pretty ghosts for poor Rankin on a night like this, I'd say!"

They went to the door, and there Tom tried the latch. There was no lock whatever, unless a bar inside. He tried the latch, and the door jerked open with the pressure of the gale.

"That confounded wind!" said Rankin, rising from his knees beside the stove, into the fire box of which he had been stuffing wood.

He turned toward the door, dusting the splinters from his hands, and there he saw the two dripping forms against the dark, their faces looking white and wet, no doubt.

"Gosh!" breathed Rankin, and stood transfixed.

18

THERE WAS no gun on Rankin, and his eyes flashed to the corner, where his rifle leaned against the wall, and where his revolvers hung in their holsters, suspended by the cartridge belt slung over a projecting nail. But it was too far to get across the room to them. That one desperate flash gleamed in his eye, and then he looked back to his visitors with a grin and a nod.

"I'll bet you found the pass blocked with a landslide, eh?" said he. "This here rain is heavy enough to start to knockin' things loose! Come in and set down and rest your feet, will ya?"

They entered. Tom came in last, and his companion began to talk in a perfectly cheerful manner.

"We couldn't get through," said he. "We tried the main pass and it was blocked, all right. And then we went up that first gully to the right—"

"First gully to the right?" said Rankin. "Oh, I know what you mean. Why, you didn't try the gulch on the face of old Baldy, did you? That pointed right up the belly of the mountain!"

"Yes, it did." said the smooth Franchard, "but the fact was we thought that we could manage it, and that it might turn off to the left and let us through on an upper level—another pass, do you see?"

"You soon got that knocked out of your heads, I reckon!" said Rankin, laughing a little.

"We got it bumped out of our heads," agreed Franchard. "Of course, we found that we couldn't get through, and then, when we turned around, we smashed a wheel. Tom, here, was driving, and he let the mare lurch, and she bashed the wheel against a boulder half the size of this house!"

He turned and gave Tom Fuller a dark glance. Tom blinked, and endured it. He could not understand where this conversation might lead.

"Then you better teach him to drive," said Rankin almost sharply. "Mostly the folks around here don't recommend no guides as young as him! Where'd you ever serve as a guide before?"

"I never did," said Tom.

"Well, folks," said Rankin, "you might as well settle down and spend the night here. I'm glad to see you, and I'm mighty sorry that you didn't get through the pass. Maybe I spoke sort of careless to you. But the fact is that people got through the pass about six months back, and so I thought that you'd have a good workin' chance. Otherwise, you'd have to go back mighty nigh to Orangeville before you could get south."

Tom, watching him, noticed that the color was returning to his face, and he could not help admiring the manner in which the man had talked himself back into a courageous and satisfied state of mind. In the meantime, Franchard went on:

"While we were stuck up yonder in the gully, with our broken wheel, and sitting in the rain to wonder what on earth we should do next, we saw a number of men coming up the gulch. Tom jumped onto a rock and tried to get their attention. There were so many of them that we thought they might help us to get our things back to your cabin. Then we could go up there and repair the wagon the next day."

"You saw them? And they didn't see you?"

"Apparently not. There was a good deal of rain. We only saw them through the rifts."

"Well, I'll be darned!" said Rankin under his breath. Then he added, aloud: 'I'll wager that they would have been glad to see you, and they would have taken care of both of you, too!"

A flash of a smile appeared on his lips and went off again.

"Maybe they would," said Franchard. "They appeared to be riding hard. Presently they came down again, and it was perfectly plain that they had tried the pass and had missed it. We shouted to them again, but it was thundering and storming like the deuce by that time. We couldn't draw an eye."

"Well, that was pretty hard luck," replied Rankin, wandering toward the farther corner of the room.

A fit of coughing seized Franchard, and in the intermission between two spasms, he said to Tom: "Get ready to cover him!"

Aloud he added, wiping tears out of his eyes: "We've had a hard day, Rankin, and we're mighty glad to get back to your cabin. Although I'm afraid that I'm imposing on your hospitality."

"Not a bit, not a bit," said Rankin, rather absently.

"And the eleven good men who came out with you," said Franchard in the same suave voice: "I'll wager that they cursed and swore a good deal when they found that they had had their ride for nothing."

Rankin turned quickly, and stiffened a little.

"Particularly Henry Plank?" said Franchard.

Rankin's mouth twitched.

"I dunno what you mean," said he.

"I didn't think that you would," said Franchard. "You don't find it easy to follow such talk as this. It's a great deal simpler for you to arrange your ideas when you have print under your eyes—offerings of rewards, let us say?"

He smiled, and Rankin, with a gasp, sprang for his rifle. He had it grasped by the middle, swinging it into position to shoot, when he saw the revolver in Tom's hand. It had winked into view in a single flash.

"Drop it!" said Tom.

Rankin did not hesitate. The businesslike manner in

which that gun had been produced meant a great deal to him, an expert in all these affairs of powder and lead.

He dropped the Winchester and slowly turned until he was squarely confronting his two visitors. Franchard sat down on the side of the table and embraced a knee between both hands.

"Look here," bawled Rankin, "by gravy, I dunno what you take me for, you gents!"

"We take you for a fairly good fellow," said Franchard, with a wave of his hand. "We take you for a very good fellow indeed. But the truth is that every man is apt to reach his price. And when the law is offering a good fat sum, and Plank is offering a still larger sum above it, and where there's a bit of reputation to be gained by the way—why, any man other than a fool would take a chance at such a thing!"

Some of the desperate tenseness left the face of Rankin.

He said: "I'm glad that you got sense, Franchard. I didn't want to do it. You'd come here as a guest—but, well, a man don't want to slave away in a dirty hole in the ground the rest of his life!"

"Certainly not," agreed Franchard cheerfully. "That was exactly as I felt about life in prison. Five more years would have completed my term. But I couldn't wait. Strangely enough, the first half of the term was not the longest part!"

Rankin sighed.

"I made a big bust of this," he said. "I hope you'll call it square, partner!"

He stepped forward, his big hand extended. Tom saw Franchard nod, and then a little thrilling line of red flame ran across his eyes, and seared deeply into his brain.

He moved forward and stretched out his arm, intercepting the advance of Rankin, so that it was his hand that the miner clasped, and instantly the grip of Tom Fuller contracted with inhuman force. It crunched the bones in the back of Rankin's hand. It pressed the life and strength out of it, and Rankin's knees suddenly bowed with pain as he cursed and jerked back.

He nearly dislocated his own shoulder, but he did not move the boy, who remained steadily watching him, with a set, fierce face, and with the fingers of his left hand twitching ominously.

Rankin, desperate, whirled up his left hand to strike.

"Don't," said Franchard. "He'd kill you, if you touch him."

Rankin saw those twitching fingers at the same time, and he found it easy to control himself and that intended blow.

Tom released him.

"I'm mighty sorry," he muttered to Franchard. "But it sort of choked me—to see him comin' up to shake hands with you!"

"That's all right," said Franchard. "The best of men make mistakes, and Rankin made a few today. The worst of them was the last one. He thinks that he's easily out of this—unless the little handshake with you has undeceived him. Do I see red on the ends of your fingers, Rankin?"

Actually, the blood oozed from beneath a broken finger nail; the tips of Rankin's fingers still were purple and swollen, and the rest of his hand was a deathly white.

He nursed the bruised and nerveless hand and grinned with savage pain at Franchard and the boy. .

"Blood on your hand, Rankin," said Franchard; "but, after all, it's a great deal better to have blood on your hands than to have blood on your soul, and to break the rule of hospitality, and to betray a guest, eh?"

Rankin said nothing. By inch and inch, he backed away from the two, until nearly the length of the hut was between him and them.

"In the first place," said Franchard, "I want to warn you that this young guide of mine, as you call him, will often lose his way, as you pointed out, also; but he never allows one of his bullets to go astray. And even if

109

we don't tie you hand and foot, it's because we understand that we have you in the grips of our hands—ready to break with a pinch, as it were!"

Rankin moistened his white lips, and still chafed his crushed hand.

"Now, then," said Franchard, "it's only fair that we should get down to business. Business consists in an exchange. I can tell you what I have to offer you, and I know what you have to offer me. There's no reason why we should not transact some business, my friend Rankin. Do you agree?"

"I dunno what you mean!" said Rankin.

"Well, then, I'll tell you in clearer words. I can offer you your life. Is that something?"

"You mean that you've been thinkin' of murderin' me?" asked Rankin bluntly.

"I should not call it murder. I should call it the execution of a public duty and a private pleasure to put out of the world a yellow dog; a poisonous, yellow dog, like you!"

"Would you?" muttered Rankin savagely. But then he bit his lips and was silent.

"You'll want to know what could keep us from doing that duty—that pleasant duty? It's this—that we know you have information which we want. Rankin, we'll have that information, my friend."

"What information?" said Rankin, his head bowed, and his voice reduced to a whisper.

"Rankin," said Franchard, "we want you to be our guide, and we want you to take us to the house of your good friend, Henry Plank. Will you agree to that?"

"Plank?" said Rankin. "Plank?"

His jaw began to sag. He looked old and sick in an instant.

"Gosh!" breathed Rankin. "You wouldn't mean that, would you? Not that I should double cross Plank!"

19

WITH A MOST acid smile, Franchard regarded his victim.

"No doubt that hurts, Rankin," said he. "It's a more painful matter than to double cross your guests and feed them lies, and try to drag them into a net so that you can put your hands on a parcel of money. But I'm going to ask you to hurt your conscience just in that way. Now, what's your answer?"

Rankin's mouth twitched. He looked toward the door as though he were about to hurl himself at it and try to escape, but then he encountered the mild, curious eyes of Tom Fuller, like the eyes of a child, and Rankin shook his head.

"What'll you have from me?" he rasped.

"I want the way to the house of Henry Plank," said Franchard.

"I dunno it," said Rankin.

"Don't you?"

"I mean, I don't know where he lives. Nobody knows. Plank is just floating. I don't suppose that he's got any house."

"Then why were you so cut up a moment ago by the thought of double crossing him? Why should you be afraid if you didn't know? You can't tell a thing that's not in your head."

Rankin did not hesitate. He said confidently: "You can see why for yourself. The fact is that I was scared to

111

death. I still feel shaky. You turn loose this bear man onto me, and then you hold Henry Plank under my nose like a gun!"

"But you don't know much about him after all?"

"I know enough to be afraid of him! Everybody knows that that's ever really heard of him!"

"That's the point, Rankin. Not very many people have heard of him. He can walk in and sit down and chat with a sheriff, and the sheriff's glad to see him. Now, what do you know about Plank that scares you?"

Rankin hesitated a bit for the first time.

"Where did you learn his name?" pursued Franchard.

"I picked that up."

"Now, go carefully," said Franchard. "I think you're lying when you say that you don't know much about Plank. I'm reasonably sure of it, in fact, but I want to make absolutely certain before I go ahead. You're on trial, now, as I may say, and the subject of the trial is your knowledge of Plank. Guard every syllable. I have a keen ear for lies. Speak with care. Don't become confused, and don't deny your own statements. If you make me feel that you do know Plank very well, I'll have the rest of what I want to know out of you—if I have to feed you into the mouth of that fire yonder!"

As he spoke he slowly raised his arm and pointed toward the fire box of the stove. It was still open, as Rankin had left it, and the fire was glowing furiously. The top of the flimsy stove was beginning to redden.

Rankin flashed a glance in this direction, and then he scowled back at his judge and questioner.

"Fire away," said he. "I don't have to stop and think. I can't tell you what I don't know."

"Let's go back to this," said Franchard.

He took from his pocket the snapshot of the two mountains and the little valley between them and laid it before Rankin.

"About this," said he.

"I've told you about that."

Franchard lifted his eyes with a smile.

112

"You were lying when you talked about it before!"

"All right," said Rankin shrugging his heavy shoulders. "I guess maybe you know all about this, eh? You know all that's in my head?"

"No, but I expect to get part of your information away from you!"

"Fire away."

"You said that these mountains were south."

"They are."

"They're not, and you know it."

Rankin lifted his brows, but he said nothing.

"Where are they, Rankin?"

The miner said quietly: "I've told you the truth about that."

"How long have you been mining here?"

"Coming on five months."

"Is it hard work?"

"Yes. There's a quartzite—"

"Get much out of it?"

"A little color. Not much. Vein pinches out and comes in again."

"Make a living out of it?"

"About."

"But you have to stick close to the job?"

"Yes."

Tom Fuller glanced from one to the other in great excitement and suspense. He could not follow the course of these questions—that is to say, the hidden point at which they must be aimed—but he could see a white spot at the base of Rankin's jaw where the set muscle stood out against the skin, and he knew that the miner was an anxious man indeed.

"You're a fool," said Franchard. "I knew I could trip you up if I kept you at it fast enough."

"I ain't tripped up," said the other. "I've told you the truth."

"You lie," said Franchard, without passion, almost gayly. "The fact is that you've been up here fooling around the mine to cover your face and give you something to do."

113

Rankin dropped his head a little forward, his brow covered with loose wrinkles, like the brow of a bull.

"One man, working briskly, could pile up in two weeks as big a dump as you've left there in five months."

"Working quartzite?"

"It isn't quartzite in the dump. That was made while you were cutting down to the hard ground. Now, Rankin, confess. You've been lying like a ticking clock!"

"Well," said Rankin, "I have, but not about Henry Plank."

"What's the reason, then?"

"You ain't a judge or a sheriff, after all."

"No, you can talk out to me."

"The truth is that I've been dipping off on my own and helping myself to things that I needed."

"Rustling an occasional cow, and that sort of thing?"

"Yes," said Rankin, and the boy noticed that he did not blush, but spoke rather with a thoughtful air.

"The fact is this," said Franchard: "Plank has to have a few trusty fellows spotted around the country, and you're one of them. He's used you before, and you've gone in deep for him. Now you wait here to be called again. He's going to make your fortune, one day. He's always going to do that! But you've been in so very deep with him, that he's even talked to you about me, given you the poster, promised you a great reward if you should snag Franchard. Is that right?"

Rankin, after a moment of silence, muttered: "You think you know it all. What's the use of me talkin'?"

"Because you can tell me what I don't know. Rankin, will you admit that you've been caught lying?"

"No," said Rankin.

"I'm the judge, though. What about you, Tom? Has he lied?"

"Yes," said Tom.

Rankin swayed toward the door, but it was only a movement of his shoulders. He saw Tom between him and flight, and his feet remained rooted to the spot. The handclasp had crushed his spirit. Franchard said nothing. After chatting so briskly, he now became silent, seated on the edge of the table, smiling a little at Rankin, and never taking his eyes from the miner. Rankin endured this silence, ill at ease.

He again looked to the door, then hastily back at the glowing surface of the stove. His face began to shine with moisture and Tom could see that his breast was heaving and laboring hard.

"Well, what d'you want?" he gasped at last.

"A guide who knows the way," said Franchard gently.

"Great guns!" cried out Rankin. "Whatcha want? To be taken where you'll be eaten alive?"

"Yes. Right up to the old lion's cave."

"He'll swallow the three of us. That's what would happen! Why, Franchard, you ought to know him!"

"I know him. I'm willing to take the chance."

Rankin slumped into a chair. He was trembling from head to foot in a horrible, loose fashion, as though his flesh were jelly.

Then, as Tom began to be mastered by disgust and sympathy at this sight, Franchard slipped from the table and went to Rankin. He dropped a hand on the thick shoulder of the miner and looked down into his face.

"Rankin," said he, "why is Henry Plank taking such particular pains to keep me away, to stop me at a distance?"

Rankin suddenly jerked up his head and stared inquiringly into the face of the other.

He seemed to feel a touch of hope and amazement together.

"That's true," said he. "He's wild to stop you!"

"Why, man?"

"I dunno. Who'd ask questions of Plank about what was in his mind, or what his reasons might be?"

"Then ask yourself, Rankin. Would he want to stop me so badly if he were not afraid?"

"Afraid? Plank?" echoed Rankin in greater amazement than before.

"He's afraid of me. Here I am, a stranger in this land,

unable to shoot straight, with only a boy to help me, and with every chance of being picked up by the law, and yet Henry Plank is more frightened now than he's ever been before in his life. And he has reason to be!"

"How could he be?"

"You've seen for yourself that he is. As for the reasons, I'll tell you this: They're as profound as reasons can be. Now, Rankin, you have your choice to make. Will you go along with us?"

Rankin hesitated another moment.

Then his battered and shaken manhood suddenly reasserted itself. He stood up from his chair and stretched himself, spreading out his long arms, and yawning a little.

"Well," said Rankin, "I'm cornered. You've seen through me, Franchard. And perhaps you're right. Perhaps you have got a ghost of a show against Plank. Anyway, what's the use in talking? You're holding the cards, and I'll have to play your game!"

20

ONCE RANKIN had thrown himself upon their side of the scale, he appeared to do so without stint. He forged straight on with his plans to help them, and was thorough in everything. "Because," said he, "once Plank finds out that I've left this here place and sent no word to him, he'll know that I've gone over to your side. And after that, they's nothing in the world that he'll want so much as to cut my throat!"

He advised the abandonment of the buckboard at once. It was true that they could follow wagon trails a great part of the way, but before coming to the end of the journey, they would have to give up the buckboard. Furthermore, every wagon road was sure to be watched by the men of Plank, and by the men of the law, whom Plank was certain to advise.

The next morning, in the early light of the dawn, Rankin built a small model on the ground before the cabin door, and in that model he sketched the country over which they would have to pass.

First he scattered a number of small rocks, and drew a stick among them, knocking a passage clear and furrowing the ground.

"Here we are," said he. "Here's the cabin; here the gorge; and yonder's Orangeville, southeast. No, look at here. These stones are rough mountains—the Timber Mountains—all spilled up north of us, and cruel, bad going. But that's where we gotta go. And that's where Plank knows that we're going!"

He paused, and frowned speculatively at his companions, as though wondering how they would endure the labors that lay before them.

"You go along north through these here, until you come to the Big Yellow."

Here he made another trench in the ground with the end of the stick. "The Big Yellow ain't so big except in the spring, when the snows melt. We could ride right across it, and so it don't make any difficulty. Now, on the far side of it, you get to the Candle Plains. I dunno how they got that name, and I don't care, unless it's because they're pretty much on fire most always. A couple of times in the winter a blizzard flattens out those plains with ice, but the rest of the year it's just blow sand, so light, that if you stub your toe, a ton of that there sand is likely to go blowin' away to the edge of the world. And Plank'll be watchin' the Candle Plains. An easy thing to do, too! Half a dozen gents, with good glasses, could keep a hundred miles of it swept clean, and when they spotted us, they could gather us in. I'd say that crossin' the Candle Plains would be just about like walkin' up and throwin' ourselves into a fire."

"There must be some other way," said Franchard. "Let's see another way, my friend."

"Well, here's where the Little Yellow branches off from the Big Yellow. The Little Yellow, it backs off toward the Candle Mountains, and all the way it cuts a road for itself. It's like the Big Yellow, and it don't run very deep with water, except when the spring floods come rippling down it and chuck around boulders bigger than you and me! Them stones have cut out a gorge for it. Straight as a ruler they are! A dry bottom, this time of the year. And nothin' to do but to dodge along among them boulders, in a place so narrow that two men could be put to watch, and they'd sure see everything that was worth seein'. Now, how else is there to get at that place of Plank's, unless you was to take a lot of time and ride clean around the Candle Plains and come in over the Candle Mountains from the north? That would take the best side of a month—"

"I would be in jail by that time," said Franchard calmly. "There's no use thinking of that. It would diminish my chances, and my chances are already so small that they can't stand being cut down. I had one chance in fifty, before I had the good luck to meet with you, my friend, and now I have, perhaps, one chance in eight or ten. We must go straight ahead, and not let time tell against us, along with the other barriers. You know Plank, Rankin. We mustn't let time become his ally!"

Rankin nodded, and grew a little pale as he looked off over the hills. The morning was bright. From the deluge of the day before, every inch of the valley sides was bursting with water, and the valley, where the shadow fell, glimmered faintly, and where the sun fell it was of a shining silver.

"Then it means the Candle Plains, or the gorge of the Little Yellow River," said he. "You can take your pick."

"Which one would you choose?" said Franchard.

"I'd choose the river, because it's where they won't expect us. It's sure to be watched, but it may not be watched by gents that have their eyes open. Them that think watching ain't needed don't see things, even when their eyes is open! But—I'm gunna ask you one thing."

"Ask it, then. I'll answer if I can."

"We got slim chances of breaking through to Plank's place. But supposin' we do, you're sure you could do something worth while there? You could paralyze him?"

"Have you seen a wasp paralyze a spider, a great tarantula?" asked Franchard.

"I've heard about it."

"Very well. Then, I undertake to handle him as efficiently as the wasp handles the spider."

Rankin stared, incredulous.

"Every man has some weak spot," said Franchard in a philosophical tone. "So has every animal. The rattlesnake can let out the life of a grizzly bear with a tap of his fangs. The bear can break the neck of the bull. Everything runs in a circle. There must be some broken link somewhere. So it is with our friend, the great Henry Plank. There is a flaw in his wonderful armor. I know that flaw, and through it, I intend to sting him. You will see him," said Franchard dreamily, "sitting like a child that doesn't know its lesson. You'll see him sitting like a child about to be spanked!"

He laughed softly. Then he started up.

"We have to begin, Rankin. We might as well begin now!"

The buckboard they pushed into the farthest corner of the horse shed and pitched down enough hay from the mow to cover it.

"If he finds the wagon he'll know everything. If he don't find it, maybe we'll have a few more days' head start," said Rankin in explanation of this device, which he had suggested.

In every way, Rankin seemed to have given up hope of escape, and to have identified himself totally with the others. As Franchard explained to Tom: "His very reli-

119

gion is the fear of Henry Plank. All men who ever have worked under Plank have the same feeling—with one exception." His eyes flashed, and he did not need to explain who formed that one exception.

"Now, then," said Franchard, "Rankin has turned against his master, and he knows that his neck will be broken if Plank ever can lay hands upon him. Watch him like a hawk for a few more days. Then we can treat him as though our interests were his interests!"

Tom did not answer, but he nodded. He felt his inability to follow the mental windings of this serpentine Franchard, but he was willing to follow on blindly and do the work which was allotted to him. That work, in the first place, was to remain constantly near to Rankin, and he lived up to the letter of the task.

For four days he never was ten feet from the miner and former ally of Plank; but day and night he haunted the big man while they worked their way through the Timber Mountains. During those days they saw not a soul, or a single human trace, except, on a hilltop, a circle of stone where, in some other day, a band of Indians must have made a death stand against their enemies. It was wonderfully rough country, and the buckboard could not have lived in it for a single day, but they forged ahead, eating up the miles slowly on horseback.

This was a painfully unfamiliar method of transportation to Franchard, and caused him a good deal of suffering from exhaustion and from the chafing away of the skin on his legs. However, he did not complain, but kept his seat with compressed lips and a frowning brow of determination. There were no trails, except cattle trails, and these were as devious and as difficult as could well be imagined. The cows of that wild land seemed as agile as mountain sheep, and willing to take ways almost as precipitous. The timber which had given the range its name, was all second growth. Those small trees—largely lodgepole pine—interspersed as they were with big, rotten stumps, obstructed the way, but never could have given a sufficient shelter against observation. They had to be constantly on the alert, and every hilltop that overlooked their way they examined with care and with fear, lest it should hide spies who were on the lookout for them.

Once in the middle of a hot, steaming afternoon, Rankin broke out:

"It's like as if he was holdin' off till he'd got us fair between his teeth, durn him!"

The same thought was in Tom's mind. His only glimpse of the great Henry Plank had seemed to show him a sufficiently harmless fellow, but the talk of Franchard and Rankin gradually built in his mind the conception of a demi-demon. He prepared for the battle which he was sure must come. Every day he was allowed to spend an hour making as much noise as he chose with his guns, shooting off quantities of ammunition with both rifle and revolver. Rankin refused to join in such practice.

"I never was a great hand," said he. "I done the shootin' that come my way, and luck pulled me through with nothin' much more than a slug through the calf of my leg. But if I started to practice, I'd simply learn to lose all confidence! I never would be like Tom, here. He could think a gent dead, and the gun would do what he was thinkin'!"

This tribute, Tom accepted mildly, as he always did all compliments, for it seemed to him that his deficiencies were of such importance that no amount of smaller accomplishments could make up for them.

So they came through the Timber Mountains to the last long ridge, and from a hollow between two peaks they could look down on the northern foothills, and beyond these, they could see the long line of the Big Yellow River, winding between its banks, fringed with straggling willows in the low places, and with sparse groves of poplars at others. It was the one sign of verdure in a great, flat, naked landscape.

"There you are—bare as the palm of your hand!" said Rankin. "And if we—"

121

Franchard had leaned down to tighten the cinches of his saddle, but now he gasped: "Look behind, for Heaven's sake! They're on top of us!"

"The trap!" said Rankin. "I knew all along that we was ridin' into the throat of it!"

And, down the hollow behind them, between the two hills, Tom saw a drove of half a dozen armed men riding toward them silently, but at a furious pace.

21

THE THREE horses of the pursued staggered as they felt the drive of the spurs, and then got into a racing gallop; but Tom, glancing behind them after a few seconds, felt his blood turn cold. That glance told him that the six behind them were gaining fast, and it also told him that they would continue to gain. For the six horses moved not with the pounding lope of cow ponies, but with a long, raking stride which told of blood!

Well enough to chance a mustang against one of these during the long grind of a ten-day journey under weight across western mountains and burning western sands, but this was not a ten-day race. It was a single burst of speed which would tell the tale, and those six behind him were controlled by riders who seemed willing to risk their necks over the uneven footing of the valley floor.

It was a tough mustang which big Rankin rode, and a fast one, too. After the first moment he was struggling for the lead beside Franchard, who was on the cream-colored mare. And she, plainly, had the foot of the trio. As for Rusty, he ever began slowly. And now, with his ears flattened, he grunted as he reluctantly gave himself to his task, letting out link after link, unlimbering his muscles for their work. He would take up with the two before him, Tom felt confident, if only the race last long enough, but in the meantime, they were opening a big gap.

The downward pitch helped the mustangs to lengthen their stride. It would help the thoroughbreds behind them even as much, unless their knees gave with the increasing shock of the impacts.

Tom looked back once more, and he saw that the rangy animals behind him were eating up the ground with wonderful ease.

Then Tom slid the long Winchester out of its leather holster beneath his right leg. He took a firmer grip with his thighs and knees, and let the reins hang loose, so that he would be able, at any time, to swing about in the saddle and plant a few rapid shots among his pursuers.

He had no scruple about it. Whether they were men of the law or men working for Henry Plank did not enter his mind, but he only knew that he was a hunted animal, and that they were the hunters. And so he urged Rusty on, guiding him to the best footing by the sway of his body.

Rusty, suddenly, was pricking his ears, as though he realized that a fight was toward, and this was the sole thing that gave a spice of happiness to his strange soul.

There was time for Tom Fuller to wonder at himself. He was as different from his expectations of himself as a man in a dream is to his real self. Always, before, the mere thought of taking a life had been abhorrent to him beyond speech to express it, but now he was feeling a singing happiness that swelled in his breast and trembled in his throat.

The horses, first of all! He would aim low for those. But afterwards, for the riders themselves.

So he told himself, and actually laughed into the teeth of the wind of the gallop, which blew his throat cold in a moment and howled inside his hollow cheeks.

It was a bright clear day. There were no clouds in the sky, only a thin horizon mist, and the valley rocks on either hand shone brightly about him. Among those rocks he searched, hoping for a break in the valley wall on either side, into which the three of them could dodge. Such a gulch, with badly broken ground, might give them a defensive position from which they could hold off even twice their number. Yet the odds were greater than that. Rankin, he had no doubt, fighting for his life as he would now, might give a good account of himself, but Franchard would be more than useless.

However, the walls of the valley, though broken repeatedly, were never yielding back into a real canyon in which they could ride toward higher ground, and take shelter among the trees or the rocks. All was bare. And the indentations were shallow things which held out little hope.

Gallantly the three mustangs worked, never abating their pace, and lengthening their strides to take advantage of the downward slope which swung them ahead— and yet the six riders in the rear were still gaining.

These were experts at their business. They had not bothered to draw a gun, but spent all of their energies jockeying their horses along, taking advantage of the best ground for the running, hurling their weight well forward, getting the most out of their fine mounts. Men who could ride like this were sure to shoot straight, and suddenly Tom was sure that they were indeed the men of Henry Plank. He, alone, would have been able to muster six such men and six such horses! The law had not the time or the money to spend in making such selection.

In the meantime, Rusty was gaining gradually on Rankin, although the cream-colored mare still stretched away in a comfortable lead. But suddenly Tom saw Franchard throw up a hand, with a yell that floated dimly back to him above the rattling of the hoofs. Off to the right swerved Franchard, bouncing in the saddle as the mare changed direction, and instantly the boy saw the reason.

Before them, and to the left, was exactly the thing for which he had been waiting and watching; the shadowy mouth of a canyon which cut back from the valley in which they were riding and undoubtedly climbed up to the western highlands. But now, out of the mouth of this canyon, like so many shot out of the mouth of a gun, came four riders who bade fair to cut straight across the race and end it then and there.

Tom caught his breath.

He could remember, now, all that Rankin had said, all that Franchard had inferred about the invincible brain and the invincible power of Henry Plank. He could remember what Rankin had been saying that very day, about their riding into the throat of a trap.

And here it was!

He looked behind. The six riders were drawing rifles, sitting straighter, and preparing to open fire as they saw the mouth of the bottle about to be blocked. The four who were cutting in from the side already were weapon in hand.

They were not pushing their animals. There was no need, for they had the game in their hands. To shoot at six was a hopeless thing, to shoot at four was not. Besides, they were the nearer target! Tom hesitated no longer, but pitched the butt of his rifle into the hollow of his shoulder.

He held it fairly loosely, so that all the shock of the galloping hoofs of Rusty would not necessarily be transferred to the rifle itself. But it was a difficult business; more chance than skill, one would have said, to shoot from the back of a galloping horse. The targets jolted suddenly into the sights and out again. Sometimes Tom was pointing the gun at the floor of the valley, and a moment later the blue sky was his field of vision.

For an instant he studied the swing of the gun's muzzle as it jerked up and down in regular sequence, and then he steadied it a little on the leading rider of the four, a tall man on a tall gray horse which flashed like silver under the glare of the sun. Into the sights and out he swung. Glancing down the rifle barrel seemed to give the boy the eye power of a field glass. He could see the very face of the man, and the fierce joy in it, though he was still a furlong off. Then, catching at a centering of the sights upon the target, Tom pressed the trigger quickly.

He lowered the gun, as Rusty shied around a black rock that reached at them like a tooth out of the valley floor; and when he looked, he saw that the magnificent gray was down, and spinning head over heels—a dead horse from the fall if not from the bullet.

The rider, arms outstretched like a man diving into water from a height, landed well ahead of his mount, twisted rapidly over and over, and lay still.

Dead? said Tom to himself. And the word and all its meanings rang through his brain. No matter what he felt about it, that bullet might have made him a murderer in the eyes of the law, and he could see suddenly only one picture—that of the other murderer, Cressy, with his hands held together by irons, and the proud escort riding around him, leading him toward the jail, and afterward toward the gallows!

There were other matters to think of now, however.

The effect of that bullet had been as magic. If it had been the second or the third shot, it would not have counted so heavily, but at the first pull of the trigger, Tom had sent a man down with his horse. The other three did not stop to figure what part chance might have had in the triumph, but they split to either side like an Indian charge before a stockade where rifles are thrusting out through the loopholes, and a chief already has gone down at the forefront of his galloping men. Tom could see them pulling frantically at the reins.

They were too busy pulling up and swerving to either side to try to get in a return fire, and in that critical moment, the three fugitives drew level with them and whirled past.

Then guns began to bark. Twice in quick succession

126

waspish hummings flicked at the ears of Tom and disappeared. He saw Franchard duck low in the saddle; he saw the head of Rankin jerk around, and had an instant's view of a darkened face of anger and hate.

Then he looked back again.

In those few and vital seconds, both the three from the left and those in the rear had unlimbered their rifles and were pouring in a fire made wild by the fact that their horses still were galloping, even if more slowly. That would have been the moment, Tom thought, for a wise leader to give the order to halt them all. Then they could fire with precision, and from such a range that they could hardly fail to bring down at least one of the quarry of three.

The shooting ceased as he looked back. He saw a broad form among the first six pursuers swing to the front on a grand black horse with the head and neck of a stallion, and he saw this fellow swing a hand and wave the others forward.

Instantly, Tom's heart was in his throat, for though he could not be sure, something told him that this was the same figure he had seen through the hotel window, and the same which he had seen again, riding with bent head down Rankin's valley through the dusk and the rain. It was Henry Plank himself, come out to lead the cream of his forces. And he was not halting his followers for a volley. He was urging them forward to catch and swallow all three of his foes!

In the same instant he saw another sight which was welcome to his eyes. Already far behind them, the gray horse lay sprawled where it had fallen, but now its rider staggered to his feet, with both his hands clasping his head.

It was not murder, then!

Tom turned once more, and bent to the work of shooting Rusty more rapidly down the slope.

22

Now RANKIN drew even with him, falling back little by little, and the mare under Franchard was only half a dozen lengths in the lead. She had plenty of foot, but the awkward riding of Franchard was telling heavily against her.

Rankin turned a face contorted with fear and with savage satisfaction.

"Good work, kid!" he shouted. "You split 'em up! You split 'em up!"

And he laughed, with the wind of the gallop tugging at his face and parting his beard.

Half a length he fell to the rear. Obviously, either his weight was beginning to tell, or else his mustang had only early foot. Tom looked back.

Nine men were now coming behind them like arrows freshly off the bow, and the rider of the black horse was in the lead. Tom stared at the man, and felt sure that it was indeed Plank. He rode with a higher head than the others. There was about him a nameless presence of command, and an utter fearlessness which Tom could tell even from the distance. It was Plank, and Plank played his hand like one who has no fear of losing!

What fear was there, after all?

For the nine riders kept together in a close bunch, only two lagging a little to the rear, while the rest thronged in a compact mass, the black horse galloping strongly in the lead. Every rifle was back in its holster now, and every man was using spur and quirt to maintain his place in the hunt. And although a stern chase is a long one, as sailors say, still the whole body was drawing up.

Tom looked across at Rankin, as the latter fell behind, and he saw that the face of the miner was white and set. He was falling back into the jaws of a dreadful death, for there was no doubt in Tom's mind that the miner would not be given a mercifully swift exit from life if ever he came into the grip of his former master. He was more than an enemy in the eyes of Henry Plank; he was an archtraitor, and as such he must be paid off!

Franchard gave not a single glance back, but, bouncing up and down and from side to side in such a manner that it was wonderful that he could keep in the saddle over such a rough course, he bent his body still forward and tried to get greater pace from the mare.

He failed to do so!

Little by little he was coming back to his two companions, and now a scant two lengths separated him from the others. So Tom saw, suddenly, that by their horses they could not win. There was simply not enough speed in the tough little animals to rate them against the blood horses in their rear. Like sleek panthers those beasts were bounding over the ground, apparently at ease, unpressed, and they could be driven on for a long time at the same rate. They were simply another breed, another race, and the mustangs could not hold up against them.

He drew the rifle from its case again, and swinging around in the saddle, he jerked the butt into the hollow of his shoulder.

The result made his heart leap! For every one of those nine riders suddenly pulled to one side or the other, and drew in on the reins. Even Henry Plank had veered sharply to the left, and so doing, had lost vital ground, for the mustangs ran straight on, with never a break.

"You got 'em in your hand, kid!" yelled Rankin, new hope in his eyes.

But Tom knew better. No man in the world can shoot accurately to the rear from the back of a running horse, over rough ground or smooth. And though the first threat might work, the second one would not. It had been merely an instinctive flinching from fire, since they had seen the result of the first shot he had sent. But they would not flinch again.

He glanced back once more, and he saw that Plank was again in the lead, turning a little in the saddle, and doubtless cursing his men. They would not turn again!

Like great greyhounds behind tiring rabbits, the pursuers were gaining now. The valley began a long bend toward the east, and rounding that bend, Rankin and Tom, side by side pulled up level with Franchard for the first time.

Tom looked at him curiously. His face was pale, but it was thoughtful rather than afraid, and he gave his most careful attention to his work of keeping in the saddle. Such clumsy riding, however, had told heavily upon the mare. She was darkened by sweat, and foam that had flicked back from her gaping mouth was like a lace shawl over her breast and shoulders.

Franchard called out with wonderful cheerfulness: "Go on, boys. I can't keep up!"

"Spur, spur, for Heaven's sake!" shouted Rankin in answer. "There's the last chance ahead of us!"

Shooting around the broad shoulder of the valley, they saw before them a mass of cattle being driven up the way toward them. It looked to Tom far other than a means of escape. It seemed to him as though Fate had stepped in, at this point, and had reached down a hand to block their way, with this untimely herd.

Franchard, too, actually drew in upon his reins, and only instinctively loosed them again at the command of Rankin.

But that man, like one gone wild, rushed straight upon the herd!

The cowpuncher who was riding upon either point of

the head of the band, waved his hands frantically to warn back this mad rider, but Rankin went on, with his hat in his hand, waving it above his head, and shouting like a wild Indian.

Tom, not knowing in the least the purpose, imitated that example out of sheer desperation. Rankin was the entering wedge. The cattle, fortunately, were not too compact, and could give way to either side before the horsemen. They were a lean, long-legged rout of longhorns, wild-eyed, nervous, savage. They winced aside, and Rankin, as he passed, still yelled, and slashed at their flanks with his quirt.

That was more than enough.

The cattle before them shrank away, but those that they had passed began to gallop forward as though three terrors with clouds of fire and brimstone had just whirled by. Tom dared not glance back.

He was too busy with the grim task of twitching Rusty to one side or the other out of the danger of those sharp horns, but Rusty was an old hand with cattle, and he did his work well.

Poor Franchard was equally well mounted, but the jerking from side to side was too much for him. Dropping the reins, he simply clung to the saddle, while the mare dodged wildly here and there among the steers.

It seemed to Tom that they never would come to the end of that herd, but at last he gasped with relief, for the rearmost cows split to either side, and he saw daylight before him—daylight, and the furious faces of four cowpunchers, who were making at him full tilt.

He cared not for them. His concern was with what might be happening behind him, and the progress of Plank and his men through the milling cattle.

His first glance satisfied him. There was no sight of Plank or the rest of the nine. All the throat of the valley was alive now with tossing horns, dim in the shadow and bright as steel in the sun; all the valley was choked with the thunderous bellowing of thousands of strong steer as they plunged forward like a river, in full stampede. Henry Plank was not among them, or, if he

131

were, he could say his last prayer, for no horse and no man could continue in that mass for five seconds without going down!

Tom looked across at Rankin and Franchard, and it seemed to him that in their faces he saw the same expression of sickness and of relief which he knew was in his own heart. It was like a miracle. The dumb beasts were charging up that valley and carrying away with them all the intelligence and the fine horses and the keen men of Henry Plank, while these three, like men saved without reason, stared at one another.

He had something else to think of at that moment, for a burly cowpuncher rushed at him and caught him by the arm.

"You—" began the cowpuncher.

And then all words were lost in a roar of sound, vague imprecations looming through the mist.

Tom smiled gently on him and laid a finger on the fellow's breast.

"You better go pick up your doggies, stranger," said he. "Because they'll never come back here to pick up you!"

That word of advice was oddly successful.

The cowpuncher changed color, reined back his horse, and stared. Then he turned straight off after the disappearing tails of his cows. Rankin and Franchard, similarly beset, were similarly freed from disturbance, for they had seen their leader fail with Tom, and they rode hastily after him, as though they were anxious to learn from him what had happened.

The three went on, Franchard laughing outright with relief and with joy; Rankin smiling a little sourly to himself, and the horses jogging comfortably. They had done their work, and after the nine riders had been harried up the valley for a few miles by the crowding mass of furious longhorns, they would have little heart and not very much strength to renew the chase with vigor.

"You see how it goes?" said Franchard. "Heaven gives a man only a certain portion of good fortune, and I think that Henry Plank has had the last of his. Yonder in the valley, if you could see the heart of that man, you would find fear in it, my friends. For he knows that he has played strong cards. He knew that his hand was good enough to win. And yet he has collected only a dead horse—and some saddle sores, I hope!"

He turned to Rankin.

"It was your idea that pulled us through," said he.

"Me?" snorted Rankin. "We wouldn't've had any lives to save, Franchard, if it hadn't been that the kid turned the four back, and that he split the nine of 'em a minute later. Me? What I done I've done before. Besides, I rather have wild bulls get me than Plank. All they got is horns to split you, and hoofs to stamp you flat!"

The valley widened suddenly. They saw before them the muddy waters of the Big Yellow, streaming down meagerly among gravel banks and sand bars. To the right stretched the limitless Candle Plains. Far to the north they could see the brown and blue of mountains, cloudlike and indistinct.

"We'd better stop here a minute to give the hosses a breath and us a chance to look. Somehow, this here old world never looked so good to me before," said Rankin. "I been ridin' for the last hour with my sins sittin' on my shoulder and whisperin' into my ear!"

23

FROM THE high bank of the river, the trio looked back, but the mouth of the valley still was empty. Far away they could hear a murmur like that of thunder below the horizon, and they knew that the herd was yet in full stampede, brushing before its horns all the courage, all the strength and the cleverness of Henry Plank and his men. They could not help glancing at one another with a smile, as they listened and thought their own thoughts.

Then they started zigzagging down the bank.

As they reached the level of the stream, the horse of Franchard stumbled and threw him against the pommel of the saddle. Tom heard him stifle a groan, but he thought little of that until afterward.

In the meantime, they turned up the stream, keeping their horses in shallow water so that all signs of the trail should disappear. Rankin arranged this, and in all their march he was the guiding genius and more full of resource than the other two put together. It seemed as though his fear of Henry Plank had filled him with a new intelligence.

For half an hour they continued in the bed of the stream, until Tom began to fear that the men of Plank might appear at any moment upon the bank and open fire upon them. But only at the end of a half hour did Rankin suggest climbing the farther bank. That they did, taking the horses up a rocky place where the hoof marks would not tell. It was so steep that they dismounted and the mustangs were led, and it was as they mounted again at the top of the bank that they discovered the further handicap under which they must ride. For as he reached for the pommel and tried to draw himself up to the saddle, Franchard suddenly groaned and fell almost exhausted in against the side of his horse.

Rankin took him by the shoulder and shook him.

"Franchard, are you sick? Are you sick?" he shouted.

Franchard rolled at the big man very sick eyes indeed.

"By grab, you were hit!" yelled Rankin.

"I was only scratched," said Franchard.

It was along his right side. A bullet had raked his ribs, and his clothes and his side were dark with congealing blood. It was such a thing as would have been hardly more than a spurgall to a young and powerful man, but Franchard was neither young nor strong, and the drain on his strength and his nerves was more than he could bear. In the shelter of a grove of willows, they dressed the wound as well as they could, Franchard making light of it and trying to jest about the shallowness of the scratch, but all the while with his face yellowish-white.

Afterward they rode on once more, Franchard with his shoulders squared with unusual precision, and his back unnaturally straight. Tom found a chance to talk to black-faced Rankin during the ride that afternoon.

"He can't be badly off," said Tom. "It ain't much of a hurt."

"Ain't it?" said Rankin.

In his own fear and savage bitterness, he glared at the boy as though he would have liked to strike him.

"Look here," said Rankin, after fumbling for a long time to find the right illustration: "It takes a lot to crack a tin cup, don't it?"

"Sure it does."

"You and me are tin cups, Tom. But Franchard, he's fine china, and the flick of a finger nail, it would crack

135

him! Mind you what I say—he's pretty nigh ready to fall out of his saddle, right now."

Tom stared at that erect back before them, and was inclined to agree. Franchard was using all his nerve, strength and his courage to support him in the saddle. It did not seem possible that that strength would last very long.

"What'll happen, then?"

"Who knows? Not I," said Rankin. "What'll we do if anything happens to him?"

"We'll stick by him to the finish, I guess."

"Yeah, we'll do that. And after the finish, what then?"

"Why, we'll cut and get away, if we can."

"We'll cut and get away?" sneered Rankin. "You talk like you were crazy! The fact is that we'll never get out of this here net we're in. Our only chance is to stay inside and work to the center of it, and there let Franchard cut Plank to bits, as he says that he can. I dunno how, of course! But if anything happens to Franchard, you and me, son, are out of luck. Darn the day that the pair of you ever showed up at my shack!"

Tom did not answer; he was too convinced of the truth of what Rankin had said.

They entered the gorge of the Little Yellow, and since it pointed toward the west, the sun flowed into it in intolerable strength, reflecting back from the rock walls, and turning the chasm into a furnace.

The effect of that heat was amazing upon Franchard.

He began to breathe hard, with his mouth twisted to the side and his body bent toward his wound. Presently Rankin pointed to the feet of Franchard, and Tom saw that they were hanging loosely in the stirrups. His weight was supported upon his hands, which clasped the pommel of the saddle.

Then the sudden shadows rolled out from the side of the canyon and covered them from the sun, but still Franchard seemed in no greater ease.

"And him to break up Henry Plank!" said Rankin through his teeth. "I'd as soon tackle quartzite with a

136

wooden chisel! We gotta get this brittle gent into cover. Then I suppose we'll sit by and watch him cash in! That'll be about our size!"

Tom agreed. It was clear enough that Franchard was working on his last strength.

"We're going to camp," said Rankin, riding up beside Franchard.

Franchard turned to him gravely.

"We had better keep on, Rankin," said he. "Now that the fire is out of the air, you can see how it lies on the ground. You wouldn't want to lie in camp on ground like that, Rankin; we'd be burned to the bone in no time!"

Rankin gaped at him and then glared significantly at Tom.

Suddenly he said to Franchard: "You're right. But we'll climb up there through the rocks and get to a cooler spot."

"A cooler spot for you, perhaps," said Franchard in the same manner. "But the fact is, Rankin, that while the yellow flame was falling through the air, I breathed of it, and now it's rankling in my heart and lungs. It's burning me slowly—"

He reeled in the saddle, and Rankin caught him under one arm.

Tom took the mare by the bridle, and leading her in this fashion, they conducted the delirous man up the first ascent to the right. Deep among the rocks they paused. The boulders closed them in like fantastically shaped houses in a village, as thick and almost as huge. There they pitched down a bed for Franchard, and laid him upon it. He was quite out of his head by this time, and kept murmuring and moaning, and sometimes he would break out into a light laughter that sent flecks of snow into the veins of Tom.

They looked to the wound. The whole of Franchard's side was inflamed, and Rankin turned white as he looked at it.

He said to Tom: "Maybe there's an infection started in that wound. Maybe not, I dunno. And maybe he's only irritated from the riding that he's had to do. But it looks to me like he's on his last legs. Feel his forehead. It's burning hot. He's breathed of fire, all right, as he said. He'll die. And then we'll die, too, Tom, as sure as shooting."

The sky was turning to rose and pink above them as the sunset began. And they heard Franchard laughing cheerfully, and then talking to himself.

"Look, Henry, look! The faster you run the faster I go with you. I'm riding in your shadow!"

"He's goin' dippy," said Rankin. "He's gonna be out of his head the whole night, maybe. And what if Plank's men should hear him yellin' as they ride up and down the pass? Wouldn't that be a sweet mouthful for them to find all at once? Plank, and me—and you and your guns. What could you do in the middle of the night, with a dozen of 'em? Or else, they'll make a circle, and sit back on their haunches and laugh at us, till they've starved us out into the open—"

He paused, with a groan, and Franchard in his delirium groaned at the same moment. It made a grisly harmony.

"Look here," said Rankin, "he'll never pull through without a doctor."

"Then we'll have to get one," said Tom. "Where's the closest town?"

"Town? Why, fifty miles down the Big Yellow is Holliday. Who'd ever chance that ride, kid? Fifty miles, and Plank's eye on you all the way?"

"He can't see everything," said Tom slowly, after consideration. "Besides, I'd like to try."

"You would," growled Rankin. "Sure you would like to. Like candy, you'd like it!"

Tom waved to the rocks around him.

"I'd rather ride out and take the chance," said he, "than to sit here and wait. I'd rather be doing something than—"

He paused.

"I think you would!" exclaimed Rankin suddenly. "Doggone me if I don't think that you would!"

He looked anxiously up to the sky. Then he pointed. "With that agin' you, too?"

Pale as a bit of cloud, and like a cloud seeming translucent, Tom saw the round face of a moon near the full hanging in the center of the sky. He knew what light that moon would throw through the thin mountain air. It would be almost like a sun. And all the difficulty of crossing the open country would be increased a hundredfold.

Rankin explained, almost bitterly:

"Stick to the cover of the river bank and the trees there, and you'll be two days following its windings. Take to the open and there's the moon plastering you all the way, almost as clear as the sun. What do you say, kid?"

Tom stared fixedly at the moon, and then he shrugged his strong shoulders.

"I'd rather be riding than sittin' here," he murmured at last. "I'll start when the night comes!"

24

IT WAS NOT full night. It was only the heart of the dusk when Tom left the camp. Behind a pair of great rocks, Rankin was struggling to make the smallest of fires to boil the coffeepot which he himself had filled with water, by venturing down to the stream that escaped from the higher side of the valley not fifty yards away. His face, showing by that light, was desperately set and grim. One would have thought that he was fighting for his life. And this, in a sense, he really was doing.

Just out of the gleam of the little fire lay Franchard on his bed of blankets, and his murmuring sounded on the ear of Tom Fuller drowsily, like the running of water. All sense had left the mind of Franchard, though the life still remained coursing in his veins. His face was fiery hot to the touch. His pulse raced and faltered, alternately, and Rankin was gloomily of the impression that even a doctor might come too late.

Yet, there was a chance. Something might be done which would lower that temperature almost in a moment, and give Franchard another chance for life. In the meantime, he lay in the throes of delirium, and Rankin was only grateful that the ravings of the wounded man were hardly more than moanings and groanings. It would be hard for one passing up the almost dry bed of the Little Yellow to disentangle these vocal murmurs from those of the thin trickle of water which went down the slope of rocks.

"If I get to Holliday, what doctor will I go for?" asked Tom.

"How do I know?" snarled Rankin. "First place, you ain't going to get to Holliday. You'll be snagged on the way. Second place, if you get there, no doctor would be willing to come. They've heard about us before this, and folks don't take chances with the enemies of Henry Plank—not in this neck of the woods! No doctor would come."

"One has to come."

"Sure, one has to come. But one won't!"

"Is it full fifty mile?"

"No. It's closer to thirty."

"I could make that by nine or ten o'clock."

"You might make it then. Unless they snag you on the way." .

"I'll try!"

"Get out, then, and stop talkin' about it," said Rankin.

The boy went to Rusty and prepared to mount, but Rankin followed him suddenly.

"Listen!" said he.

Softly, and sounding very far away, Franchard was singing.

"What's that?" whispered Tom, overawed.

"That's the Frog language. I been up to Quebec, and I learned enough of the chatter to recognize that. He's singin' French, kid. He may be singin' in heaven before you come back, and if that's the case, I'll be singin' at his side. Listen to me. If you get to a doctor in Holliday, which likely you won't, take him by the back of the neck and smuggle him away with you. I dunno how you'll do it. That's up to you. Heaven help you, and Heaven help the rest of us!"

Tom hesitated.

"Rankin," he said, "are you sort of tempted to saddle your hoss and ride away with me?"

Even through the semidarkness the eyes of Rankin flamed.

"I been turnin' that back and forth in my mind for two hours," he said. "Leave me alone. No, I'm agin' Plank now. And I'm gunna stay agin' him. I won't try to go back to him, crawlin' on my knees. Besides, it wouldn't do me any good. There's nothin' that he likes so much as kickin' a man in the face. Now get out of here, and don't talk no more foolishness!"

Tom left.

He and Rankin, together, had wrapped around the iron-shod hoofs of Rusty some pieces of buckskin, and tied them firm. It might be that one of the bits of leather would become untied, or that the sharp edges of the shoes would cut through the soft binding. In that case, the clink of metal against the rocks would be almost sure to alarm such a guard as Plank's men must be keeping upon the valley at this time.

However, he must have a horse, and there was only that one way of getting him up the gorge to the mouth, where it dipped down to the wide gorge of the Big Yellow. And Tom rode the mustang down with care. He was as ready to fight, now, as any desperate, cornered animal. A naked revolver was in his hand; in his left hand he kept the reins, drawn tight, so as to keep Rusty on the alert.

But the mustang seemed to know that there was danger about them. He went forward with pricked ears. All his usual sullen hostility and mulishness had gone from him, and he went like a big cat, stepping with care. Once, when his footfall turned over a stone, which fell with noise, he paused, one hoof lifted, and seemed to listen to the sound which he had caused. And as Tom glanced from side to side, guessing at every shadow beside every one of the great rocks, the horse stared, also, so that Tom felt almost as though he were going with an extra guard.

He went a furlong down the chasm when Rusty froze like a pointing dog, and through the murk of the evening, Tom, looking straight ahead, saw dim figures drawing toward him. He pulled Rusty into the black steep shadow of a rock and waited, gun ready, teeth set.

The figures came nearer. Tom heard the clink of shod hoofs upon the rocks, and then the puffings of the horses which, no matter how slowly they were going now, had evidently been ridden hard not long before.

Then, peering around the corner of the boulder, he saw four men riding side by side. Next, he could hear their voices. And, finally, one speaking in caution: "Not so loud! Might as well go along carryin' a lamp!"

They were very close, and Tom could hear the more quiet answer: "They's four of us!"

"How many bullets is there in a Colt?" asked the first speaker.

This pregnant reply caused the other to laugh a little.

"Only them slugs that are labeled fly true," said he.

"The kid they got with them can shoot."

"Callow found that out."

"His head is cracked, they say."

"Aw, it always was! He always was loco."

"A ridin' fool he was."

The four drew abreast of Tom's boulder, and in a desperate effort to hide himself from their obstruction, he pressed against the surface of the boulder. Even Rusty seemed to understand, and he, as it seemed, pressed as close as possible against the rock in turn.

But bad luck was dogging Tom at the very start. Here, beside him, all four of them stopped their horses. They looked about. One of them, on the nearest side, looked straight in the direction of Tom, and that look nearly drew a bullet. It seemed a miracle that the fellow did not see, but Tom forgot that the light of moon and dusk had mingled, filling the valley, as it were, with a mist. Also, the shadow of the rock was steep; and perhaps he was more shielded than all else by the fact that though they were looking for suspicious objects, they were hardly looking for objects standing still, and so near at hand.

They talked together, keeping their voices cautiously low, and a strange feeling it was for Tom to realize that their voices were lowered for his sake, no matter about what they talked.

"You heard how Callow rode the Brinsley roan?"

"I never heard tell."

"You know the Brinsley outfit?"

"The toughest doggone outfit that ever I seen. I worked for 'em, I rode that range six months."

"Then what happened?"

"Well, I quit."

"You got run out, you mean?"

"You think so? You go back and ask, will you?"

"Anyway, about Callow. That gent could ride."

"Sure he could, and maybe he will again."

"When he buys himself a new head!"

They laughed at this remark, laughing softly, guarding their voices.

"Callow could ride, but he was just out of hospital from havin' the knife of a greaser lodged too fast in his lining. Well, when he got pretty well he went out to the Brinsley ranch to ride for 'em, and he asked for an easy string, because he didn't want to get his insides stirred up too much."

143

"I know the way he felt."

"This here hard-boiled foreman, he said sure, and he gave Callow a long-headed roan that looked half asleep."

"I know that kind. The kind that play possum are the worst, a lot, ain't they?"

"Shut up, and lemme tell my story. Callow, he climbed onto this here roan and he talked to him, and the roan just pricked up his ears, and Callow tickled him with a spur. It was like droppin' a can of nitroglycerine. The roan, he busted right up into the middle of the sky and come down on one leg. Callow managed to hang on, though he was most cracked in two. And for five minutes he had to ride like he'd never rode before. He's a proud gent, is Callow, but that day he pulled leather, and he pulled it good. He wasn't workin' in no rodeo then! He rode that roan to a lather, and a thick one at that, and then he come back to where the foreman and the rest of them boys was standin', with a broad grin on their faces.

"Callow, he felt pretty sick, and he felt pretty mad. As I was sayin', all of his insides had been mixed up by that no-account bronc, and when he seen the grin on the face of the foreman, he says to him: 'Here's your quiet hoss back for you, and when I get off him, he ain't gunna bother nobody no more.'

"Then Callow, he heaved himself out of the saddle, and as he fell, he lurched forward, and he grabbed that bronc around the head, and took a hand hold under his chin, and the whole weight of him jerked on one side, like a hangman's knot.

"Well, he snapped that mustang's neck for him, and the roan dropped dead.

" 'There,' says Callow, 'is what I call a real quiet hoss. He was nice and smooth before, but now even a lady could ride him. Has anybody got any remarks to make?'

"Nobody had no remarks to make, and when the boss heard about that job of Callow's, he says that that's the kind of a gent that he wanted to have workin' for him on his ranch. And he sent for Callow and give him bang-up pay, and Callow's been workin' here ever since."

"He won't work no more, for a while. The kid spilled him right on his bean. That's what I call shootin'."

"You talk softer, or you'll be able to feel some of it. Callow, he's gunna get well, all right. Drift along, boys, they ain't nothin' around here!"

25

THEY RODE on, but to Tom it appeared that they went at a snail's pace. The horses seemed to pause and falter at every step. So keenly he watched them, that he saw the inward sagging of the horses' hocks. Softly he prayed to himself that no one of them might look back, because the moon had shifted a little, and the shadow was now thin that covered him in his shelter.

He heard them talking as they went.

"That kid is a dead shot."

"They ain't such a thing. They ain't such a thing as a dead shot, except a gunman that's dead, and they's plenty of them."

"You think he had luck?"

"I know he had luck. He took a chance, and the chance worked."

"All right, but that's the kind of luck that I don't want to run up agin'. It wins lots of poker games."

Their voices grew fainter. And Tom, breathing more deeply, kept pulling softly on the bridle reins to keep his

145

mustang occupied. For he feared lest Rusty might stamp or snort. However, the tough little horse stood still, and the riders gradually vanished.

He breathed deeply for the first time in minutes. These, he knew, were fighting men. Of such the whole force of Henry Plank's followers doubtless was composed. He had selected picked men, here and there, and paid them their price.

Tom waited until the four were out of sight among the rocks, then he let Rusty go ahead down the valley. And like a very wise little animal, the mustang went slowly, stealing his way, literally testing the loose pebbles before he put his weight upon them. However, in a few moments, it seemed safe to go more rapidly, and he let the horse strike into a jog trot. This raised what appeared to Tom a prodigious clangor, like the sound of the anvil in the blacksmith shop. But he could guess that these echoes were magnified in his imagination, and that they were not audible very far up the gorge.

Very soon he came to the mouth of the canyon—surprisingly soon, considering how long it had taken them, as he remembered, to come up to that place. There were no guards stationed at the mouth of the canyon. Even the brilliant mind of Henry Plank, apparently, had devised no better scheme for guarding the chasm than to have a patrol ride up and down through it. A patrol which rode carelessly, talking as it went!

He felt a fierce leap of his heart when he thought that he, even he, could have devised a better scheme than this, and so he rode Rusty at a canter through the soft sand at the side of the valley mouth, turned a naked boulder—and fairly crashed into three men!

Two stood on the ground. One was holding a match, lighted, while the third member of the party leaned from his saddle to get the light for his cigarette.

There was no chance to turn back and mask his approach. He heard a curse that moment, and saw the unemployed member of the trio reach for a gun. So he leaned far forward on Rusty and drove him straight ahead.

Much was related about that incident in after days. It was, above all, the thing that gave Tom Fuller the greatness of his reputation. But that repute was based upon a misconception. Men took it for granted that he had attacked the trio with malice aforethought. They could not understand that he had been committed to the action partly by carelessness and partly by accident. Also, they could not understand how greatly he was advantaged by finding them as he did, with two of the three occupied, though by so small a matter. The flare of a lighted match, in fact, was in the eyes of all three when the form of Tom rode upon them through the shadows. He heard a yell; he saw the others startled; but he, in the meantime, had used the vital second.

In the earlier days of Rusty's career, men said he had been tried out for polo. He had failed because he had not sufficient foot, but in that education, he had learned a great deal. He had learned contempt for all men, except for this one rider. Furthermore, he had learned contempt for those of his own species. One quality he had which Tom knew, and which he used now. That is to say, he drove him straight at the broadside of the horseman in his van, and Rusty, with a practiced skill, and with all of his concentrated weight behind it, gave his shoulder to the other pony.

It was not a big horse. Even if it had been, it is doubtful if it could have stood up against the shock of that impact. At any rate, it was knocked fairly from its feet, and involved in its fall the holder of the match of a moment before. Two of the three were rolling in the sand, half choked by it, but valiantly striving to curse and regain their feet.

There was only the third left, and he put a bullet half an inch from Tom's ear. Then Tom rode him down.

He wished, afterward, that he had used his Colt. If not a bullet, then a blow with the long steel barrel would have been enough to prostrate the man. But he did not think. He had used Rusty once, and now he used him as a weapon again, and hurled him straight at the unlucky cowpuncher.

147

The poor fellow went down. Tom had a ghastly sense of Rusty's hoof slipping on something soft, and then a cry, chopped short by the very extremity of agony, cut into his brain from beneath.

Catching his breath, he spurred Rusty wildly ahead. Again the yell of pain rang behind him, louder, more piercing, but when he glanced back, already the sprouting rocks had blotted out the scene. They, and the treacherous moonlight, and the remaining dull glow of the dusk, veiled him from sight, and there was not a single shot fired after him.

He did not keep up the pace. He dismounted at once, and removed the muffling from the feet of Rusty. Then he remounted and turned the mustang out toward the left, across the Candle Plains.

If there was a pursuit, and of that he could be assured, he might hope that it would fly straight down the course which he had apparently been taking when he left the mouth of the canyon of the Little Yellow. Surely, they would not suspect that he was bound actually for Holliday, where doubtless there were waiting agents of the law!

He rode on, keeping Rusty at that lope which he could maintain without tiring, day and night. With wolfish ease the little mustang ran, and the rocks swayed past them, and the western sky darkened to livid obscurity, and the stars rose.

The sky seemed to brighten as the last light of the day departed, and only the moonlight remained to rule the world. Brighter and brighter it grew, until the boy was shifting in his saddle, now and again, and scanning every group of trees that he approached, and every outcropping of the rocks.

They were all upon his right. They were his guides upon his course, that night, for they represented the line of the Big Yellow. Keeping just off of this, so as to avoid the windings of the river bed, he could ride straight into Holliday with the least loss of time, as big Rankin had assured him.

His heart began to rise to his work. He felt, moreover, his first contempt for his fellow men. They who all his life had seemed as demigods, compared with his weak and failing self, now were of another nature. They had shrunk, and he had gained what they lost. They might perform better with rope, or branding iron, or with a pencil behind the ear, but they were not to be trusted altogether in a fight.

He thought of the nine heroes of Henry Plank, led by that famous man himself, turned back by one rifle shot and a herd of steers! And he thought of the blindness of the four selected men who had gone by him in the river gorge. Last of all, there were the three. There they had loomed before him, and suddenly they were gone again! They had been blotted out of the picture, and by the hard shoulder of Rusty alone!

It was hardly a wonder that he laughed a little as he rode. Though, back in his mind, there still rang the wild cry of the trampled victim.

He rode onward for a full hour when, as Rusty trod through a bit of very soft sand, he distinctly heard the clangor of hoofs upon rocks behind him.

He turned sharply about, and was in time to see a rider disappear behind some brush on the river course!

That jerked the triumph out of his mind. It was a shining gray horse, a silver horse, like that one which Callow had been on when Tom's bullet had jerked the mount from beneath him. Now it was gone behind the trees. And it did not come out again.

Alarmed, he pulled the mustang farther in toward the river and its procession of shelters in the way of rocks and trees, but for a half hour, though he looked constantly behind him, the apparition seemed to have vanished.

Then, once more the sound of hoofs beat faintly upon his ear, and again there was the silver horse, sliding like a ghost through the moonlight far to his rear. His heart leaped. There were tales of phantom horsemen. Suppose that Callow had, in the day's course, died from his fall—his skull had been fractured, the men had said—might that not be his haunting spirit riding across the night?

He moistened his lips and gave Rusty the spur. For a mile they rushed ahead, and during all that time Tom would not once glance behind him. But when he looked, there was the phantom again!

Tom grew desperate.

Before him, to the right, nearer to the river, he saw a cluster of trees, and for these he made. When he had gained the shelter of them, he drew rein to wait, but when he looked back again, the phantom rider had disappeared once more. Five long minutes he rested there, listening to the heavy, regular breathing of Rusty, but the silver horse was no more in view.

At last he started on again.

He was more than a little desperate as he rode Rusty on over the plain, but though he looked repeatedly behind him, the silver horse was no longer there, though the moonlight made the whole width of the plains lie clear beneath his eye.

Then he saw other lights before him, lying in a long, depressed line across the plains. They were yellow. They blinked and altered like the gleam of glowworms, but gradually they grew more distinct beneath the moon. They were the lights, he knew, of a town of some size. From a thing that he could have held in his hand, it gained in size, until he could have stretched out his arms to it, and then it ran still farther from side to side, a true straggling town of the western plains.

He was on the verge of it now. Its size gave him an added confidence that, somewhere in this place, he could find the help of which he had need. What he would do, he could not tell. He felt that he must wait for inspiration until he faced the doctor that he selected. Then something might come to him.

So thinking, he turned in the saddle, and looked back for a last time across the level plain.

And he saw the silver horse striding smoothly up behind him, glistening beneath the moon!

26

Ghost or no ghost, Tom Fuller had endured enough.

He whirled Rusty around and spurred that gallant little mustang straight at the stranger. Well and valiantly did the mustang go, his ears flattened, his head jerking in and out like the head of a snake, in his efforts. But it was of little use! The stranger had turned at the same moment, and though Rusty ran his hardest and best, the gray horse faded out into the moonlight, and glimmered away, diminishing at every stride.

Tom, wondering that such a horse should be, wondering, moreover, who that mysterious spy could be, turned back again toward the town and entered it, as he had hoped, not long after nine o'clock.

He wanted a doctor, first of all. After that he was commissioned by Rankin to get some food. It was almost as essential as the doctor, because they would certainly have to camp for some time among the rocks of the valley of the Little Yellow, and, while there, they would need food which could not be brought down by the rifle.

Both commissions were sufficiently dangerous in execution, and the getting of the food was apt to prove almost as hazardous and difficult as the getting of the doctor.

Up the street he went, wondering how he should set about it. It was a pleasant little town, this of Holliday, though it had been laid out upon a scale a good deal too big for the houses which were in it. It was one of those towns sketched upon the desert by the brain of an optimist. It had huge streets, wide enough to have served as avenues, with trees planted upon either side, and with enormous squares, tree-planted, also. The waters of a little tributary of the Big Yellow flowed through the town and gave a moisture to supply the trees, but since they had come up, Holliday looked more like a forest than a city. Vacant lots were now covered with dense, lofty brush, and with fairsized trees. The streets themselves would have been worthy of the park of a great city. And it was only by peering under their branches, as it were, that one could make out the modest little fronts of white-painted houses, with neat gardens and lawns before them.

An air of peace extended over Holliday. It entered into Tom's own mind and made him smile a little. The long width of the plains was far behind him, and the dangers through which he had passed in the canyon, and above all, the wounded man in the gorge of the Little Yellow.

However, he could not go dreaming through the town. He saw a pair of men jogging their horses up the street and he accosted them.

"Hullo, partners."

"Howdye, stranger."

"Not so doggone well," said Tom. "I'm lookin' for a good doctor in this town. Who you recommend?"

"They's all kind of doctors here," said the nearest of the two riders. "But what's laid you up?"

Tom had prepared his answer.

"Rheumatism in my left arm," he said. "It's got hold on me pretty bad, and I ain't much good handlin' a hoss. I gotta be on the back of a household pet, rather than a real man-sized broncho like you'll have in your string on pretty nigh any man's ranch."

"That's a true thing. Well, lemme tell you. Most of the folks goes to Doc Holmes. But I wouldn't. They's the old colonel."

152

"I want a doctor, not a soldier."

"He ain't a soldier. Only, he comes from Kentucky. You know what I mean, maybe."

"Yes," said Tom.

"The old boy, he's the one in town that knows rheumatism. Had an aunt laid up with it mighty bad. She'd had it for nigh onto ten year, and tried all the medicines. But the colonel, he fixed her up. Another thing is that he don't charge much when he sees a puncher down and out. He collects his money out of the rich gents!"

"Where could I find him?"

"If he ain't playin' poker at the hotel, you'd likely find him right down there at that big corner house."

Tom thanked the informant and rode on. He did not want to stop at that corner house, because he had no wish to fall in with some keen-eyed "colonel." However, he saw that the two were sitting their horses and looking after him to make sure that he stopped at the right place. Therefore he felt compelled to pause in front of the colonel's house. He dismounted. He even pushed open the gate, just as a tall, shadowy form came down the drive.

The glow of a cigar showed a pointed silver beard, a long, aristocratic face.

"Do you want me, young man?"

"Are you the colonel?" asked Tom.

"I am Colonel Forbes."

"Why," said Tom, "the fact is—"

There was a soft pounding of hoofs in the deep dust of the street, and then a cheerful voice hailed them: "It's me—Joe Murphy, Colonel Forbes. The gent said that he was laid up with rheumatism. I just sent him along to you."

"Thank you!" called the colonel. Then he added: "You come along with me. Where's the rheumatism?"

"In the left arm," lied Tom, wishing with all his might that he were far from there. But, somehow, he was drawn up the driveway behind the other.

"The best arm to have it in," said the colonel. "In

that arm, it doesn't interfere with the dealing of cards, eh? And you can throw a rope and draw a gun, just as well!"

"Yes," said Tom rather faintly, not relishing the importance of the last phrase in the colonel's remark.

They went up the long, wide steps of the colonel's house. It was the pseudo-colonial type, with narrow pillars grouped around a semiclassic porch. The big front door opened. They stepped into an atmosphere of musty rugs and carpets on which their feet fell silently, and went down the entrance hall to the colonel's office.

There, for the first time, Tom could see him, and he was greatly upset. The colonel had an eye that was filled with the most penetrating light, and which sifted through to the very core of his soul. For a moment the man of medicine did not speak, but merely stared. Then he said:

"Rheumatism, eh? You're young to have that. Let me see your arm, young man."

"They's no rheumatism in my left arm," said Tom.

The other frowned.

"What sort of a dodge is this?" he asked. "What do you want with me?"

"I don't know," said Tom, "that I've come to the right place."

"What sort of a place do you want, my friend? And what sort of a doctor?"

Tom stiffened with anxiety and shifted his weight. He could not help but stare at the other in a haunted manner, and wonder how he could begin to talk. Suddenly it seemed monstrous that he should broach such a scheme as his to a respectable physician. But then he saw, in a flash, that one man would probably be as difficult to handle as the next, and that he must fight out the battle on this battleground. As he hesitated, his color changing, the colonel stepped a little back from him and watched him with a frown of caution, but not of fear.

Then he said suddenly: "Young fellow, you're broke and you need money. Is that it? I may tell you that I've never yet turned any stranger away from my door. But you need not have come to me disguising your motives. I thank Heaven that I have known poverty myself!"

Still Tom hesitated, and the other said, rather impatiently: "Come, come, young man, speak up, what is it that you want?"

And at last an answer blurted forth.

"I want a brave man," said Tom.

"Aha," smiled the colonel. "A brave man, and not a doctor?"

"I have a friend that's sick."

"Where?"

"Thirty mile out."

"In what direction?"

"I could show you the way," said Tom.

Suddenly the colonel smiled. "With my eyes blindfolded?" he asked.

"Oh, no!" said Tom, his simple eyes widening.

The colonel frowned. "My young friend," said he, "whatever your mystery is, don't you think that you'd better be frank with me?"

"I can't be," said simple Tom, and he shook his head.

"You want me to go blindly? Who is your friend?"

"A—a man named Smith."

"A—a man named Smith," mocked the colonel, not unkindly. "This fellow named Smith—what's wrong with him?"

"He has a fever," said Tom.

"What sort of a fever? How did he catch it?"

"He was hurt."

"By a bullet?"

Tom was silent.

"By a bullet?" repeated the colonel, his eyes sharpening.

"Yes," murmured Tom.

"I thought so. And who are you, young man?"

"I'm a friend of his."

"You're a friend of Smith. You come to me in the night and ask me to ride thirty miles. You won't tell me the direction. And you expect me to go? Why, my young friend, for aught I know, you and your friend

155

Smith may both be outlawed men, whom it is prohibited that I should help."

His teeth actually clicked over the last word, and Tom groaned aloud.

"Colonel Forbes," he said, "I sure don't want to make you no trouble, but I'd like to beg you to—"

"Hold on a minute," said the colonel, "perhaps I may be able to guess where your sick friend is lying."

"Could you?" asked Tom, amazed.

"The gorge of the Little Yellow River, let us say? Or out in some hollow of the Candle Plains?"

Tom was fairly staggered.

"Does your friend Smith," went on the colonel, "sometimes call himself Franchard?"

The blow had fallen. Tom, instinctively, took a backward step toward the door.

And then another blow struck him in swift succession.

"And are you, by any chance," went on the colonel, "the youth about whom every one in the town is talking on this day? Are you Tom Fuller?"

27

Now, IN THAT crisis, it seemed to Tom as though his vision were widened and made at the same instant more acute, for he saw not only the lean face and the keen eyes of the colonel, but also he saw every detail of that room in which he was standing—the brassbound book on the center table, the formidable desk which looked to weigh five hundredweight, at the least, some flowers under a glass globe in a corner, and two or three great faded enlargements of photographs upon the wall, together with the colonel's chiefest pride, which was a colored print of Salvator on the day when he won from the great Tenney. The legs of Salvator looked slender as pipe stems and seven feet long. The jockey on his back appeared tinier than an infant, and the shoulders and hips of the famous racer seemed as ample as those of a Percheron.

These details the boy saw as he stood before the colonel, at that moment feeling that the end had come for him. Near Forbes' hand there was a bell pull. He watched it, fascinated, expecting each instant that the hand would grasp the cord and pull.

After that, what?

A frantic retreat, gun in hand—or a crashing dive through the window in the hope of reaching the lawn beneath without a broken neck! He thought of these things; then he looked back straight into the eyes of the colonel, and he was astonished to see that Forbes was smiling a little—a dry, quiet smile which was rather in the eyes than on the lips.

"You are the desperate Tom Fuller, my lad?" he asked.

At the sound of his voice, Tom's fear departed. He took a great breath. "You're not gunna send for the law, then?" he asked.

"No," said the colonel. "I'm not. I've obeyed the law long enough and often enough to relish the privilege of breaking it, now and then. I have an idea that this may be one of the instances. That is, if I can make anything out of you, Tom. We hear a thousand rumors. The celebrated Plank, it is said, is after you. Is that so?"

"Yes," said Tom.

"He hunted you this very day?"

"Yes."

"He was there in person?"

157

"Yes."

"But you got away. Something about a lucky herd of cattle which blundered along there—"

"Yes."

"And then a rifle shot, I believe, that dropped poor Callow on his head and cracked it open for him?"

"Yes."

"Did you fire that shot?"

"Yes."

"You're not a great talker, Tom," said the colonel, still smiling.

"No," said Tom. "I'm sorry, sir."

"Why should you be sorry? I want to know what Franchard is after. Can you tell me?"

The boy hesitated.

"Can you tell me?"

"I've only got part of an idea."

"And what may that be?"

"I can't talk behind Franchard's back."

He expected the colonel to grow angry at this, but, instead, Forbes put out his hand and rested it on the shoulder of the boy.

"You seem to me a straight enough lad," said he. "What mixed you up with Franchard?"

"He hired me," said Tom. "That's all that I know. He hired me. I was to be a sort of roustabout, and the pay was pretty high. So I went along."

"And when you began to get into trouble?"

Tom stared at the ceiling. "It was hard to turn back then," he said.

"Very well. Now, then, you go about your business. You'll have no harm from me."

"And Mr. Franchard?" asked Tom eagerly.

"Is it Franchard who's wounded?"

Tom flushed. It was plain that this man was much too clever for him, and therefore he finally said with a faint sigh: "Yes, it's Franchard. You seem to know everything about everything, Colonel Forbes. But will you help him?"

The colonel laughed a little. He had received many

158

compliments in his life, and he had an appetite for them. Now he fairly beamed upon Tom.

"Deduction, Tom," said he. "A little gift for deduction. That's how I spotted you. Not from a description, mind you. There's not a photograph of you posted in the town, to my knowledge. Only Franchard, the escaped robber. Now, one more thing. You were seen to come into my house by two men."

"Yes."

"Could they have seen your face?"

"No. For I couldn't see them."

"Very good. They'd have hard work connecting me with Tom Fuller, then. What are you to do now?"

"I have one more errand, and then I'm leaving the town." He hesitated. "With you, Colonel Forbes?" he asked.

"What?" exclaimed the colonel, in pretended wrath. "Leave the town with a man the law wants? I should say not. However, I've often fished the pools in the bed of the Little Yellow, and it might be that I would drive out there and arrive early in the morning. It's not so serious that Franchard can't hold out that long?"

"I think he could, sir."

"Run along about your business. But be in the gorge by morning, and keep your eyes on the alert for a fisherman who will have something more than fish in his basket. That's all, my boy. I'll be there!"

He followed Tom to the door and talked to him a moment there. He felt that Tom was perfectly safe. To be sure, he had recognized him, but that recognition was very largely guesswork. He wished Tom a good journey, and the boy went back to Rusty at the hitching rack in a very cheerful frame of mind.

It now appeared that he had done a very simple thing in coming to Holliday. He could wish for only one thing, and this was that he had not had the rider of the silver horse behind him so closely all the way to the town. However, he was willing to allow for that ghost. Once he could secure the necessary food, he would be ready to start back, but the getting of the food appeared a more and more difficult matter.

All the stores were, of course, closed at this hour. He almost wished that he had opened this need of theirs to the colonel, while he was talking with that kindly and shrewd man; but he was ashamed to return and bother such a man again.

There was the hotel. He could buy something there, no doubt, and without creating suspicion. He could not be the only man who had ridden into Holliday late and asked for provisions to cart away with him at once. He wanted such things as they could eat without cookery—jerked beef or venison, for instance. And the hotel, in such a place, was certain to have quantities of it on hand.

So Tom jogged the mustang down the street to the hotel. It was a long-fronted building, with two low stories, and since the evening was warm, and supper already was over, there were a dozen men lounging still in the chairs which were tilted back against the front wall of the veranda. A great gasoline lamp blazed over the entrance and cast a glaring light up and down the porch.

Tom regarded that light with an unpleased eye, and going to the stable behind the hotel, he bought enough crushed barley to fill a feed bag for Rusty, then hitched him in front of the hotel and tied the bag over his head. Instantly the bag was on the ground, and Rusty, with mouth agape, was trying to cram the entire contents down his throat in a single mouthful.

With that attended to, he went straight into the hotel by the side door and groaned inwardly when he saw that it was crammed with guests, particularly with a party of noisy, newly arrived cowpunchers who were just then flocking into the dining room for a late supper. They had just come into town, and the kitchen had been put to work to feed them.

On second thought, Tom was pleased by this accident. It should give him a chance to hide himself in the crowd and to get a meal at the same time. Afterward, he could arrange for supplies through the waiter.

So he went straight into the dining room.

It was a big room, and it ran straight through the depth of the building, from the front to the back, a fact which was presently to prove of importance. The party of punchers who had just come in were occupying the total length of a big table which ran down the center of this room, and around the walls were other tables. But the cloths of these had mostly been removed. Only one in a far corner was laid, and accordingly Tom went for it and settled into a chair. He could not have been better placed if he had designed the scheme of things, for he was facing the entire table, and he could watch both the doors which led into it.

At the farther end of it were two small doors, in addition, which opened upon a veranda over the river—for the creek which watered Holliday and flowed on into the Big Yellow at this point cut across behind the hotel. There was little chance to hear the flow of the waters, but now and again the long, still murmur rose and filled a pause in the noisy talk of the cowpunchers—as when every plate was freshly filled, and there was only the clinking and the clashing of busy knives and forks.

There were only two waiters to serve that crowd and Tom besides. But they worked with wonderful speed. With a great crashing and rattling, they brought in stacks of plates and dealt them out like cards at a poker game. Then vast platters of thin, greasy steak were slid onto the board, and huge bowls of soggy, boiled potatoes, bread three days old, and unappetizing butter.

However, the punchers were not particular, nor was Tom Fuller, for it seemed to him that he never had tasted anything half so good, and he was well on with his meal when a sudden hush fell over the room. He looked up, and at the door he saw the prettiest girl that had ever come under his eye. There she paused a moment, with the big sombrero pushed back upon her head, and her frank eyes drifting down the long table, from place to place. Finally she saw Tom at his table, and to his bewilderment, she nodded, and smiled, and started straight across to him!

161

28

HE STOOD up, not controlled by good manners, but really because he was startled. And as she came closer, his alarm grew greater. She was dressed roughly, like a girl of the range, in divided skirts, a mannish coat, and a huge sombrero, but her beauty shone through undimmed. She was as brown as a berry, with cheeks red-stained by the open air, and her eyes shining; and when she came to Tom and held out her hand to him, he was staggered to speechlessness.

"May I sit down at your table?" she said.

"Oh, yes," said Tom.

And, as she sat down, she went on: "You'd better sit down, too, and try to smile a little and look glad to see me, because every one is looking at us."

They were. As Tom sank unnerved into his chair, he saw that the whole battery of attention from the long table was fixed upon him. He tried to smile, and the result was a very dim effort. He managed to say: "I don't know that I've ever—I've ever—"

"You've never met me, and you've never known me," she answered cheerfully, "but you're going to."

She turned to the waiter and gave her order; as the man disappeared she went on: "I'm Kathryn Lane. Does that mean anything to you?"

"No," said Tom. "It doesn't mean anything. I'm sorry."

"Are you? You shouldn't be," said she. "It won't worry you that I know who you are?"

"You do?" said Tom, fidgeting in his chair.

She laughed.

"Oh, what a lot they'd give to know what I know— all of those jolly cowboys," said she. "To know that Tom Fuller is sitting here in the same room with them, and the price he bears like a halo around his head! They'd be mighty glad to know you, Tom, but I won't introduce you, if you don't mind."

Hastily he passed a handkerchief across his forehead.

"Is it as hot as all that?" she said, chuckling. "You don't have to be afraid. I'm a friend. I'm not apt to fish up the Little Yellow with something more than fish in my basket, but still I'm a friend."

He moistened his white lips.

"You're a friend of Colonel Forbes, then!" said he.

"I'm not a great friend of Colonel Forbes. But I like him very well. I liked him better tonight than ever before."

"I don't quite foller this," admitted poor Tom.

"You look tortured, in fact," said she. "Well, I'm going to explain everything. You remember a gray horse behind you on the Candle Plains tonight?"

He stared at her harder than before.

"I remember," said he.

"I was wandering about and saw you start. I wasn't far from the place where the three of them were when you crashed into them. I should think that was rather a dare-devil thing to do, Tom Fuller."

"I didn't mean—" he began.

"Oh, no, you didn't mean to," she said, nodding at him with very bright eyes. "You didn't mean to, until you saw the chance to make some mischief, and then you were forced to go ahead. You couldn't keep from the temptation. It would have been an easy enough thing to ride around those sleepy fellows, wouldn't it? But no! You couldn't keep away from them any more than a cat could keep away from mice!"

163

No matter how much sternness was in her words, there was nothing but laughter bubbling in her voice, and Tom could not help but feel more at ease. He no longer feared her, but he began to wonder at her more and more, and as he listened to the quick, musical voice, the very heart of Tom Fuller took wings and leaped forward; only to fail and fall again as he remembered what he was—stupid Tom Fuller, fit to be a blacksmith, and no more. A failure even at that!

So the joy of having this beauty near him was blended exquisitely with sadness, and with a sense of distance which separated them to the ends of the world.

"One of them was hurt," he said.

"One? Jerry Loyd was knocked silly. He won't be the same for a month. And poor Dave Meany had his leg broke. You must have heard him yell when Rusty stepped on him?"

He stared again, and then shuddered.

"I remember," said he. "I'll never forget. I—I didn't mean that. I could have knocked him out of the way with a gun. Somehow, I didn't quite think fast enough. But I felt Rusty step on him. How come that you know Rusty's name, ma'am?"

She smiled at him with her usual frankness. The waiter came hurrying with her dinner, and she began on that with a great appetite.

"We know a lot about you, Tom Fuller," said she. "Questions had to be asked, you know. They began to ask questions in Orangeville, and they've been asking them ever since. Pete Stringham told something. Charlie Boston told a lot more. Charlie thinks a lot of you, doesn't he?"

"Charlie Boston?" repeated the boy sadly. "Well, Charlie fired me—if you call that thinking a lot!"

"He knew that you were too big to stand in his shop that was all."

"I don't foller that," said Tom. "I ain't so very big, you see."

"No?" she asked him.

164

Then the smile faded and froze on her lips, and he saw the darkness of thought in her eyes.

"You can see that I ain't so big," said he. "I dunno what Charlie meant. I thought he was mighty angry with me. I'd always tried to do my work for him."

It was her turn to stare, and stare she did, with a perfect frankness that put Tom to the rout.

"You're stringing me," she said suddenly.

"I? No, indeed!" he protested.

"You're lying low, and taking me in," she persisted.

"I dunno what you mean," said Tom. "I never took anybody in my life!"

"You weren't sitting tight at Boston's place?"

"Sitting tight!"

He echoed the words hopelessly, and still she looked through and through him, with that same dark lightning in her blue eyes.

"You about beat me," she said. "Charlie Boston said that you beat him, too!"

Tom drew a long breath. He was more and more at sea. And suddenly he felt that he could not breathe at all, unless he told her the truth.

"I'm pretty simple," he confided, leaning a bit forward. "That's the fact. Maybe you've heard something else, but it's not true."

"Simple?" she said in a sharp challenge.

"I guess you've surely heard that before," he urged.

She stopped eating and rested her chin on her hand.

"Would any simple man have fifty hard-riding people strung out across the hills trying to catch him, while he drops through their fingers? Oh, Tom Fuller, you can't go on playing possum forever. You played it long enough, but now we see the facts about you!"

He considered that remark with a downward eye, puzzled, struggling to find an answer.

"You see," he said, "I never could do anything right, and—"

He paused.

"I'd give a lot to know what you've been hiding," she

broke in as his voice failed. "You are a rare one, Tom Fuller. You are a new kind! Here you sit playing your game, laughing up your sleeve at me! I've tried to show you that I'm a friend. Why, I could have brought the town down on you! Not that you wouldn't have been able to slip through them, as you've slipped before! But I could have made trouble for you. I didn't. I was too interested!"

She laughed.

"When I saw the light go on in the colonel's office; and climbed up to the window sill, I laughed till I nearly fell off the sill, seeing the way you turned the colonel around your finger. Poor old Colonel Forbes! And he thinks he's such a great reader of human nature! He's proud of his cleverness. Deductions! Deductions! What a great deducer he is!"

She tilted her head back and laughed merrily, while Tom watched her, half smiling, and half in despair. It seemed impossible that any person as intelligent as she should persist in such a false idea of him. For, gradually, he was beginning to see what that false idea was. She thought that he was a very brainy man who had lived a life of pretense, a life of assumed simplicity, all the while with a dark and dangerous power hidden within him, waiting for the right time to show it.

Studying that problem, he wondered how he would be able to correct this false impression.

But he could not see a way, except to protest again, and such protests meant nothing to her, apparently. She had her own idea of him, and to that idea she was clinging with all her might.

When he thought of the boldness of this youngster, pursuing him across the wide sweep of the Candle Plains, he thought of another thing, and shuddered: Suppose he had followed his impulse, once or twice, and fired on her?

She went on, rapidly, merrily:

"Poor Colonel Forbes! He really was patronizing you, wasn't he? He had worked up quite a fatherly interest before the end of the interview!"

166

Laughter choked her.

"Oh," she broke out, "weren't you ashamed, Tom Fuller, to deceive such a good man and fool him so perfectly?"

Tom Fuller rubbed his knuckles across his chin, quite desperate.

"I see something in your eye now," said she. "I do wish that you speak it out loud. Tell me the truth about it all."

He was silent.

"If you don't," said she, with a flare of wild light in her eyes, "I'll jump up and tell these fellows who you are—and then you'll be in a hot swarm!"

He waited, silent. And suddenly he heard her stamp lightly beneath the table.

"You are a clever scoundrel, Tom," said she. "Of course, they would not believe, after seeing me sit here laughing and talking with you. They'd take it as a joke! And here I am, just as helpless and foolish before you as the colonel was!"

She stared at Tom, and he stared at her, and then looked back to the table cloth. He saw that it was useless to try to convince her of the truth. He had no words. And she was so armored with her own beliefs about him!

"But do you know what everyone is eating his heart out to know?" she said.

"No," he answered truly.

"They want to know some of the things that you've done before this one. How cleverly you've hidden everything, Tom Fuller! On your trail, your back trail, they've all run against a blank wall!"

29

To Tom, the revelation of the girl's mistaken idea of him was enough to make his brain spin.

He felt a sort of miserable joy in it. For it was plain to him that she was highly excited by the role into which she had fitted him of her own accord.

There was more than her own opinion behind this. Apparently there were still other people with whom she had talked, who had held exactly the same idea about him. He was a cunning rascal, in their estimation, who, as she said, had played possum until the time came when a high adventure and a big reward were placed ready at his hand, and this was the theory to which she was grimly sticking.

He looked back to the fumbling, numb stupidity which he had shown in the presence of Colonel Forbes, and wondered how she could have mistaken him there. But no—she had laid all his apparent stupidity down to consummate acting. His blundering, his tongue-tied stupidity—these were qualities which he had assumed in order to win the generous colonel to his purpose!

Now, as he saw the picture which the girl had substituted for his real self, he sighed. Here she sat opposite to him, her eyes dancing, and her heart beating, with admiration in all her face, her voice, her gestures. She was electric with emotion.

To her he was a terrible tiger of a fellow, who could not resist the temptation to rush down upon three armed men and scatter them as the wind scatters dead leaves. To her he was a man of mystery, of steel-cold nerves, of dauntless bravery. And because she had made up that picture of him, even Tom Fuller could see that she was close to love. She was on the trembling verge of it. Aye, her glance opened to him, and admitted him to her heart.

No, it was not he whom she admitted. It was the other man, the shadow, the ghost, the false spirit which she had put into his form and endowed with his name! What pleasure could he take in that? A melancholy pleasure, to be sure! It was as unreal as the loves and passions which appear upon the stage, all assumed by weary men and women to amuse the crowd beyond the footlights.

How much those cowpunchers envied him, around their long table! What glances they threw at him, narrowing their eyes as they scanned him and asked themselves what there was about him to so obviously fascinate such a girl as this!

And she herself? How did it happen that she was riding alone over the Candle Plains at such a time of night? What was she doing unescorted here in the dining room of the Holliday Hotel?

"They went to Pete Stringham," she said. "Pete's a smart enough fellow. I've danced with Pete and know him pretty well. But Pete's idea of you was really something to make one laugh. Do you know, he really thinks you're just the sort of a man you've been posing to be? He said that you were actually not much better than a half-wit?"

She laughed again. The very thought rejoiced him.

She made a little gesture, extending the fingers of one hand and slowly closing them.

"Oh, to think of having everyone in the palm of your hand, everyone completely baffled and fooled, and never for an instant seeing just what you are! How really wonderful, to do it for years, and keep your true self a secret for your own eye, alone!"

Admiration flamed hot in her face again.

169

"Why, there's nothing like it, even in books, not even in the wildest books! Dumas never dreamed of anything as clever as that! Even he would have said that it was impossible for a man to keep in his role for such a length of time. And then you're young, too! I'd like to know what put the idea into your mind!"

She paused, searching his face eagerly.

"No, of course you won't tell me," she said almost bitterly. "You'll let me guess as much as I please, but the secret's to remain your own."

"I want to say one thing right now," said Tom.

"Ah, say it, then."

"There's nothing in what you've heard about me."

"Don't!" she said, and stiffened in her chair angrily.

He shrugged his shoulders, and waited for a blow to fall.

"Ah, you're clever!" she cried softly. "When I see the way you step into your part, and make your eyes wide and stupid—why, I almost disbelieve my wits and take you for what you want to be considered. But, then, though you've covered your trail very well indeed, some things have leaked out. You must not think that you've played your part as perfectly as all that!"

"What have you picked up, then?" said Tom, resigned, and strangely excited, too, to see the erection of his new self, which had no being.

It was like waking from a deep trance and having one's history for ten unknown years recited.

"You want to know, really?" she said. "Oh, well, chiefly it was made up of hints, here and there, and fragments. You tried to play the part of the coward, it appears, among other things. But now and again they picked up the truth. Why, even Pete Stringham had to admit that he'd rather creep into a lion's cave at night than walk up to you and ask for trouble in broad daylight! And Pete's one of those who were pretty completely hoodwinked by you. Charlie Boston seemed to see nearer the truth than any one."

"Charlie Boston?" he exclaimed.

170

"Ah, you thought that he was completely blinded, did you?" she demanded with a sort of hungry interest.

"Yes," said Tom, "I did."

He checked himself, and would have put this speech in other words. For, as he had said it, it implied that she was right from the beginning, and that he had been leading a double life, and had been fooling those about him with an affectation of simplicity.

But what she said about Charlie Boston fascinated him. He would gladly have learned more.

"I'd like to know just what Charlie said."

"I can remember, I think, in another minute. Let me see. It went something like this: 'Nobody in the world knows what that kid can do. Maybe he don't know, even himself!' That's what Charlie said!"

She leaned back in her chair once more. She had forgotten her food, and all her attention centered about him, so that he could see the thoughts flick like shadows across her eyes. And the longer she was close to him, the greater became her beauty, and her eyes were a deeper and a richer blue, and the slender grace of her brown hand was laid, as it were, upon his very heart.

With all the power of his will he fought against the emotion that began to rise in him; but still it mounted like a tide and filled his soul with music and with sadness.

"I'd like to ask you a little about yourself," said he.

She smiled suddenly, greatly amused, it appeared, by this remark.

"Go on," she said. "I'd like to have you ask me questions. What do you want to know?"

"Who are you, Kathryn Lane?"

"I'm the daughter of a poor farmer in the hills," said she. "I'm Jim Lane's daughter. I was just out riding, to-night, and I happened to come by the valley and heard them shoot at you. That was all!"

Still her eyes danced at him, and shone. Until Tom found himself smiling, too, for no reason other than the reflection of her own mirth. But this smiling of his had a

171

great effect upon her, and she broke out with a sudden laugh:

"You can't help showing that you see the truth," said she. "Oh, you're letting down the bars, a little, now. Well, I'm glad of that. It makes me feel that I know you a little better! But oh, Tom Fuller, to pretend that you didn't know all about me! And to stand up like a gawky stick when I came up to the table, and then to sit down and stare at me like a silly child! Well—I've never seen such great acting in my life, and I'll never see such great acting again, unless I see you!"

Her face grew more serious.

"And I suppose I shall see you again?"

"Yes," he said suddenly, "you'll see me again."

Her eyes closed; she drew a quick, deep breath. Then, leaning a little forward, she said slowly: "I'm not trying to beg off for him. I know that he's done a great many bad things. But—I wish you'd think it over again. No—no," she broke in upon herself, "I'm a fool for even dreaming that you could be influenced. You'll go straight on, as a tiger goes—as a tiger goes—"

Excitement rushed into her face.

"Why shouldn't I run out of the room and give the alarm? If you break through the net, I'd have the pleasure of seeing you smash the meshes!"

He hardly understood anything that she had said, in the last few moments, except that his relentless purpose, as she described it, would lead him to see her again, on the way. He could not put two and two together and make a whole out of this thing, but as she sat there with excitement and anger in her face and her eyes, the words which he would have kept back spoke of their own accord.

"You're beautiful! There's no other girl half so beautiful!"

He felt his eyes burning as he looked at her.

The words caused a strange effect upon the girl.

She caught at the edge of the table with one hand, and the color was struck from her face.

"That wasn't fair," she said slowly. "That wasn't a

172

fair thing to say to me! But—but I've been a fool. I've opened the door to that—to almost anything, I suppose."

She turned in her chair and stood up. He rose with her, numb with horror and regret.

"You can pay my bill—that's a part penalty for such a speech," she said.

And he saw the tears in her eyes, and somehow he knew that she was leaving her bill to him for the very reason that she feared those tears might be seen if she lingered another moment.

She went from the room, and Tom saw all eyes trailing after her; and he saw the cowpunchers look at one another when she had disappeared. Then, in a flash, every eye was fastened upon him. Aye, they envied him with all their hearts.

He, for his part, sat for a long time over his coffee. From the waiter he ordered a small stock of such provisions as they would need in the valley with the sick man. They were brought; he paid for them. And while he waited for change, still he was trying to decipher what had happened.

She had not been entirely angered. Otherwise there would not have been tears. And in her last speech there had surely been an emotion that was capable of a friendly interpretation. What if he were to follow her and speak to her again? Would she be entirely hostile to me?

His heart leaped at the thought, and as he stiffened in his chair, he heard a girl's voice, Kathryn's voice, whispering from the window: "You madman! They're surrounding the hotel! Do something now, for the love of Heaven!"

30

Tom LISTENED with a sharpened ear of horror. They were surrounding the hotel at that moment!

The plan of the place flashed through his mind. There was the broad street in front, and on either side there was a vacant lot, and both spots, no doubt, were populated, by now, with sharpshooters!

Behind the hotel was the river, with steep banks, such as lined it all the way through the town of Holliday. How was he, then, to escape?

The cowpunchers were breaking up from their dinner now. Rolling cigarettes, and yawning with weariness, they were strolling toward the door. And it seemed obvious that no one of them had been warned as to the identity of their fellow in the dining room. Certainly they could not have disguised their information so well!

The voice went on behind him, panting with anxiety and haste: "Do something quickly!"

He saw the waiter returning toward his table, with the change upon a plate. But he could not move. It was patent to Tom Fuller that he was surrounded upon every side, and that he must surrender. After all, he had tried to do his best. He had launched a doctor toward the scene of need, and if he were captured after having done so much, he was reasonably sure that no man could have held it against him.

What was the shame of a surrender to overwhelming

odds? There was no shame; and it was the thing that he would do!

The voice of the girl, Kathryn Lane, stammering with excitement, again hurried on behind him.

"I know that you despise them and their numbers. I know what you love—it's fighting battles against odds —but the odds are too great now. Run, Tom! Run, for Heaven's sake! It will be enough of a miracle if you can get away. I've taken the gray horse down into the gulch behind the hotel. Nobody will suspect that he's there. I don't think they've posted any one there, because I don't think they imagine that any one could get down the bluff! But there's a way to get down. I've estimated the distance, and you've got a chance, if you can tie this rope to one of the veranda windows and get down it. Only—quickly—don't sit there, scorning everything. Some day you'll have to fail, and this may be the day. Listen! I'll ride your mustang out the river road, if you get clear. You can have him again, there—"

The voice stopped, choked off, as it were.

He took the change from the plate which the waiter held, fascinated by the quivering of the man's hand. And then he understood why. The cowpunchers at the central table had not been told the secret, but the waiter had gathered it, somehow or other. His face was a face of death, as he held that plate!

Remembering himself, Tom put a liberal tip upon the plate.

And he saw the man turn and go hurriedly toward the kitchen door.

He leaned, then, and picked up his package. That would seem a natural thing to do, if any eye were watching, and that some eye was watching, he had no doubt whatever.

And, as he leaned, he saw a coil of rope lying inside the window. She had dropped it there, making no noise! She, in spite of her faith that he was able to work miracles, had dropped the rope within, that he might use it if he chose. Doubtless, she expected that he would not

175

need such a thing, wonder-worker that she felt him to be!

Rising to gather the last of the parcels, he gathered the slick, hard coil of the rope, also, and thrust it up under his coat. Then he advanced toward the door. There was one thing which they must not suspect until the last moment, and that was his probable line of retreat. So he remembered himself, and summoned a tune to his lips and whistled it cheerfully, softly. If any were listening, surely they would suspect nothing.

At the door which led out into the lobby, he ceased his tune, and with long, swift steps, he walked toward the entrance to the veranda over the river.

Would any one be there?

He gained the nearest door.

No one was there! Salvation, as he felt, was before him there! But to what should he fasten the rope as he descended by it toward the water side?

He leaned out the window, and beneath him he saw plainly the back of the gray horse, glimmering in the moonshine, with tall, black brush all around him; and beyond, the river flowed past him in steady interchange of light and shadow. The opposite bank rose high and stiff, a perfect bluff, and upon the edge of it, he saw two erect forms with rifles in their hands, like thin pencil strokes of light.

They were the sole guard, as it appeared, upon that side. It would not be hard to shoot across at them. Perhaps to bring them down with two quick shots!

But as the grim thought entered his mind, he saw them turn and walk up the bluff. Their minds, for the moment at least, were occupied. But behind him?

He seized on a bench which stood on the veranda and tied the end of the lariat around it. The loose end he cast out of the window, and it fell with a twist and a jerk. Behind him, at the same moment, a voice shouted:

"He's taking the river way! Watch the river, men! He's tryin' the river way!"

He sprang back toward the nearest door onto the veranda and saw half a dozen men spilling through the lobby entrance into the dining room. He sent one bullet among them, heard a man yell, and the whole group fell prostrate in their frantic effort to turn about at once and bolt back whence they had come.

They would bother him no more from that direction. As far as they knew, he might be barricading himself in that final stronghold of the veranda porch. Certainly, they had fled fast enough!

Then he slid himself over the window sill.

Far beneath him the river gleamed, and the black brush, but once he was committed to the rope, it seemed as slender as a thread, and as feeble, and the bottom of the ravine appeared a mile away. The very murmur of the river was more distant and dim.

And now he swung by his hands above the void, grappling with his legs at the rope, farther down. He turned his head and then he saw the two watchers from the opposite bank top turn, and one of them pointed.

Guns were lifted in their hands—

He waited to see no more, but slid rapidly down the rope.

A bullet hit hard against the wall past which he was falling, and immediately afterward, he heard the clang of the report. Another, and another bullet followed. They crunched into the wood about his head, and then they were clicking sparks off the surface of the rock wall beneath. But still he slid down the rope with unabated speed. He heard a distant yelling. It seemed above him, and looking up, he saw the heads and shoulders of men crowd into the windows of the veranda.

Then his feet struck solid ground!

Never was anything more blissful to Tom Fuller. It was as though he had been striving to walk the thin air for half of his life, and now he was restored to the ground again. Shrinking back into the shadow of the first bush, he felt the whizz of bullets about him. They were like invisible fingers of sound, prying to find him out, and with his Colt he sent a bullet at the riflemen on the farther bank. Suddenly they disappeared beyond its lip. He fired upward at the crowded window nearest to him on the veranda; and from both the windows the heads and shoulders went back.

So simple it was to frighten men from their purpose!

He turned, and there was the gray horse beside him!

He ceased to wonder now that the girl had been able to follow him as she would, and disappear into the moonshine when she chose, for the long, sleek line of the thoroughbred proclaimed his quality at once, and when he swung into the saddle, he felt the strength of the loins that would carry weight, and carry it far. To such a horse the burden of Kathryn Lane was no more than thistledown!

So he mounted that charger, after untying the lead rope. And he felt that already he was sitting in the midst of safety.

But he was wrong.

The way up the canyon was winding, broken with many rocks, and extremely narrow. Twice he had to leave the way altogether and crash through the water. The gray horse took it with flattened ears, but courageously always, trusting to his rider and to his own great heart.

Straight over his head a beam of light flashed, wavered on the brush, and then, centering, found him.

They had brought out some strong bull's-eye or searchlight to spot him in this moment of danger, as though the light of the moon were not enough!

The river beside him was a steady roar, but above it he could hear the voices of men shouting wildly from the banks. But he must escape quickly from the deadly, prying light that played upon him.

Up the bank, upon his left hand, he saw a narrow path, winding in and out with the contours of the river side. It was not a horse road.

It was hardly a precarious footpath for boys that wanted to get down to the water by the quickest route, but at that way he put the gray, and gallantly the gray answered.

It was no question of galloping, or even of trotting. It

was a matter of laboring up by strong heaves, with fighting hoofs that struck away the earth and gravel almost as fast as he put them down, but nevertheless, he mounted rapidly, and the roar of the river's water grew more faint and sullen, and the shouting of the men grew nearer and more dangerous.

They twisted through a screen of brush. For an instant they hung on the verge of a bank that yielded before them and under them, seeming to cast them out into the air, to fall back in one disastrous crash the entire distance they had climbed!

The gray gelding fought like a cat, and held his own. In another moment he was lurching forward on the level.

They were not out of the town. That had been the fond hope of Tom Fuller, and that he would be able to ride off across the open fields, but now he saw that he had simply ridden into some man's back yard, unfenced, because the river bluff was fence enough!

Well might they talk of that ride in later days. He himself, seeing the place many a year hence, would swear that no horse and man ever could have passed that way. But, at the time, he dared not think of marvels accomplished, because more marvels lay before him to do, and, not the least, a high board fence directly in front.

He tried the gelding straight at it, but even that good horse refused. Tom circled him for a second attempt, and as he did so, a window was jerked up, and a rifle blazed at him.

Night light, moonlight, is not for marksmen. The bullet flew wild, and now the gelding, as though inspired by the hum of the lead, rose nobly, and took the barrier in a great bound. He hung in mid-air, and then dropped down into the soft earth of a rose garden. Before them lay a low hedge, and beyond the street, and beyond the street was the pleasant darkness of the open country!

31

THE GRAY did not seem to need telling. He went for that open country like a flying bird, and topping the hedge, he landed with muffled hoofs in the middle of the dusty lane, and stretched away for the reassuring dimness beyond.

What a horse was this!

As they swerved out from the street, Tom could see behind him a down-headed throng of twenty horsemen coming at him in a thundering charge, each rider getting the best out of his mount. But the gray, half winded though he was by his strenuous run up the river, and his climbing of the bank, held them even. In another moment they were striding across country, and he was getting his wind back, with a resultant increase of stride and speed.

It was a district used, apparently, for pastures for cow and horse by the townsmen, and therefore, it was constantly checked across by fences of barbed wire. There is no more dangerous obstacle in the world for man and horse to jump, and Tom Fuller knew it. But he wanted to get rid of his pursuers quickly.

He swung to the right, and the good gelding took one gleaming barrier after another in his stride, flaunting on with tremendous ease, fairly bounding over the dangerous wires.

Behind them, guns began to crackle, but they were at a hopeless distance for moonlight shooting. Only once a bullet darted dangerously close to Tom's head, and in five minutes he was by himself, in a low swelling of hills which shut him off completely from the sight of what was happening behind him. But he did not need his eyes to tell him that he was not pursued. He drew the gray back to a walk, and he could hear nothing.

So he pulled the gelding around to the left and headed back for the road which hugged the bank of the Big Yellow. On the river road she had promised to meet him, and to bring Rusty with her. He wondered how she would manage that. There was only one person in the world reasonably at home on Rusty's back, and that was himself. And yet from the first he never doubted that she would live up to her word.

Arrowy swift, the tall horse flew across the intervening country with the lights of Holliday gleaming upon the left, and the moon haze over the Candle Plains on his right. The trees and rocks of the river region rose before them, and finally the hoofs of the gray rang loudly upon the metal of the river road.

He slowed down to a trot. It might be that she was waiting for him in any of those nooks and corners among the trees and the rocks, and he wanted almost more than life to have another glimpse of her face, and to hear her voice once more.

Then, before him, between two tall poplars, with the glimmering face of the river making a background, he saw a small horse and a figure standing beside it. The figure waved, and Tom rode straight at it and swung down from the saddle before Kathryn Lane.

She was breathing hard, as though from desperate work, and there was a dark spot on one side of her face. She was laughing, too, and panting at the same time.

"I knew you'd make it, of course. But I can't help wondering. What would you have done without the rope and the gray?"

"I couldn't have done anything," said Tom honestly. "I would have been helpless!"

"Helpless? You?"

She laughed again.

181

"You would have walked right out through them and managed to get away on Rusty. Oh, I know you! I know you, though you think you're still pulling the wool over my eyes! Tom Fuller, why do you try such crazy things?"

He turned away from her, fearing that even by the moonshine she might be able to see more in his face than he wanted her to know. From the saddle pockets of the gray he took out the provisions which he had taken with him down the rope.

"Ah, I see," said she. "You wanted food. And you wouldn't do a dull, stupid thing like breaking into a grocery store and carrying off what you wanted. You had to go into the hotel and sit there under the eyes of all men! But you don't see? They didn't know your face, before. Nobody did! And now they'll all have you spotted!"

He could realize the chilly truth of this, but he could not answer. She was still talking not to him, but to her desperate dream of what he was.

He crossed to the mustang again and passed the articles into the pockets of the saddle.

"The gray worked pretty well for you, Tom?" she asked him, cheerfully, breaking into her own trend of thought.

"He ran like the wind!" said Tom truly. "He flew. I never was on a better horse."

"He's the best in dad's string," said she. "He ought to be good!"

He stood foolishly before her. He wanted to say something graceful and gay and full of gratitude, but the words would not come to him. He could only stand and stare helplessly down at her, with every nerve in his body quivering and jumping, and a pulse thundering at his temple.

Then, as he watched her, it seemed to him that the dark spot on her cheek was spreading.

Suddenly he cried out: "You've been hurt! Kathryn, you've been hurt! What happened?"

"This snaky brute jumped out from under me a couple of times," said the girl carelessly. "Once, I landed on the side of my face. It jarred me a little and broke the skin, I suppose, but it's nothing. What's a scratch—in the sort of a life that you lead, Tom? Oh, don't speak of it!"

But the knowledge that the stain was indeed blood, that it had been spilled for his sake, and was spreading over her face—and the whole overwhelming sense of what might have happened, stunned the boy.

At last he said, in a shaken voice: "I should have told you. I never should have let you try to ride him. He's a brute. Why, he might have savaged you—he might—he might have trampled you—Kathryn—"

He came closer to her, and he noticed that she did not shrink away from the hands which, instinctively, he stretched out toward her in a cherishing gesture.

"You're not laughing at me now?" she asked him rather sharply. "You're not still making fun of me, Tom?"

"Making fun of you?" he cried. "Of you? When you've saved my life—"

"Oh, stuff!" said Kathryn Lane. "You had to overdo it, and put a trembling in your voice. Tom Fuller, d'you think that I'm an absolute simpleton? Don't I know what you care about life? And—and now you stand here and pretend to nearly weep over me! Why, what sort of a flabby idiot do you take me for?"

He was thrust back from her again, and suddenly, as he felt the full force of the manner in which she had tied his hands by her mass of preconceptions, he began to laugh, not in mirth, but in a sort of despair.

Here she was, making light of the services which had saved him from prison or a lynching party, and laughing to scorn the attempt he made to thank her. It was as though she had saved the life of a dog. It was as though she had done something less than that—as though this was merely a gay, jolly, foolish game, which they had played together and which was not worth serious consideration.

183

She was nodding at him while, with her handkerchief, she touched her bleeding face.

"That's better," said she. "Of course, I know what's really in your mind. You thought that I was trying to make a melodrama out of it—young girl saves desperado's life—and all that sort of stuff. Oh, I'm not so silly, Tom. I knew that you could save yourself whenever you chose, and you were just playing the game the way that you had planned it. I suppose you only used the rope and the gray to please me! To give me a greater chance to make an idiot of myself!"

She laughed in her turn, her voice soft, and floating musically toward him.

Tom, stricken dumb, pressed his lips close together, and felt a great swelling of the heart. And suddenly he muttered to her: "Do you think that it's all play-acting for me, Kathryn? Look at me! D'you think it's all playing?"

He stood fairly before her, so that the moon beat into his face and his eyes. And she, close before him, drew still closer. Her head tipped back a little, he distinctly heard the catch of her breath.

"Then you're not all wild, Tom? You do care a little?"

He began to tremble again in an odd manner. And such words as Tom never could have dreamed of before, suddenly were born in his brain and flowed upward to his lips.

He took one of her hands, gingerly, because he had been taught that he must not trust the strength in his fingers. He was apt to do harm when he least wished it.

"If my life was made of a diamond, Kate," said he, "I tell you what—I'd close it in one of your hands, and trust it to you forever. There's nobody like you! You're more'n breath to me. You're more'n life and air to me!"

He saw the laughter die out of her face, and a great curiosity widened her eyes. She stood perfectly still, studying him.

And at last she said:

"Tom, it's not all acting, you clever rascal! It's not all a sham. I—I almost think you're making love to me!"

He tried to speak in answer to that, but the word, somehow, unnerved him, and sent weakness through brain and body, like flowing water, or like thin, piercing fire.

"What do you mean?" asked Kathryn.

"That I love you," said Tom suddenly. "By heaven, that I love you!"

She did not change the steady, piercing gaze that was fixed on him.

Then she said: "You're breaking my hand."

He released it and stepped back with a catch in his breath. Before his brain had cleared, she was in the saddle on the gray.

"I don't blame you much," he heard her saying. "I suppose that all the girls that break their hearts about you expect you to talk like that. You do it well, too. Even a great actor like you needs practice, and I can see that you've had a good many rehearsals. But—I hoped you'd see that I was a little different. I hoped that you wouldn't want to make a fool of me, as you have of the rest. But—it's been a grand party, anyway. And—good night, Tom!"

32

HE WANTED to call out after her, and stop her retreat, but he found himself unable to move or to speak, and presently the tall, gray gelding swept away like a form of silver under the silver moon mist, and was gone. Only the rapid beating of the hoofs came back to him in pulses, and then died away.

But even if his heart ached, he knew that it was better this way. Otherwise, she would have been sure to find out the truth about him, and that would have ended their friendship, he felt, as with the stroke of a knife.

He watched her disappear and heard the last throb of the hoofbeats on his ear. Then he mounted.

He could see, as he looked back upon the scene, that there were many interesting questions which he could have asked her, as, for instance, how did she manage to get possession of the mustang, when surely it was being closely watched. And there were a hundred other things which he might have said, if he had not been benumbed in the brain by the beauty and the strangeness of this girl.

More strange even than beautiful, he felt her to be, for even in that land of free, brave, and careless women, she seemed peculiarly her own mistress and without fear.

He looked at his watch. It was after midnight, and so he must start straight on toward the gorge of the Little Yellow. Even now he might have to hurry a little, if he were to get in before daylight. His thoughts turned back to the wounded man, and to Rankin, wondering if the latter might not be tempted to betray his present employer just as he had betrayed the first? However, that was a thing from which he resolved to keep his mind. He would have difficulty enough in penetrating to the heart of the valley without worrying about the possible trap which might be waiting for him at the spot where he had left Franchard.

The way was long, Rusty was tired, and, therefore, he let the mustang jog softly on at a dog trot which ate the miles up slowly. He himself grew sleepy. He found himself half in a dream, with Rusty following the windings of the river road, and odd shapes of trees and rocks drifting past them, dawning suddenly upon his eye, startling him into complete wakefulness, and finally fading away beside him again.

186

The moon, by this time, was hanging very low in the west, and her circle was beginning to puff out at the sides, and she herself to take on a russet-golden color, but still there was ample light upon the way when, with a jerk, he was roused from one of his weary trances by a barking voice. Rusty stopped with a jolt, and Tom found himself staring stupidly down the bright length of a rifle so held that not a quiver appeared upon the barrel.

Behind the gun was a masked face, and behind the mask spoke a rough voice in Mexican. Tom knew the language perfectly well, but it by no means reassured him to hear it.

"I greet you, señor," said the other. "I should have known that my luck is with Alicia, and when she went lame, it was because a little fortune was coming my way. Put up your hands, amigo!"

Tom, obediently, thrust his hands above his head. He was still only gradually coming to full wakefulness, and now he could curse himself for having traveled along the river road, when, as a matter of fact, it was almost certain to be watched by the men of Henry Plank. And yet this fellow did not have the look of such an employee. All the others of Plank's men, so far as he had been able to distinguish, were white men and Americans.

He sat stiffly, foolishly, in the saddle, and gaped at the other.

"Have no fear, amigo," said the Mexican pleasantly. "I am no murderer, unless you drop one of those hands too quickly. Be at peace, but be careful with your hands. I mind them more than your voice. If you have much money on you, you may curse, rage, rave, and it will be nothing to me. But if you wish to keep silent, so much the better. Only, I care for what you do with your hands. You understand, señor?"

"I understand," said Tom.

A bell jingled among the rocks.

"Be still, Alicia. Be still, Maria. *Dios, Dios,* you have still left a little luck in the world for a poor muleteer."

As he spoke, one of the mules put her ugly head into

view from behind a rock, and it seemed to Tom that there was laughter in the face of the beast. But he began to have a great new hope, which was that the muleteer, who apparently did not recognize him, would merely empty his pockets and let him pass on.

"Put your leg over the pommel of the saddle. Your left leg, señor, and kindly slip down to the ground."

Tom did as was directed. The courtesy of this robber did not disguise the fact that his hand was steady on the gun as a rock, and that he was grimly attentive to every move that his victim made.

"All right," said Tom. "You'll find my money in the wallet in this righthand coat pocket."

"Good," said the Mexican. "I see you're a man of sense."

He approached, and, resting the muzzle of the rifle against Tom's stomach, he managed the weapon easily with one hand, keeping a finger on the trigger, and his eye fixed burningly upon that of Tom. In the meantime, with his free hand, he fumbled in Tom's pocket, and brought out the wallet. This he opened, and dropped his glance for a single instant to examine the thickness of the sheaf of notes. There were a number of one dollar bills, and these made the prize seem something worth while. Tom could veritably feel the bulging smile behind the mask of the muleteer.

"Now," said the Mexican, stepping back, "I suppose, since you are so much lighter, you will not mind going ahead on foot? You understand, señor, that a poor muleteer grows weary in the legs. I cannot be expected to walk forever!"

"Are you going to steal my pony?" asked Tom.

"I never steal," said the other. "I borrow from time to time, but always in the full expectation of returning the thing which I have taken. You will understand, amigo, that a man of brains must eventually find his fortune. Perhaps this very night puts my foot on the first rung of the ladder, and presently I shall climb higher and higher! If you should meet me at some other time, I have no doubt but that I may be able to repay you, and with interest. In the meantime, if you please, face about and walk toward those trees."

"What do you mean to do?" asked Tom.

"No murder. I borrow money, and a horse or two, but never a life unless it is forced upon me. I am going to tie you safely to one of those trees and leave you there. The night is not cold. Before long, the day will come, and you will not be gagged, so that you can call to the first man who passes up this river road."

Tom answered nothing.

"Very well, then," said the other. "Face about!"

Tom obeyed and marched off toward the trees with a vague fear that he would be shot in the back, in spite of the assurance of the Mexican.

The other followed, talking in his usual cheerful way.

"We must find a good, thick tree," said he, "so that you can put your arms comfortably around it, and your legs also. I am one of those men, señor, who wish to do everything in the best manner. But such a conscience as mine goes unrewarded in the world! There is no return, and my talents have been almost wasted. Here, now, is a proper sort of a tree."

He directed Tom toward it, and the boy obeyed. He was thinking of one thing, only—and that was the sudden explosion of his reputation for daredeviltry, so newly acquired, and now to be lost when the first passerby in the morning discovered him tied to a tree.

And suddenly he thought of the face of beautiful Kathryn Lane, when she heard of the shameful news. Would it not cast a bright light upon him, by which she could read all the truth of him, and all the folly of her own preconceptions? Her face would grow hot indeed, when that word came to her!

"Here," said the muleteer, "we may halt. Examine the tree, señor. Is it to your liking?"

Tom obediently looked it over.

"It will do as well as the next one," said he.

The muleteer chuckled a little.

189

"I see that you are a simple soul, and not critical," said he. "So that, in fact, I am sorry that I should have to take your horse away from you. To say nothing of the money. But, at the same time, you have my earnest promise to return everything to you in due time. However, for that purpose I shall need to know your name."

Tom was silent.

"Come, come!" said the other. "Everything in the best of spirits to this point, and I hope that you won't spoil our meeting by growing sullen now? Tell me your name, my friend, or I shall have to tickle it out of you with the point of my knife."

He stood a little at the side now, apparently enjoying the expression on Tom's face, but though he made sure of his man, still the Mexican kept the rifle constantly pointed.

"I'm Tom Fuller," said the boy.

"You—*Dios!* The mustang—. The—the—*Dios, Dios!*" gasped the Mexican, and he went back half a step, the rifle swinging away from its right point at the same instant.

There was no need for a door to be opened very wide for Tom at that moment. As a cat turns, so he turned; but it was as one of the Mexican's own mules might kick that he struck the other in the midst of the mask, and felt his hard knuckles bite home through the softer outer flesh against the bone of the head.

The shock numbed the other to his very finger tips. The rifle fell to the ground, unexploded, and the Mexican slouched sidewise down, a heavy fall.

There he lay without making a stir, and Tom rapidly jerked the mask from his face.

He saw a smooth-shaven, rather round-faced man, not more than twenty-five years old, and looking good-natured even now, though the blood was running copiously from his nose. He was totally unconscious, and his hands and feet were tied, and his pockets emptied of his own and the stolen wallet and the knife of which he had spoken, before he came back to consciousness again.

When he did so, he stirred, groaned, and then wriggled into a sitting posture.

Tom picked him up in his arms and carried him to the tree. To it he fastened him with a rope that ran all the way round. Then he stood back and surveyed him.

"Are you pretty comfortable?" asked Tom.

"Señor," said the other, "I am charmed! As a result of this night, I shall become famous. The muleteer who nearly captured or killed the famous Tom Fuller! Señor, I salute you. *Dios,* if only I had shot you through the heart!"

33

HE SAID this with the same bright tone which he had used throughout, and Tom could not help laughing at the poor man. He took the Mexican's handkerchief from the ground and with it stanched the bleeding of his nose.

"I'm sorry for you," said Tom. "But what else could I do?"

"Nothing—nothing!" said the Mexican. "I would not have it otherwise. I need the rest of the night to sit here quietly and think out every word of the story which I am to tell in the morning. That will be a lie which will be worth listening to! In the first place, there are four bullets discharged from my gun. They were discharged, of course, in a battle with you. But we both missed, and then we fought hand to hand. I would have stabbed you to the backbone, but I broke the point of my knife on the buckle of your belt. You may see for youself that the point of the knife already is broken. Then we fought hand to hand. We fell upon the ground, and you were beneath me, when your hand closed upon a rock and you dashed it into my face. There, señor. Do you approve? Can you suggest anything else?" ·

Tom laughed, in spite of himself.

"I think that may be enough, as it stands," said he.

"Very good, then," said the Mexican, "but to save my life, I cannot understand how you got that rock into your hand."

"What rock?"

"Why, that one with which you spread my nose over both cheeks."

"I had only my empty hand," said Tom.

"You had—only your empty hand? Heaven forgive me, Señor Fuller! I also am a man of invention, as you have seen, but I never have risen to such a great lie as that. Well, then, it was with your empty hand that I was struck!"

He laughed, as he came to this point, and Tom chuckled a little with the rascal.

"What is your name?" he asked good-naturedly.

every man should have. There is no reason why we

"I," said the other, "have a number of names, as should limit ourselves to one coat; neither should we be held down to one name. In Boston I have been called Robinson—with a dash of old Indian blood, to account for my dark skin. I have been Taliaferro in Virginia, and Van Blicken in New York, and Jansen in Minnesota."

"Then you speak English?" said Tom.

"English? Oh, yes. Very well. I speak all the American dialects of it fairly well, I believe. However, in this part of the world I prefer Mexican, because it is my natural tongue. You were asking me for my name, and at the present moment, it is Pedro Aguillar."

"Pedro Aguillar?"

"Or 'Pete the Mule-skinner,' sometimes. It all depends. You may call me Pedro, however, because already I feel that I know your hand, and part of your heart, señor!"

This fellow was full of laughter. It bubbled in between his words and ended nearly every sentence.

"Pedro Aguillar," said Tom, "where are you going?"

"I am going to town, to tell my story to newspaper reporters and live on free drinks, and collect money from editors for ten days, unless I run out of lies, which is something that never has happened to me before."

"Where were you going, then?"

"I was going up the Big Yellow, as far as Los Parmas."

"To trade?"

"To sell what I have, which is a very poor cargo of black walnuts."

"Black walnuts?"

"Yes. I got them for nothing, and that is why I am carrying them. There is a curse on them. A strong man could starve to death on the things and break his teeth trying to eat them. However, a poor man cannot win until fortune decides that he may."

A thought came slowly into the brain of Tom.

"Have you traded much in this region?"

"No, I have not."

"Do you know the places?"

"Yes."

"The Little Yellow, say?"

"Yes. I once took a cargo up that gorge."

"To what place?"

"To what place?"

The Mexican laughed as he repeated the question.

"In all this country," said he, "is there any man so great a fool that he will talk of the place that lies beyond the gorge of the Little Yellow?"

Tom looked down in earnest interest.

"Do you think I am a safe man to tell it to?" said he.

"You? Señor, now you make a joke of me! Of course, Tom Fuller knows where he is riding as well as any man in the world."

193

"I never have been there," said Tom.

"Then," said the Mexican, "you never will learn from me. Not a word!"

"There are ways of making men talk," said Tom grimly.

"There are no ways for you," said the Mexican instantly. And he smiled in the very face of Tom. "I know you, señor. Your heart is too big for such Indian ways of dealing with helpless men. But, even if you were to peel off my skin inch by inch, I would not speak a word!"

"And why?" said Tom. "How would you be rewarded for keeping silent?"

"No reward for that, but a great punishment for speaking."

"How could it be found out that I had learned from you?"

"He is the evil one himself," said Pedro Aguillar with deep conviction. "He is, and that means that he has ears everywhere, and tongues everywhere. No, no señor, ask me any other thing, and I'll talk as freely as the wind, truth and lies. But even lies I will not tell about the Little Yellow!"

"Very well," said Tom. "But now you've given me an idea, and I have to ask for your clothes, down to your sandals, and up to your hat. You may have mine in exchange."

He dropped from the Mexican into his own tongue.

"Pedro," said he, "where I can't go in my own skin, maybe I can wriggle through in yours!"

"Three more exchanges like this," said Pedro, "and then I would only need a good name to take a fine place in the world. Help yourself, señor, and be at ease!"

In ten minutes, after Pedro had been freed from the ropes, the exchange was made. Then he was tied again to the tree and Tom left him.

"I'm taking both your packs and one of your mules," said Tom. "But if you go to the Little Yellow, tomorrow, you'll find everything there, I hope! Pedro, good night!"

"Thank you, señor," said Pedro Aguillar. "You will find that Maria is as stubborn as ten thousand demons. But there is one way to manage her. On her right side you will see a lump. Strike her there, señor, and her very soul responds. It is the magic spot. I myself made it, and I know its purposes! Good night, Señor Fuller, and fortune be with you!"

Tom, still smiling, went to the mules. From the lame one, which stood with a rear foot pointed, he stripped the pack, and from the pack itself he took a great part of the contents, replacing them with Rusty's saddle and pack. Then the pack saddle and its new load he strapped upon Rusty, who shook his head and grunted at the weight.

After this, he went to the river, and with some of the black walnuts and a little water, he rubbed every inch of his body from head to foot. The result should be, if he remembered the properties of that nut, a complexion fully as dark as that of swarthy Aguillar himself.

When he had finished this preparation, and dressed again, the moon was quite down, the road turned dark, and a chill wind began to rise out of the north and whistle across the Candle Plains. Tom returned to poor Aguillar and tossed him a saddle blanket for additional warmth, and even lingered to roll him a cigarette, which he lighted and placed between the lips of his captor.

"Señor!" said the Mexican suddenly, his heart melted by this last act of kindness. "Wherever you go, take advice from an unlucky man, and do not go up the Little Yellow tonight. I, Aguillar, know. They have doubled the guard!"

With that for comfort, Tom went off and took the road. He was not sorry to have to go on foot now in the slipping sandals of the Mexican, for he needed the exercise to keep him warm. He beat Maria and herded Rusty before him, and so they crawled slowly, slowly forward.

While they were going on in this manner, winding up the river road, he saw the first gray of the morning

195

streaked above the hills, and a short time afterward, the mountains were black against the dawn.

He watched that growing light with apprehension, knowing perfectly well that the sun could not shine upon him without leading him into peril. He would be found, but when the guard encountered him, he must be found to be a Mexican only!

He began to reflect, studying over all the ways and the manners of Pedro Aguillar. And he began to compose lines which, he felt, would be in tune with the rather sardonic cheerfulness of Pedro himself. In this humor, he felt himself fortified and ready for trouble, and he set his jaw and faced grimly forward, when the trail turned up the gorge of the Little Yellow River.

Colonel Forbes was perhaps due there before long. Tom looked anxiously at the thin runlet of water which went down the valley, connecting the ponds of water that were spotted here and there in the low places. It did not seem possible that fish were here, but he was sure that the good doctor would make a tremendous show of certainty in the matter.

In the meantime, Rusty and Maria went doggedly on, heads down, weary from the long trail which they had followed. Tom could have given himself up to sleep in five minutes. There was a slight numbness in the back of his brain, and he had to shake his head, now and again, to rouse himself to a full wakefulness.

In the meantime he had come well up the gorge of the Little Yellow. He was, in fact, not a mile from the place where he had left Franchard and Rankin when he began to hope that he had successfully passed through all the dangers of the entrance, and that he might win straight on to his goal without further interruption. But at that moment a voice called loudly before him; another sounded at his rear, and out from the rocks came no fewer than five armed men. By the first glance at them, he knew that resistance would be impossible. And he knew, furthermore, that these would be thorough questioners!

34

HE GLANCED at his battered sandals, and at his legs, naked from the knee down, and told himself that there was little wrong with that part of his disguise. And, then, as these wild men swept down around him, he looked about the valley on either side and above, as one looks in saying farewell. He saw the western rocks gilded and shining in the light of the rising sun, and the sky losing its color to become a pale blue. There where the light diminished he saw a floating speck, and knew it was the buzzard, waiting for a death. This added another shadow to the mind of Tom Fuller—it was a very little thing, and yet it seemed to point at him with a mighty dark, sinister finger.

The five riders circled about him on their horses.

"It's only a greaser," said one.

"Good morning, señor," said Tom in his best Spanish and he raised his hat and exposed hair which he had carefully tousled.

"It's only a doggone snake-eatin' greaser, Harry," said another of the punchers.

"If it's only a doggone greaser," said Harry, who was a wiry, dark-faced little man, "what's he doin' here in the Little Yellow? Hey, you, whatcha doin' here?"

"No spik Inglish," said Tom blankly.

"Talk greaser to him, Harry," said one of the men. "He ain't got a white man's lingo at all."

Harry rode up and paused a yard from Tom. There

he waited for a moment, as though gathering again his knowledge of the foreign tongue, then he said:

"What's your name?"

"Pedro Aguillar."

"Where from?"

"Holliday."

"You live there?"

"No, señor."

"Where do you live?"

Tom looked about him a little wildly. In what place should he say?

Then he pointed at the mule and the broncho.

"Wherever these are is my home, señor."

"He's a wanderin' peddler, Harry," said one of the punchers. "Looks about scared to death, don't he?"

"Shut up, Lew," commanded the leader. "He probably knows every word you say."

Tom waited. He knew that his eyes were blank. He opened them still wider as he stared at Harry. That leader regarded him for a long moment and then said:

"What you doing in the Little Yellow?"

"I am going up the canyon, señor."

"You're going up the canyon, are you?"

"Yes, señor."

"And why are you going up it?"

Tom paused. He hardly knew what answer to make, and felt that he was walking on quicksand. The mystery of Henry Plank was one which few people had penetrated. For his own part, he had gathered only bits of information, here and there, and he was only fairly sure that, somewhere beyond the end of the canyon of the Little Yellow, there was a house in which Plank lived at times. He was in hiding there, as it seemed—perhaps from the law, or perhaps only from Franchard. He wished with all his might that Franchard had been more open in saying what he knew; but even Franchard seemed to know very little. As for the men who were guarding the canyon, it was probable that not one of them ever had seen the house. They were employed by an unseen master

198

and ordered to put their curiosity in their pockets. Yet, undoubtedly, Plank was a man who would require servants about him. He even had allowed the peddler, Aguillar, to come to his place. Doubtless, he permitted this only to people in whom he could put an absolute trust. On the strength of this, Tom ventured to say:

"There is a place beyond the canyon, señor."

"Is there?" said Harry. "What place?"

Tom paused. He looked earnestly at the other, as though he wished to speak, and was rather in doubt, still.

"What place?" repeated Harry angrily.

"There is a house—" said Tom slowly, and paused again.

Harry gathered his brows. Then, turning suddenly, he said, "Lew, come here. The rest of you back up out of hearing. I gotta talk to this bird private."

Three of them fell back, and Lew approached, a large, redheaded, smiling fellow the sight of whom gave Tom more confidence.

"Lew," said Harry, "this gent says that he's going up the canyon, and that they's a house beyond it."

"What kind of a house?" asked Lew of Tom.

Tom searched his mind. How could he describe a thing which he never had seen?

"A house, señor," he finally said with caution, "that is hard to find."

"What's in the house!" cried Harry as though angered.

Tom shrugged his shoulders.

"Señor," said he. "I am not one to speak!"

"Are you one to have your skin taken off?" said Harry fiercely. "Who is in that house?"

A spark of anger flashed into the mind of Tom. It gave him the courage to answer. "Señor, I do not know you!"

"You don't know me, eh?" said Harry, his lips twitching with anger. "I got a mind to make you know me!"

199

"Hey," protested Lew. "Don't go too fast. If he was to shoot off his face when you ask him to, what sort would you put him down for?"

He added to Tom:

"What you say your name was?"

"Pedro Aguillar."

"Aguillar? Seems like I can remember some greaser like that comin' up last year. What did you bring?" he demanded, turning to Tom again.

But Tom shrugged his shoulders once more.

"Señor, I brought what I was commanded to bring."

"I'm gunna make this greaser talk," said Harry savagely. "I'm tired of hearing' him dodge."

"Leave him be, leave him be!" urged the other. "Fact is, there was one like that that came up last year. I didn't see him, but I heard about him. If you skin him, you're likely to get skinned yourself when the chief hears about it!"

"I'll take a chance on it," said Harry sullenly. Then he added: "What's he doin' with one mule and one hoss? That hoss has the look of a man-size cow pony." He said to Tom: "Where'd you get that horse?"

"I found a man walking and leading him," said Tom, inventing slowly. "My other mule was dead lame. I began to talk with the man who was leading this horse and I learned that he was walking because he could not ride the broncho. Finally, I gave him the mule, and he gave me the horse. You see, señor, it is harder to buck off a pack than it is to buck off a man."

"A bad actor?" suggested Lew. "He don't look as much as that, though."

"Lew," said Harry. "I sort of smell a lie behind this here peddler, this Aguillar, as he calls himself. He looks dirty enough and low enough. But I got an idea that something is wrong."

"Have as many ideas as you want," said Lew, "but don't get yourself all worked up over a wrong trail, is what I suggest. Bigger men than you have been broke!"

"And what if he is crooked?" said Harry. "What

200

would happen to me then? It's my neck that would be broke, Lew. You don't take no responsibility."

"He knows that there's a house," argued Lew. "That's something. He knows that there's a man there that don't like to be talked about. That's twice as much more. Now, then, when you put two and two together, whatcha got? A greaser that knows a good deal; and that's scared of us—look at his face now!—and that is still worse scared of talkin' about that house beyond the canyon than he is of us. I say he's straight. But you make up your mind for yourself."

"That Sim, yonder, he can ride a bit?" said Harry suddenly.

"Sure he can ride. I seen him—"

"Sim!" broke in Harry.

Sim, lean and gaunt, with the seat of the true horseman, loped up to them and drew rein.

"Sim, I want you to try out that mustang, there, will you?"

He ordered Tom to remove the pack, and the boy obeyed, and saw Sim cheerfully cinch his own saddle on Rusty's back. He mounted, and Rusty merely flopped one ear forward.

"Get along, mustang!" said Sim, and dug his heel into Rusty's flank.

Rusty broke into a gentle trot.

"Is that the man-killing horse?" asked Harry of Tom, his face tense with suspicion. "Is that the horse that couldn't be ridden?"

Tom stared after Rusty in despair.

"He is very tired, señor. It has been a long march—"

"A mean hoss tired, is still a mean hoss," declared Harry to Lew, "and this here greaser is a liar—"

"Hold on!" said Lew.

Sim, having ridden a hundred yards, turned the mustang, or tried to turn him, but this procedure did not fall in with the desires of Rusty. He jerked back his ears with an audible grunt and planted all four feet. Sim, well-warned, gathered himself and set himself for trouble.

201

It came at once. Rusty rose suddenly into the air, tied himself into a knot, and landed on one leg, with a jerk that knocked off the rider's hat and snapped his chin down on his chest. And having opened with this shot, Rusty began to spin in a rapid circle, bucking as he turned.

Three circles he completed, with Sim swinging farther and farther to the side. Then, quick as the snapping of a whiplash, the cunning mustang reversed.

It was too much for Sim. He was flicked clean from the saddle. Landing on head and shoulder, he tumbled over and over, to rise staggering at last, while Rusty jogged quietly back to his master.

Lew, grinning broadly, nodded at Tom, while Harry suddenly broke into a laugh.

"That's a bust and a proper bust," said he to Lew. "I guess you're right, old son, and the greaser can go on. A lucky thing for me that I didn't bust into the packs and look at what the chief is having brought up!"

He turned to Tom.

"Get!" said he, and waved up the valley.

35

Gladly Tom "got!"

And, fifteen minutes later, as he went up the trail, he saw a tall figure rise from behind a rock and exclaim: "By heck, you got through! You got through!"

It was Rankin. He helped bring the two animals into

the harborage among the rocks where Franchard lay, mumbling in his sleep.

"And where is the doctor?" asked Rankin.

"There's one promised to come."

"Promised to come?" exclaimed Rankin in alarm.

"Colonel Forbes."

"Great guns! How could you persuade him to come?"

"He recognized me. And I guess he's coming because he wants to make a game of it. I don't know why else he should!"

"Forbes, knows what's ahead—and he's comin' anyway? That's like him! Who steered you on Forbes?"

"It was only luck."

"There ain't that much luck in the world," said the other vehemently. "Kid, you've done ten men's work. And how did you get in just now? In this greaser outfit?"

"I met a gent down the road, and got his clothes, and borrowed his mule."

Rankin asked no more, but his wonder stood in his face. He looked anxiously to Franchard. It was plain that he had no thought of escape, but was keenly eager to have Franchard cured. The explanation of his good faith was not long in coming, for he and Tom took up a watchful position, from which they could see the floor of the canyon, so as to keep an eye upon Forbes, in case he passed, and from which, also, they could hear the murmurings of Franchard as he lay delirious.

Then Rankin told him he had lain at watch during most of the night, and, stealing down through the rocks, he had heard the guards passing and repassing.

From their talk he had learned all the details of Tom's escape, a matter which appeared miraculous to Henry Plank's men. It appeared no less marvelous to Rankin himself! But he had heard more than this. He had learned that Plank had sworn to have a terrible vengeance upon the man who had become a traitor to him and his cause. More than upon Franchard or Tom,

203

Plank now stored up wrath for Rankin, and had vowed to give him a death of consummate torment.

"And he knows the ways," said Rankin slowly, his face colorless. "He knows all the ways. I've seen—"

His voice stopped here, but already he had said enough to send a wave of disgust through Tom. He did not like Rankin, not only because the man had really sold himself, but because there was a very aroma, as it were, of baseness in the man.

It grew hotter and hotter still. The slim, brown lizards, which had come out to sun themselves, slid off into cracks and crevices again. And the canyon began to turn into a furnace. They spent much time over Franchard now, keeping a wet cloth upon his head, fanning him, and adjusting the shade above him. But the heat was very hard on him. His eyes were glazed continually with delirium, and his face was pale and very thin.

It was mid-morning. They were talking, anxiously, of what might be happening in the other world, the world which Henry Plank was dominating all around them, and wondering what next maneuver he would attempt, when they heard a cheerful whistling coming up the canyon, and, the next moment, they had sight of Colonel Forbes coming up the floor of the gorge with his fishing basket at his side, and his rod held tightly in his hand.

A low word and a gesture brought him in among the rocks, and in another moment he was kneeling beside Franchard. He had come with the excited face of a man who is adventuring like a boy; but when he was beside Franchard, he turned coldly professional at once.

When he had finished his examination, he talked not to Tom, but to Rankin, as an older and more responsible man.

His report was serious enough. As for the fever, it did not worry him, and the wound was nothing. But Franchard, he said, was really thoroughly exhausted.

"We have two kinds of strength," said the doctor. "We have the strength of our muscles, and the strength of our nerves. When the muscles are played out, then we can begin to use the strength of the nerves. But that is a very serious matter. The muscles, after a point, will not continue to work. They demand sleep, and sleep restores them—slowly, perhaps, and partially. Nevertheless, it restores them. But the nerves are not surface affairs. They run through the entire body, and when the brain has taken charge and is driving a man forward, not only arms and legs, but the nerves of heart, and lungs, and all the vital organs, slowly are drained.

"This man has been drained in such a manner that there is not much left to him. I would order him to go to a distant country and rest, not for a month, but for a year. He is thoroughly vitiated. He is brittle as an eggshell. As for this fever, I think I can guarantee that it will be broken an hour after he has taken this powder. But an hour after that—the man might die!"

They listened to the doctor with awe.

"Brittle, brittle!" said Colonel Forbes. "Handle him with care, or he'll fritter away to dust between your finger tips!"

He left his final directions, and after dressing the wound and seeing that the powder had been swallowed, he stood up to leave.

"There is a fellow whom they call Harry," said the colonel, "who trusted me no more than I trust a wolf. But—Harry was pacified at last. He let me through, but I think that he's apt to be flying like a hawk behind me, to see where I take to the ground. I must go back."

He beckoned Tom to one side, and then, standing close to him, he said with a stern face: "Young man, I've given you a promise, and that promise I've kept. But if I'd known about you last night everything that I've learned in the meantime—I should not have been so hasty as to make any promises."

Tom could only stare.

"What have I done?" said he.

"In Holliday?" asked the colonel. "Do you need to be reminded of what you've done there? At least, the entire town will never have to be jogged to remember that evening."

"I had to get food," explained the boy.

"You could have had a truck load from my house."

"When you were doin' so much, could I keep on askin'?"

"As for the hotel riot," said the colonel, "that could pass by without much trouble. After all, you harmed no man there. But, young man, you have wounded a woman."

"A woman?" cried Tom. "No, no! I'd never do that!"

"You've blighted the good fame and name of Kathryn Lane," said the colonel. "Can you deny that?"

"Good name?" echoed Tom, shocked and bewildered.

"Can a girl wander about with a strange young fellow through half the night, give him means of escape from the law, steal his horse away from guards and bring it to him, lend him her own flyer to get him out of the jaws of capture—can an eighteen-year-old girl do that and remain untalked about?"

Tom guilty, his heart falling, could only stare.

"Do you hear me?" snarled the colonel.

"I couldn't keep her back," said Tom.

"You tried, I suppose!" said the colonel fiercely.

"I did. She thought I was a hero. I told her that I wasn't. She had a wrong idea. She kept makin' a great man out of me—she wouldn't listen—she laughed when I told her the truth about myself. I never would've had harm come to her—"

He paused. Then a savage emotion arose in his breast.

"If I could find them that have done the talkin', I'd break their necks!" said Tom.

To this simple speech, the colonel listened with a keen, piercing eye fixed upon the boy's face; and suddenly he smiled faintly.

"I think I understand," said he. "Kathryn is an enthusiast. But you're needlessly piling up grievances for her stepfather, aren't you?"

206

"Stepfather? I don't even know him," said Tom, looking as blank as ever.

At this the colonel recoiled a little and his face darkened suddenly.

"Fuller," he said, "I think I've deserved a trifle more confidence than this from you!"

Then, as he saw Tom flush, but heard no answer, he went on dryly: "However, I see that you feel that one mind is enough to hold one secret, and, therefore, I won't obtrude. I bid you goodby, and wish you whatever luck there may be in store for you."

He did not shake hands, but turned on his heel and strode off through the rocks. Instantly, he was out of sight, and Tom felt as though a great support had been stripped from beneath him and left him floundering. The unfairness of it rankled in him. He had been at ease, more or less, with Forbes, as feeling that this man, at least, took him for what he was, and would not attribute to him great qualities which he did not possess. Forbes had accepted him not as a mystery, but as a simple youth—a very simple youth. But now, at the last moment, it seemed that even the colonel was imagining him as a cunning actor. He was troubled and distressed, and, above all, he was confused.

Who was the stepfather of Kathryn Lane? That was what he wanted to know.

But now he had the sick man to consider.

At half-hour intervals they continued to give Franchard the powders which the doctor had left with them, and before noon the skin of Franchard was covered with a copious perspiration. He fell into a sound sleep which lasted without a break until six o'clock that evening, when he wakened with a clear eye, and pushed himself up on his elbows.

It required some moments for him to realize where he was. And when the realization came, he said nothing, except to ask for food, which he ate with a good appetite. After that he smoked a cigarette and rested again, lying with one arm pillowing his head and staring up at the colored sky of the sunset. Rankin, sitting beside him, told him briefly of all that had happened, the adventure of Tom in Holliday, and the visit of the doctor that morning. To this narrative, Franchard listened without a single comment, often closing his eyes, so that he seemed to be asleep. But when the dusk had deepened, he sat up, suddenly, and said to Rankin and the boy:

"This is the beginning of our great night, my friends. Either this ruins us, and is our last night in the world, or else we win a great stake. I should stay here another day to gather strength and let the wound heal further. But we cannot remain here. By tomorrow, Plank will be combing this valley with a finetoothed comb, and we must be away. Now is our time. Help me get to the house, and by the grace of fortune, I'll be the fighting force when we reach it!"

36

IT SEEMED reasonably certain, when they pondered over the means of escape from the place they were in, that by this time Henry Plank must know that the man who had called himself Pedro Aguillar never had come through the canyon of the Little Yellow, and that he, therefore, was hiding somewhere among the rocks; and from that Plank would deduce that the fellow was an ally of Franchard, who must be in the same place. This would be true, even if the real Aguillar had not, by this time, been released from his bonds and had returned to

Holliday to make his wild story known to all. But it was very likely that Aguillar had said all that he could invent, besides the facts, and Henry Plank knew that his enemy was cooped in the rocks of the Little Yellow.

This would be a fact which would cause him little anxiety, and he would doubtless take his time to make a painstaking search of the gorge for the purpose of locating Franchard and the latter's allies. His logical procedure would be, of course, to mount a patrol night and day on either side of the valley, riding along the verge of the canyon walls so as to cut off escape in those directions. More than this, he would stop each end of the gorge, and beyond that, he would probably concentrate a strong guard in the immediate vicinity of his house, to stop the attack, if it should slip through his outer defenses.

There were two things which they could do to get out of the trap. One was to try to slip or to rush through the guard at the upper end of the canyon, and the other was to attempt to steal or charge through the patrol on either side of the valley.

Franchard made the decision.

It seemed to Tom wonderful that a man of the Western experience and the fighting character of Rankin should submit so absolutely and willingly to the ideas of a weak and sick tenderfoot, like Franchard, but Rankin merely put forward all the possibilities and allowed Franchard himself to do as he pleased. Tom, as a matter of course, was always silent when it came to these discussions. No matter what was done, it seemed to him a perilous, and a well nigh hopeless attempt.

Franchard, however, went about his decision more or less as a mathematician goes about the solution of a proposition in geometry. He said: "We must go between this point and this"—sketching on the ground as he talked—"and we must go in the direction in which my friend, Henry Plank, will least expect us. In which direction will he least exepect us?"

"Over the cliff," said Rankin instantly.

He sat on a rock with his hands gripped hard and

resting on his knees. His eyes burned with a desperate desire of life and a desperate fear of losing it. That man, Tom felt, would hardly be relied upon in a pinch.

"Over the cliff makes the hardest going," said Franchard decisively. "So he will know we're apt to take that way in order to surprise him. Therefore, he'll guard the upper lip of the canyon carefully on each side. Furthermore, that upper ground is comparatively smooth, and a mounted patrol could continually sweep up and down. The ground being level and the moon high—you see it now beginning to grow brighter—even if we succeeded in getting a little way off, we probably should be seen, followed, surrounded, and shot down."

He paused and tapped the tips of his fingers rapidly and lightly together. He had the hands of an artist, the fingers long and bony, and hair covering the first joint thickly.

"I don't favor climbing the cliff," said Franchard, "because of the reasons I have just given, though I suppose we could get up by dint of the cunning of Tom Fuller, here, who seems able to top all obstacles!"

He smiled and nodded at the boy, as he spoke.

Then he continued: "If we don't climb the cliff, at which end of the cabin will we find the largest guard?"

"At the upper end," said Rankin, "because he wants to keep us away from his house, and so he'll put the biggest guard at the end that's nearest to him."

"Doctor Forbes has been here," said the sick man in the same gentle voice with which he usually spoke. "Now, then, he managed to get through to us, but is it likely that his fish basket will not be examined when he goes out? And if the remains of the medicines which he brought are discovered there, isn't it possible that he'll be suspected of having come here on an errand, called by our great ally, Tom Fuller, whose trip to Holliday must be making a great deal of talk, by this time? Of course, that is likely.

"I should say that it is highly probable that Henry Plank now knows, or guesses, that we are held in here because one of us is sick or wounded, or both! That being the case, he will suspect that our next intention is to retreat from this trap, if possible. In other words, his first thought will be that we will climb the edge of the plateau to attack him. His second will be that we may retreat, giving up the attack for the time being. So his next greatest guard will be at the lower mouth of the gorge. His third effort will be made to close the upper mouth of the valley, and there, I think, he will keep the smallest number of men.

"Men in a desperate situation like ours are apt to imagine that their enemy has infinite wisdom and infinite resources. As a matter of fact, it is not probable that Plank will be able to get together as many men as he needs. He's rich, but at the same time he's in such a position that he can't employ any but trustworthy people. For that reason, I dare say that he will find it difficult to stretch his resources to cover all the danger points, which include both sides of the valley, the lower mouth, the upper mouth, and finally the house itself. What will he do? He is a gambler, and a gambler cannot help trying to bluff. Plank will keep a very scanty guard on the upper mouth of the valley. Of that I am sure. Very well, then, let us go in that direction as soon as we've muffled the hoofs of the horses."

"Leave the horses behind," said Rankin earnestly. "A gent can slip along and hide behind cover, but a hoss ain't got any more sense than his rider loans to him."

"That may be true," replied Franchard, "but in case of a pinch, we may need to push through and take chances with flying bullets. Horses may have weak brains, but they certainly have fast legs."

Rankin did not argue the point. He and Tom, therefore, immediately set to work bandaging the hoofs of the horses in leather and cloth rags, and when that had been done, the night was almost beginning.

They decided that this was the best moment for beginning their task. A little later and the light of the moon would be fatally revealing, but at this time the eyes of all men would be fairly dim after the brightness

211

of the day and not yet adjusted to the milder radiance of the night.

Rankin went to the edge of the boulder nest and spied up and down the gorge, but he heard and saw nothing. For that matter they had not seen or heard a sign of a patrol during the whole afternoon. When Rankin made his report, Franchard did not seem specially cheered.

"He may have cleared out," said he. "With the fire this close to him, he may have left his place, withdrawn all his guards, and let us do as we please, with a long trail to follow."

He added suddenly with a fallen voice: "A long trail, I never shall live to follow!"

They issued into the floor of the gorge, Rankin riding first, Franchard behind him, and Tom bringing up the rear guard. They carried rifles in their hands, after smearing the barrels with dust and oil comingled, so that there would be the smaller chance of alarming watchers with the glitter of the steel.

It was a strange moment in the day. The whole valley was alive with the croaking of the frogs from the pools, a sound softened and made musical by the echoes thrown back from the rock walls of the place. The sky over their heads was a dull violet, and the larger stars began to look through the skies at them.

Rankin, leading the way, went on very slowly. At every bend or angle of the way, or before they turned the shoulder of one of the great fallen rocks which strewed the floor of the canyon, he either came to a complete halt, or else went at a snail's pace; but by degrees they wound down the valley. Tom kept his lookout to the rear. Rankin held the front, and as for Franchard, he rode with loose rein, his head fallen on his chest, and his hands gripping the pommel of the saddle like a man utterly exhausted, and saving his strength for a crisis.

The valley began to narrow, as they mounted it. In two or three places they found sharp slopes in the floor, so that the horses had to scramble up with some difficulty. At one place, Rankin's horse knocked the muffling from a forefoot and the iron shoe rang loudly as a bell against the rocks. They had to pause while the bandage was secured once more, and then they pushed ahead with redoubled precaution, while they took note that the moonlight now was beginning to cast a distinct shadow.

At last Rankin raised his hand and checked his horse. Silently, the other two rode up beside him, and he said: "A couple of hundred yards ahead of us they's the draw to the right that leads off onto the upper ground. In the mouth of that draw and across the valley they ought to be a guard posted. And now we're ridin' into the teeth of the beast, Franchard. Tom, you better come up here beside me. And if it comes to shootin', shoot to kill. I know one thing that'll do you good to know. They ain't a man workin' for Henry Plank that ain't got his life in the hand of his boss. I mean, they ain't a one that ain't worthy of bein' hanged. That's just why he hires them!"

He did not seem to reflect that this implied the same accusation against him. And the three started forward more slowly than ever, crowding close to the rock wall on the right hand or eastern side of the valley, where the moon shadow fell most thickly.

The valley became smaller and smaller. The way grew more rough, and presently they crept around an elbow turn.

There was nothing in sight.

"Maybe, they've drawed all this guard off," said Rankin over his shoulder in a whisper.

When he looked forward again, it was to see half a dozen forms rise shadowy from among the rocks. Tom jerked the butt of his rifle up, but he knew that it would be useless to fight. Every one of those six guards had his gun already upon a mark! And though they might miss from the back of a galloping horse, they would never miss at this range, even by candle light, so long as they had the steady ground beneath their feet.

"Hello, Mahoney," called out the voice of Rankin. "I thought I'd never find you. Thought you'd crept off and died or gone to sleep. They ain't a thing stirrin' in the whole length of the valley. I think the suckers have blowed on us and got clean away."

"They'll never get away," answered Mahoney. "The chief has closed up his hands on 'em. I don't place you."

"I'm Tucker."

"Tucker? I thought you'd gone down to Holliday, Tucker?"

"I did, and I come back ag'in. The chief was wrong."

"Was he?"

"Sure he was. Where's your hosses, and we'll tie these here in with 'em?"

"Round there behind the rocks. Got any chuck with you?"

"Not a bit but some jerky."

"I'll take a chaw of that, anyway."

"Wait'll I get these hosses put up."

Behold, they were drifting slowly through the six men, and the six rifles were being lowered, one after another.

"You look bigger than ordinary, Tucker."

"Yep. I've laid on some weight. This sort of business is the best thing for takin' off fat, though. I ain't closed an eye for two days."

"Who has?" growled Mahoney. "It makes me sick! I was for goin' straight down through the valley right after they caught that feller Forbes. I was for gunnin' right through those rocks, and flushin' out the birds, and droppin' 'em on the wing."

"I dunno," said Rankin with a wonderful cheerfulness. "That's a right good idea, too, but the real fact is that they'd be a pretty hot nest to tackle."

"Sure they would. The kid is trouble on wheels, I guess. But two are better'n one, and we got better odds than that. Besides, that Rankin never could shoot none."

He walked now at the very knee of Rankin, so sure of the identity of the rider that he never thought of looking up through the brightening moonshine and examining the face of the other more carefully.

214

And already the other five were turning their backs on the new arrival as though confident that Mahoney, their chief, could not be mistaken. The heart of Tom began to leap with hope!

37

THE LAST remark had irritated the supposed Tucker out of caution, and he cried:

"I seen Rankin shoot circles around you. That day you both set up a tin can and rolled 'em with .45s, shootin' from the hip."

"I was full of redeye and couldn't hold my hand straight," protested Mahoney. "That sucker never seen the day when he could hold a gun with me, when I was right. He was always a measly skunk, and you know it. He run out on that forty bucks you won from him at stud last winter."

"Well—" said Rankin, choking with fury. Suddenly, he changed the subject. "Let Rankin go," said he. "He's gunna have to pay everything off in one swipe, if ever the chief lays hands on him."

Mahoney laughed brutally.

"The chief has got an old Blackfoot down from the mountains. He's gunna turn over Rankin to that Injun, if we have the luck to capture him alive. I sure hope that we do, because I'd like to see that party!"

He laughed again, with a deep relish.

Rankin, as though eager to involve Tom as well, asked at once: "And what if you land the kid?"

"You mean Fuller?"

"That's it."

"Well, that's a funny thing. I've been thinkin' that the kid had got away with something pretty much by luck, but the chief, he come down and rode the rounds himself, this afternoon. He's sure been down to your end of the valley?"

"No, he ain't been near to us."

"That's a funny thing. He's been here. He says that he'll pay ten thousand cash down to the gent that puts a bullet through Fuller's head. H don't want Fuller alive. He says that he's too dangerous to fool with. But he sure wants him dead, and wants him bad!"

"Ten—thousand—dollars!" said Rankin.

"That's right. He wants that kid out of·the way so bad that he pretty near made up his mind, he said, to let Rankin come back to us and double cross his new mates, so's to get hold of the kid."

Rankin stiffened suddenly in his saddle, and the very heart of Tom turned cold.

"But he changed his mind," said Mahoney. "Because he says that now he's got the lot of them in his hand, and that they ain't any reason for him to let any of the three get loose."

"Ten—thousand—dollars!" said Rankin, as though only that idea was strong in his mind.

"It's a heap, ain't it?" said Mahoney cheerfully. "The chief, he ain't any cheap hombre. He's a man, he is! I've agreed with the fellers here that if any of us drop him, we'll split the goods equal, all the way around. They's enough, and it'll make every one of us shoot straighter. He raised heck in Holliday, didn't he?"

"He made that a party, all right," agreed Rankin.

"Think of him standin' Kate Lane on her head! I never heard of her payin' no attention to gents before!"

"Nor me," said Rankin.

"She's growed up to the romantic age," declared Mahoney. "That's the way with a girl. She gets along to the ripe age, and then pretty near any gent will turn her head. Let alone a nervy feller like this here kid."

216

"He ain't done so much," said Rankin.

"Ain't he?" asked Mahoney almost viciously. "What else has got Franchard this far, I'd like to know? Here's the hosses, if you want to tie up your nags."

They had rounded a nest of boulders and come upon a full dozen of horses strung out in a line, tethered to a long lariat. Hay was lying on the ground before them, and at the present time, half of them had feed bags tied over their heads. It was a sign of the efficient organization of the great Henry Plank that he kept a fresh relay of horses constantly ready for his men to mount and ride.

"And what," went on Mahoney, "made the chief willin' to pony up ten grand for the kid's scalp? Just for fun, maybe? Is that your idea, you poor sap?"

He laughed and was about to add something else, when suddenly he exclaimed beneath his breath and jerked up his rifle as though to fire. At that moment the moon had shone full in the face of Rankin, freed from the shadow of the canyon wall, and Mahoney knew his man.

He had no time to act on his information. Rankin, with a grunt of savage satisfaction, swung his own rifle like a club, and slugged Mahoney along the side of the head. There was a sickening, crunching sound, and Mahoney dropped in a heap. The gun, rattling on the stones, exploded with what seemed to Tom a crash of thunder.

"Cut the hoss rope on the right end!" called Rankin to Tom, and for his own part galloped toward the left.

The boulders shut them off from the view of Mahoney's five companions, but they could hear the curses and the shouts of the guards, as though the explosion of the rifle instantly had let them understand and solve the riddle.

But they had some vital seconds of shelter, and they used them well. While Franchard got his mare to a gallop and headed her straight up the draw past the line of Plank's horses, Tom and Rankin were slashing the

217

horses' ropes and then driving them in a wild crowd before them, up the valley.

It was done in a single breath. They were through the guard, they were out of the valley, the broad, easy rolling land of the plateau was before them, the scattered horses were running like mad in full stampede, and all of this had cost the three not a stroke except that which had felled Mahoney. Not a shot had been fired, except the random bullet from Mahoney's rifle.

They scanned the plateau to right and left, but not a living thing appeared upon it, except the vanishing line of mustangs under the moon. They were alone, and they were freed from the cramping walls of the valley. Before them presently rose the shadowy outlines of trees, and Tom saw hills swelling upward, and knew that they had truly passed the heart of the Candle Plains and had arrived at the home country of Henry Plank himself!

They had by no means finished their work. The hardest part of all still lay before them, when they should find the house itself and the terrible man inside it—if, indeed, as Franchard suggested, he might not have fled long before. However, they had done much. By a miracle, as it were, they were here. They had passed the last outer guard, and they had robbed the guardsmen of their means of spreading the alarm!

Tom laughed with a nervously rich content, as he thought of these things.

They had drawn their horses down to an easy canter and then to a walk.

"We got time. It ain't far off," said Rankin, "and they got no way of spreadin' the news that we're about to arrive. We're gunna give the old man a little surprise, maybe, Franchard! Kind of a little evenin' call, this'll be!"

And he laughed, with his head thrown far back.

"Don't be stupid, Rankin," said Franchard coldly. "We still have our work cut out for us. And yet I think that there is a sort of fate working for us, and helping us through. By heavens, Rankin, you're a cool fellow! You had the right words on the tip of your tongue, and if you hadn't, they could have blown us to the door of Heaven in one half second!"

Rankin chuckled with great self-satisfaction.

"Maybe that puts me even with the kid?" he suggested. "Not that I want to take nothin' away from him!"

"I could do nothing without both of you," said Franchard. "And each of you will get the same reward. A fat reward, Rankin. You'll find it a great deal richer than the one which Plank is willing to pay, for instance, for the head of Tom, there."

"Love of Pete!" cried Rankin suddenly, and turning in the saddle he stretched out his arm and pointed to the rear.

They looked in the indicated direction, and Tom saw what looked like the bright eyes of an animal shining beneath the moon, yellow and clear, from the direction of the lip of the Little Yellow chasm.

"And ahead, too!" cried Franchard, a moment later.

He, also, was pointing, and Tom saw a similar pair of eyes of fire gleam upon a hill not far away.

He well knew what it meant, and so did his two companions.

It was some prearranged signal which would instantly tell the great Henry Plank himself that his outer defenses had been broken through, and at what point they had failed. It would tell him to guard himself against the worst.

All hope of a surprise was now lost. Perhaps hope altogether was gone!

The three said not a word to one another, but they did not turn back, and rode ahead in a dogged silence.

38

THEY CAME to the edge of a lofty wood, when Rankin drew rein.

He said in a voice which he kept low, as though even then spies might be creeping about him:

"Aw, what's the use of bluffin' any longer? We can't get through. You know it, and I know it. We can't get through, and so why not play up fair and square and admit it? We're done for if we go ahead! Tom, you know the same thing. What do you say?"

"I don't say," answered Tom. "I'm only a hired man."

"Well go on," said Franchard. "We'll go on. Rankin, don't you see that luck has brought us this far, in spite of Plank, and that it may take us in the rest of the way? We'll go on!"

Rankin did not answer. Instead, as Franchard pushed ahead, the big fellow began to curse rapidly beneath his breath, but he kept with the party, nevertheless. Then, with a louder oath, he sent his horse into the lead.

They were winding up hill and down through thick woods, with trees of great size on all sides of them. The moonlight struck through in patches and thin lance-points, often enough to enable them to find their way, but they went darkling, reining in their horses sharply, now and again. And when they did so, as a twig cracked loudly underfoot, the noise of the breathing of their own ponies frightened them.

Each time they halted, they remained still, listening,

for a longer period, and then they started forward more slowly. The very horses seemed to feel that they were marching forward to encounter a dreadful danger, and they went daintily, their ears pricked, and their heads nervous. It was as though they were entering a region of high pressure, shutting them back, excluding them from any closer approach.

At length, in the midst of a deep hollow, almost lost in the complete darkness from one another, Rankin stopped and said softly to his companions:

"Over the top of that next hill is the house of Henry Plank. Now, gents, if you want to go ahead and bash your heads agin' a stone wall, keep ridin' straight on. I won't fall away from you. But if you want to live, you'd better steer another course."

"We'll go on," said the quiet voice of Franchard. "We'll go on, of course. We can't turn back at such a time as this, with our hands on the plow, as it were. Rankin, if you're too much discouraged, turn back, man, turn back by yourself! I'll forgive you freely."

To Tom, it was as though he were hearing the voice of a ghost. So calm, so dispassionately at ease were the words of Franchard. But Rankin did not turn back. He went on, in spite of the permission he had received to retire, and they forged slowly over the hillside, the horses barely creeping.

A sudden wind sprang up with an almost human roar and went crashing through the trees. They could be glad of that. The moonlight was against them, but the noise of the wind would prove a screen under which all actual noise of their own approach would be buried.

Near the crest of the hill, where the big trees thickened, Rankin drew rein and urged them to tie up the horses. This they did in a close copse, and then they held their consultation like generals before a battle.

Standing on the ridge of the hill, they could look down through gaps in the trees upon the house of Plank. Only the roof and one lighted window showed, and as Rankin pointed out, except from that commanding spot, the place was almost invisible. One could ride

221

within a hundred yards of it through the surrounding trees and never suspect its existence.

They put their heads close together, to discuss the situation, and Rankin said: "Them that have come here before, they've always been brought. And them that have been brought, all of 'em ain't gone away again. It's that kind of a house."

Franchard appeared to pay no attention to this last gloomy warning. He merely said: "Probably three of us cannot get through at the same time. Rankin, you've been here before. Will you go scouting ahead and see if you can find a safe way to get closer?"

There was a pause, but at last Rankin said, with a groan: "I'll go! One is as safe as three, with men like that agin' us!"

He began to point.

"I'm gunna take that gully—you see where it opens up, over there? I'm gunna try to crawl down through that. If I can manage it, and find it's not too close-guarded, I'll come back and get the rest of you."

He left them without another word, hurrying forward through the trees, with his body already bent over, like a stalker striving to make himself small.

He was soon out of sight, and Tom sat with Franchard beneath the trees and listened to the bellow of the wind, and saw the tall tops of the pines swaying grandly back and forth. But he had small attention to give that. On the contrary, he had to keep his eyes chiefly riveted to the little they could see of the shadowy mouth of the gully down which Rankin had gone.

They waited an endless time. Sometimes the wind, which had ceased from its steady strength and blew now in gusts and squalls, fell off to a mere whisper, and then Tom could hear the teeth of Franchard chattering.

This filled the boy with a greater fear. He knew that their one resource, should they ever get into the house, would be in Franchard, himself, and he also knew that the man was a trembling wreck, not overcome with fear but with cold, the weakness which followed on his fever, and the long exposure which he had endured. But he kept himself keyed for the great effort. Whenever Tom saw his face, he noticed that the lips were pressed hard together, the cheeks made to appear sunken by the clenching of the jaws, and the eye burning steadily. He was pouring out nerve reserve every instant. How long would it be before that shallow well was drained?

And then a wave of despair would sweep over Tom Fuller. It seemed to him that there was only one obvious, one sensible thing to be done, and that was to get to their horses and to flee. It was no comfort to know that they had stolen at last through the mountains and come upon their prey. It was rather a terror and a horror to know that the lion's den was there!

Fire spat suddenly, like the flickering in and out of a half dozen snake-tongues in the gully down which poor Rankin had gone; and then the rattling reports came beating up around the ears of the listeners.

Was it the end of the man?

Tom, frozen with horror, leaned forward and listened. But Franchard, already on his feet, was tugging at the boy.

"Get up, get up—" he cried excitedly. "Move, boy! This is our chance!"

He did not wait for Tom to join him, but lurched forward down the hillside, dodging among the trees, now flashing into a moonlit patch, and now half lost in the shadow.

It was like the charge of a madman, single-handed against a house filled with enemies!

And then, recovering himself, Tom ran forward, half-blinded with dismay. He was almost at the bottom of the hill when he came upon Franchard, pausing an instant at the side of a creek that ran with a flash of silver among the shadows of the forest. And beyond, looming through the trees, was the house of Henry Plank.

"Where are you going? What are you gunna do?" gasped Tom, gripping at the shoulder of Franchard.

The man twisted snakelike from the great grasp of the boy, and half scrambled, half rolled down the bank.

223

Tom followed, his brain turned to ice, for he was sure that he had an insane man on his hands now. Across the creek went Franchard, his feet slipping on the surface of the stones, as he leaped from one to the other. It was not until he had staggered up the farther bank that Tom regained his side and gripped his arm with a more secure power.

But there seemed no further desire in Franchard to press forward at full speed.

He dropped down on one knee behind a large bush and stared at the broad, lighted flank of the house before them. Then he gasped: "That was our chance to break through. Rankin—poor fellow!—he was our forlorn hope, or feint—while we deliver the real attack!"

"I dunno how we got here!" said Tom, only vaguely understanding what this strategy had been.

"You don't know," said Franchard, laughing softly and fiercely. "But, you see—the sound of the shots must have pulled in the others who were watching in the woods. They must have crowded to the gully to find out what the shooting meant. They'll never dream that we've broken through and are now—"

He ceased. Out of the darkness before them two tall forms stepped, and loomed big above them. It seemed to Tom that they were walking straight upon the two at the bush, but, at the last moment, they swerved aside, as though the force of the sudden gust of wind had deflected them from their original line. In another instant, they were gone, and Tom and Franchard exchanged glances.

"Look!" said Franchard in a whisper. "There is the treasure house. We're at its door. Once inside, nothing can drive me out. Not Henry Plank himself! But what can we do now? How can we possibly enter? By the cellar? By the windows? By the roof?"

He looked wildly upward. It was a tall, two-story building, yet in spite of its tallness, the great trees among which it was lost, overtopped it. And one, a mighty elm, swayed its branches above the roof at this end of the dwelling.

"Tom," said Franchard, "you are young, strong, ac-

224

tive as a cat. Suppose you were to get to that tree and climb it to that branch which swings above the roof. Do you think you could drop safely down to the roof itself from that place?"

"The roof may be guarded," said Tom.

And he stared unhappily up at the huge tree. The thing was possible, but it would be a most simple matter to break one's neck in making the experiment.

"What other chance is there, in the name of fate?" said Franchard.

"If I could get in that way, it wouldn't help you," said Tom. "How could you climb that tree?"

"If you can get into the house," said Franchard, "I can give you a key which will, I think, open that door which is directly before me. Climb up the tree, Tom, and try. Take this package with you and hunt through that house for a beautiful woman. A woman of forty years. Perhaps her hair will be silver, now. You can know her especially by a white, round scar near the center of her left cheek. It is her one blemish. You can tell by that. Find her, Tom. Give her this package. If fate intends me to win, she will open that door for me with her own hands. Go quickly, go carefully—"

His voice choked away, and Tom, half maddened with excitement and with despair, started up and went straight toward the elm.

225

39

HE DID NOT go slowly. It appeared to him that his one chance was to make a bolt for the great tree while there was some sort of an opening before him, and, therefore, he ran at full speed, gained the trunk, and swarmed quickly up it, getting toe-holds in the roughness of the bark. He was at the second fork above the ground when he saw a pair of men turn the corner of the house. One of them halted and pointed straight up at where Tom was climbing.

He could not hear what was said at that moment, for the sound of the wind was very loud, but when it died out, the two were at the foot of the tree. Tom had flattened himself against the great branch and lay there, extended at full length. He could hear their voices, and they were saying:

"I saw somethin' move on the branch up there."

"A squirrel."

"This time of night? I seen something, or some shadow—"

"What would be doing up there?"

"I dunno, but I'm gunna shin up and see."

The heart of Tom Fuller stopped.

Distinctly he could hear the scratching of shoes, scraping to get a toe-hold, but presently the second voice said:

"Aw, quit it! You ain't gunna get up. And nobody else could. I'll flash a light up there!"

The beam instantly swept through the branches, and centered on that one where Tom lay, but with the shadow striking up from beneath, this was in itself an added shelter.

"There ain't a thing!" he heard the second man say.

"Maybe it was only one of the small branches swingin' in the wind."

"You're so set on some of that blood money, that you'd see things in the dark," said the other.

And they moved off around the side of the house.

Tom waited until they were out of sight, and then he crawled farther up the branch until he came toward its end.

It was not easy to keep his place. The force of the wind, coming in puffs and gusts, tossed the limb of the tree up and down, and swung it boldly over the gutter of the roof of the house. It was almost like the bucking of a horse, and he had to keep a firm grip.

From this position, he could look through the upper branches and see the sky, scoured clear of clouds, with a few of the larger stars showing, and all the rest of the heavens flooded by the light of that most untimely moon. Looking down at the roof itself, half a dozen feet below him, he saw a still more unwelcome sight, for there sat a pair of watchers, with their rifles gleaming brightly in their hands, and their backs against a chimney pot.

It seemed wonderful to him that he had not noticed them at the first glance, but now in a falling of the wind he could hear their voices as they spoke to one another. This way of approach was shut off, and he must get down if he could and try another. Though what other remained?

For the instant, he feared to move. At one moment, he swung within half a dozen steps of their heads, and surely it seemed that they must see him plainly!

However, there are only eyes where there is an expectation of beholding; and the guards saw the swinging branch, but not the man who clung to it.

He heard one of them say:

"—muffled in onions. That's my style."

"They got an aftertaste," said the other. "Gimme a half dozen eggs on top. That'll do."

"You ain't got no taste for quality," said the first speaker. "You want quantity—it wouldn't take no less than a couple of bushels of stuff to fill you."

The other, bearded and vast, laughed till he shook. What he said, Tom lost in the next roar of the wind, but presently he saw the man stand up and could hear his companion warning him:

"You better not. If the chief caught you off your beat—"

"He ain't gunna catch me. He's too busy raisin' heck with Rankin."

"Aye, what'll they do to Rankin?"

"Why, Rankin's a lot worse'n dead, by my way of thinkin'."

"He is, and the chief'll make you wish you were dead, too, if he catches you off your beat!"

"What does he care? What could come up here? You'd think that Fuller was a bat, or something, the way the chief is actin'. He can't fly, can he?"

"They's some in Holliday say that he can."

"A town full of pikers, is what that is. I'm gunna go have a shot of that coffee. I can get down the backstairs, and the cook will keep his mouth shut, I reckon."

"Will he?" said the companion. "You trust him, then, and get trimmed. But go ahead, if you wanta be a chump!"

"You scared of bein' left alone?"

"Aw, shut up, will you?" advised the other. "Go drown yourself in coffee, for all of me."

"So long, Casey!"

Tom, fascinated, watched the big man leave, and saw him lift the trap of the door to the roof, and disappear. The other guard, rising, stepped to the gutter, fearless, in spite of the cuffing of the wind, and looked down at the ground. That instant, as the limb of the tree swung away from him, he lifted his eyes and saw Tom.

The effect was amazing. The moon was full in his

face, so that Tom could study him. He saw the fellow's
mouth open, and his eyes; but the rifle did not stir in his
hand as the branch lurched back with the kick of the
wind behind it. Loosing his hold, Tom was hurled forward with wonderful impetus. He struck the guard with
his shoulder, and together they crashed upon the roof.
The guard, lying beneath, collapsed. The shock obviously had knocked both sense and wind out of him.
And Tom's own head rang with the blow.

One instant more, and he was up; the man beneath
him groaned and stirred.

"Fuller—by gravy!" he exclaimed.

Tom gripped his shoulder.

"Partner," he said, "you're half an inch from death."

"I been there for ten years," said the other, with unusual calm. "It ain't anything new to me."

It had seemed to Tom a necessary slaughter, the instant before, and his fingers had curled instinctively
around the barrel of his Colt. But now he paused; that
touch of humor had made the two of them kin, and it
would be murder, now.

"Stranger," said Tom, panting. "I got you cold, I
guess."

"Sure," said the other. "You got me chilled plumb to
the marrow."

"It is you or me," said Tom, faltering with the horror
of the thing that lay before him to do, and failing at the
thought.

"Why," said the other, cool as ever, "if you could
trust to the word of a gent that has told his share of lies
—suppose you let me set here and keep my mouth shut,
while you skin down and raise as big a ruction as you
please?"

A wild gust of wind howled about them, and as it
died a little, Tom suddenly held out his hand. It was
gripped hard, and keen eyes searched his face with
wonder that was almost awe.

"The word's been around that you was white, Tom,"
said the guard. "But I never dreamed of nothin' like
this!"

But Tom did not wait for further thanks. He ran up the slant of the roof to the trapdoor, and there he paused, listening. He could hear nothing from within; there was still only the wind. So he plucked the heavy door open. He was almost frightened into letting it fall again, as he heard the whistle of the wind pass in before him. But he told himself that this was his only opportunity. He must go forward. There was nothing else except to remain on the roof and be taken at the leisure of Plank's men.

So he raised the trap again and this time boldly entered and went down the steep steps before him. They were dimly lighted by the reflection of a lamp in the narrow hall beyond, and so he was able to fumble his way safely to the bottom.

There he paused again, pressed close to the wall.

He wished that he knew a thousand things, now. Above all, that he could have learned what Rankin knew about the disposition of the inside of the house. But now he must carefully fumble his way about, blinded by his ignorance!

So deeply was he breathing that the package of papers in his inside coat pocket rustled with every lifting of his chest; and suddenly he felt that he was mad beyond all computation. For he should have seen that it was like leaping from a cliff, to enter this house. Destruction could not have been more sure.

Madness, at least, he was certain possessed poor Franchard, who had such great hopes, he had said, of destroying Henry Plank, and could only offer, as a key to the house, a package of papers to be given to a woman with a scarred cheek!

Tom had no plan. He went forward merely because he dared not go back, and, as he went down the hall, his hand extended and touching one wall as though he half expected to gain protection from it, he passed a door behind which a voice was saying loudly:

"How could I know?"

It was not the words that stopped him, but the sound

of the voice, which he knew at once for the deep tones of Charlie Boston, the blacksmith. Frozen in his tracks with astonishment, he pressed his ear closer to the crack of the door, and in this manner he was able to make out what followed, though all was said faintly.

And there seemed no more peril in waiting there in the hall than in pressing forward!

"You couldn't know!" said an answering voice, smooth, easy, but somehow terrible. "You could not know!"

Said Charlie Boston, apparently trembling with fear: "I'd talked it all over with my wife. We figgered—"

"You're one of my men," said the other, "but still you're taking the advice of your wife?"

"We didn't have no idea of who Franchard was," said Charlie Boston. "We didn't even dream who he was, or I would've tried to grab him then and there, Mr. Plank."

Mr. Plank! The breathing of Tom ceased; he listened intently, with staring eyes.

"That's a lie, and a palpable lie," said Plank. "The fact is, Boston, that Franchard picked out the boy, asked you about him, won you over to his side with money, and got him away from you—"

Charlie Boston broke in with a literal groan of terror:

"Listen to me, for Heaven's sake! What you tryin' to say? Would I take the side of Franchard agin' you?"

"Ah? Wouldn't you?" asked the calm, sneering voice of Henry Plank.

"Mr. Plank, I been with you for a long time. I've done some good jobs for you," protested the blacksmith.

"And that's why I have you here now, to be questioned. Otherwise, do you think that I would have troubled my head about you, in a time like this, when the mischief is loose, as it appears?"

"He never could get here," said Charlie Boston in haste. "He never could get through the guards!"

"We've searched the place where Rankin left the two

of them, and they're not there. How can I tell? They may have gone back; they more likely have come forward."

"If they come forward, they'll simply be steppin' into a trap," declared Boston.

"That was what was said when they came through the mountains into my own hands. But they slipped through. That was said when Fuller went to Holliday. But he slipped through! That was said when the three were cooped in the gorge of the Little Yellow. But they slipped out once more. In the very beginning, Rankin had them trapped, but the two used the same trap to close on Rankin. They made him into their man. The deuce is in them. Not Franchard alone. But the boy—the black fiend of a boy!"

His voice rose, not high, but with something in it that chilled the blood of Tom Fuller.

"And you," went on Plank, "turned that avalanche loose on me, and now you're trying to lie out of it!"

"Will you lemme go back to the beginning?" asked Charlie Boston. "I gotta tell you the whole story."

"Go back to the beginning then—and tell the truth, Charlie, I caution you!"

"I'd rather lie to Heaven than to you," said Charlie with emotion. "It was this way. Along comes the kid one day and I try him for an apprentice. He has the strength of three men. I see that. I never seen anybody so strong. I was kind of fond of my own strength, but it made me look sick, the way he could slug with a hammer! So I try him out. Y'understand? I work him hard. I rub him down to the quick. I've seen the red run down the hammer handle. But he stuck with the job."

"Why?"

"Because he didn't have no other place to go. That's why. He was scared of starvation, which is a pretty good reason for a gent to put up with sore hands, I'd say! He fought along, and set his teeth, and didn't say nothin'. That kid was like a lion. I took him home into

232

my family. Me and my wife, we loved him like a son. Ask her, if you doubt it!"

"I'm talking to you, not to your wife."

"He was brave, and steady, and plumb quiet," said Charlie Boston. "But my wife hit on what was wrong with him. He was afraid of no man, but he was afraid of the world. Like a kid is afraid of the dark. It wasn't one man that scared him; it was a lot of men. I mean it was because he couldn't fit himself into the rest of the machine, if you know what I wanta say. It's sort of hard to get it out."

"I understand."

"Well, my wife seen that was true about him, or thought she seen it. She said that he would stay with us as long as we lived, and never change, and never get his mind hardened. But she said that he had to be pushed outside into the cold, as you might say. Well, we thrashed it out, till I agreed with her. I swore that I'd send him off the first fair chance that I had. I'd push him out where he'd get a chance to wake up, to be took along by some adventure, to be hammered and smashed about, you see. I wanted him to find out that there was nothin' to fear about society, that there was nothin' mysterious that other gents had that he hadn't. He thought everybody was sneerin' at him every time that they smiled. Well, I wanted him to get over that, too."

"And so you gave him to my friend Franchard?" asked Plank, with a purring sound in his throat.

"Look what happened! Along come a gent that sure didn't talk like he was a part of the outfit that he was wearin'. He was dressed West, but he talked East. He looked sick, and they was trouble in his eye, so that I seen he was on the trail of something, or else something was trailin' him. Well, it come to my mind that there might be the open door to push Tom through and hope that he'd fall on his feet safe, and wake up, and be the kind of a man that Nature intended him to be. I figgered it out that way. And when I'd done with the figgerin', I seen that Franchard was watchin' the kid with a kind of a hungry eye. He said one word to me. Then I fired Tom, and before long, off he went with Franchard, and hatin' me for the way that I had shoved him off. Them are the facts, so help me, Hannah!"

There was a pause.

"What are you gunna do with me?" asked Charlie Boston huskily.

"I don't know," said Henry Plank. "Probably this is a magnificent lie that you're telling me. But I'll keep you with me for a short time, Charlie, and look into what you have said. We'll go downstairs, now. Mind you, Charlie—I want to believe you. But if you've lied to me—"

He paused. A chair scraped back and footsteps came toward the door, while Tom fled down the hall as swiftly as he might.

40

HE HEARD the door creak behind him as he reached the head of a flight of stairs, and down this he ran as lightly as he could, thanking his fortune for a specially heavy blast of wind which, at this moment, struck the house, and howled through the trees outside.

So Tom came down into the lower hall, and could not believe that, so far, he had not encountered the eye of a single soul in the house. But the woman of the scarred cheek—in what room might she be?

He opened one door upon utter darkness, and then

the sound of footsteps on the stairs made him flee again, as well as the murmur of Plank's voice. They were coming straight behind him.

He hurried on down the hall until he came to a door across which long, blue curtains hung. Rather, it was an open arch, curtained to make it serve as an entrance and to exclude the draft, which now made the heavy cloth belly like a sail. There was no other exit before Tom, and he slipped into this at the very moment, as it seemed to him, that Plank and his companion must have turned from the last landing of the stairway and gained a complete view of the hall.

He did not pass through the curtains, however, for at the moment of parting them, he saw a woman seated between the window and the fireplace, reading. He had only a glimpse of her head, turned away from him toward the flames of the fire, but that glimpse was a little familiar.

Slipping aside, he stood where the curtain did not cover the arch, but extended down the wall for a distance beside it. Here he could hope that the dangling fringe would hide his feet, and that the draft would not sway the cloth so far out that he would be discovered.

But the inexorable footfall of Henry Plank came steadily down the hall, and brushed aside the curtain!

By the grace of happy chance, he did not glance aside or he could not have failed to see Tom, as the curtain was parted in the middle and thrust more deeply into the room. Instead, he stepped lightly into the room, saying, "Hello, Kate!"

"Hello!" said the voice which Tom would never forget. "How's the party coming along, Uncle Henry?"

There was an eyehole in the curtain just before Tom's face—a thin slit in the material through which he could look and see the fireplace group. He looked now, eagerly, and saw Kathryn Lane putting aside her book.

Kathryn Lane, and in this house—

All the connotations of that fact struck through his brain like distant thunders; he could not have moved, then, if he had been confronted with a leveled revolver.

235

Big Henry Plank, standing before the fire, his feet braced well apart, looked down at the girl, and she was smiling up at him.

"It is a party to you, Kate, I think," said he.

"Well, young people love excitement, you know," she retorted.

"I suppose they do," answered Plank. "And particularly the sort of excitement that may bury Uncle Henry Plank?"

The smile was rubbed from her face.

"That's not a fair thing to say, I think," said she.

"We ought to begin to be more open with each other," said Plank.

"Just as you please," answered the girl. "But you mustn't try to read my mind."

"I wouldn't try such a hard thing, Kate. However, you've let me see some of your cards, recently, you know."

"You mean that ride to Holliday, of course?"

"Naturally. You haven't wanted to talk much about that, I've noticed."

"Well, it was a queer thing to talk about. People say that I'm compromised and disgraced. Why, then let me be! I'm not going to defend myself, because I've done nothing that I'm ashamed of!"

She stood up lightly and faced him, as though he were in person accusing her.

"I've never had such ideas about you, my dear," said Plank. "You ought to know that. Only it seemed a little curious that you took such a lot of pains to cherish my dear friend, Tom Fuller.

She winced, but still she looked at him steadily.

He went on: "Be frankly aboveboard with me, Kate. You hold something back. What took you out of the house on that crazy ride, in the first place?"

"I went—because I was nervous," said she.

"Nervous about what?"

She hesitated, then went on:

"I'd heard so many whispers going about. Then the whole countryside knew that an enemy of yours was

236

coming this way through the hills, and that you were trying to stop him, and that you had failed, so far! Then —you had a pretty sick look, when you came in the other day. Well, I wanted to go out and see what I could see."

"You hoped that you'd have a chance to chat with the outlaws?"

"I don't mean that. I didn't want to go to bed, that evening. I went out for the ride—well, the miles jumped away behind me and that was how I found myself at the mouth of the Little Yellow when Tom made his break."

Remembering, her eyes wandered to the corner of the room, and she laughed a little.

"So you followed, eh? Followed him on into Holliday?"

"Yes, all the way. Heard him even talk to Doctor Forbes."

"Forbes, Forbes!" cried Henry Plank. "I'd almost forgotten him. Everything falls away from me. There's something in that boy corrupts them."

He muttered this rapidly, and then he went on: "Kate, wasn't there a malicious desire to see me harmed?"

"Not a whit! I didn't want you harmed. But I wanted to see him saved."

Her eyes filled suddenly.

"What are you crying about?" asked Plank more gently.

"I'm not crying," said she. "I'm not crying, or making any disturbance. I'm merely standing here like a dolt and a coward while Tom is wandering about through the woods, trying to get into this house!"

"You'd go out to save him if you could, I suppose?"

"Go out to save him if I could? Great heavens, of course I'd go out to save him if I could! Is there any other man in all the world like him?"

"How about that young blacksmith's apprentice?" asked Plank, chuckling in turn.

She looked at Plank with a sudden wonder. "Has he pulled the wool even over your eyes?" she asked him.

237

"He's fooled every one else, but I thought it was impossible for any one to bamboozle you, Uncle Henry."

She laughed, almost exulting over him.

"This wonderful boy of yours has apparently fooled every one, as you say. He was generally considered a half-wit, or very little better."

"Of course he was."

She laughed again, and looked to Tom so startlingly beautiful that he could scarcely keep from crying out, though she wrung his heart the next moment by drawing once more her own, untrue picture of him.

"Think of it!" said she. "A man who could hold himself back for years, waiting for a chance to use all his strength and to surprise the world! Think of it, Uncle Henry! And think of the way he's played havoc with everything the instant that he started. You've tried to catch him. You've had scores to help you. You've had the law fighting for you. And yet he's broken through you all as a bird breaks through a spider web! If you'd seen him, as I saw him, calmly sitting there in the dinning room of the hotel there in Holliday—oh, I tell you. I was almost choked with admiration—and then to see how he galloped up the trail on the creek bank, and faded out of town and—"

"On your horse, yes!"

"If I hadn't lent him my horse, he would have managed, some way. But—you don't really want to talk to me about Tom Fuller, I expect?"

"Kate," said Plank slowly, "It's not exactly about Tom. It's about your attitude toward me. I'm afraid that you've been acting a part, and that all these years, you've really not liked me! Isn't that true?"

She did not answer.

"Kate, I must have an answer—or else I'll bring this up before your mother—"

"Oh!" she cried at him, in horror and in rage. "Is that always the whip that you're going to shake over me?"

"No whip, Kate, no whip," he said smoothly, "but I

think that a mother ought to know when her daughter goes careening about the countryside at night."

"I'm not a whit ashamed of it."

"Your sense of shame is not being tested, Kate. I'm speaking of your mother's sense of shame. But first of all, I want you to tell me, truly, why you really dislike me so intensely?"

"I don't—not intensely," she said, half frightened, half angered, and wholly honest.

"Not intensely?" he echoed.

"Because I know that you're the man who fought to save my father's life. I'd never forget that under any circumstances. I never could."

"That's kind of you, and generous of you too," said he. "But may I ask you, Kate, what it is that particularly has displeased you?"

"Otherwise you take it up before mother?" she demanded.

"The time has come when I must know where you stand," said he, "because I stand in danger of my life."

"I'll only say this," said the girl, "that if you stand in danger it's probably because people have a reason for threatening you."

"Your young friend Tom Fuller, for instance? What had I done to him?"

"Why—hunted him through the hills like a deer! Is that nothing?"

"Lawful posse, pursuing lawful quarry," said he, and smiled on her in a manner which Tom thought was peculiarly disagreeable. Then his smile disappeared, and he said briskly: "To brush aside the veils—you, my dear girl, believe that I married your mother for the sake of her money. That's the first count against me."

She raised her head higher; but she did not speak.

"The second count is that I am a mysterious criminal, Kate, performing crimes which you cannot tell. But no matter what they may be, one thing is certain: before morning comes, this phase of our life will be at an end. In the meantime, I ask you to remain neutral to the end,

239

to reserve judgment—and to keep silent! If you talk, I'll have to bring up my side of the case—or, rather, let me call it the side against you."

He turned his back on her without any further speech, and walked straight from the room, brushing through the curtain beside Tom.

41

AFTER CRISIS there should be a sharp reaction, but when he had left her, the girl did not blench, or fall into her chair. She remained as proudly erect as before, looking after her enemy as a man looks after a foe. And seeing her courage and her poise, Tom saw a golden door of chance opening before him to achieve even the impossible.

He stepped from behind the curtain and stood before her.

"Kate," he said in a whisper, "they're saying wild things about me, but I want to tell you that I'm not here to do harm to anybody. I only want to—"

She went past him. He almost thought that she was leaving the room without a word of answer to him, but at the cleft of the curtain she paused, parting it a little and looking down the hall.

She whispered to him:

"Henry Plank has gone wild. He's pacing up and down the house like a cat. Now, what is it?"

She was as direct as a man.

"I have something here for a woman Franchard says is in this house. There is a white scar on her cheek."

"My mother."

"Your mother?"

"Yes. What is there for her?"

"This."

He showed the packet.

She looked at it; she looked wildly up to the face of Tom.

"Is there any harm in it?"

"I don't know. I only know that Franchard said it was the key to unlock the house."

"You don't know—you don't know!" she repeated fiercely. "Are you still going to cling to that farce and pretend ignorance? Oh, Tom, what a little, useless creature you think I am!"

He wanted to speak, but the sight of her emotion overawed him.

"Give it to me, then," she said suddenly. "I don't care. I'll do what you tell me. I'll take it to her."

"I must take it to her myself," said he. "Where is she?"

She hesitated only a moment, her glance wavering from his face to the door on the farther side of the room. Then she nodded briefly to him and went across to it, while he followed at her shoulder.

He had a feeling as though eyes were looking from behind him, through the curtain, fixed upon the small of his back, and when he fought off this sensation, it was only to start with the apprehension of another door on the opposite wall falling open before him, and of other eyes staring at him from this.

It was the fear of Henry Plank, he knew. And though he had penetrated to the heart of the house, it still did not seem possible that he could win against such a man.

"My mother—you know about her?" said the girl, in a whisper, as they reached the door and her hand was on the knob.

"No."

241

"Be gentle. Whatever there is to say or to do, be gentle, Tom."

Then she tapped. A clear, small voice answered, and she at once pushed the door wide.

Tom, astonished by his own calmness, walked into the room, and found himself before a woman with a very pale, thin face; on one cheek was a white scar; and from her forehead, silvery hair was drawn back. Life in her seemed tenuous as a spider's thread; her wrists and her hands looked so extremely feeble and thin that it seemed wonderful she had been able to support the book she was reading. She lay in a big invalid's chair, stuffed out with pillows, here and there. Lowering her book, love flashed in her eyes as she looked at her daughter.

Kate went toward her quickly, saying: "This is Tom Fuller. I've told you a little bit about him!"

Upon Tom rested those weary, quiet eyes, and he knew that they were looking steadily through him, and finding his soul.

"This is my mother, Mrs. Plank," she finished the sentence.

"Are you that wild young Tom Fuller?" asked Mrs. Plank. "Are you that clever and daring young man who has been trying to reach this house so long? And now that you are here, what is it that you want, Tom Fuller? What dreadful thing are you now prepared to do?"

He could not speak. Her quiet, her perfect poise, tied his tongue. And he could only take the packet from his coat pocket and present it to her.

She glanced a bit askance at him, and then unwrapped the oiled silk which covered the packet. There was only one thin, long envelope within, and this she opened in turn and shook out one piece of paper, covered with large, sprawling writing.

At the sight of the handwriting, the frail hands of Mrs. Plank sank, and she looked in amazement at Tom. Then she studied the date line at the top of the page. Next, she was reading feverishly.

It was not a long letter. It was so brief that Tom

could hardly believe that so few words could have such an effect. For Mrs. Plank, scanning the page, turned deadly white and her head fell back.

"Kate," she muttered.

Her daughter instantly was beside her.

"Kate, read it!"

And Kate read aloud, in a faint, rapid voice:

"Dear Franchard: The style is too careful. You ought to make it more careless and ragged, especially toward the end. Remember, it's supposed to be from a man dying by inches, and toward the end of the rope. He wouldn't be apt to form his letters so very carefully, as I think you'll agree. I wish you would notice, too, that in the specimens I gave you he forms his 'e's' in two manners—one the ordinary form, and the other like a Greek 'e.' Please use that form, also. Little details, as you know, make up the mass effect. Your idea of having the last sentence say that he is going to recover is a master stroke. It even gave me a chill, when I read it!

Yours to the crack of doom.

Henry."

The letter fluttered from her hand and fell unregarded to the floor.

"I've guessed it!" said the girl fiercely. "I've always guessed it. He knew what Franchard was bringing; and he wanted to stop him for that reason. Mother, mother, it's true!"

Mrs. Plank looked fixedly at the ceiling.

Then she said: "If you and I were accused of some terrible thing, we would want to have a fair trial. Henry should have a fair trial, too!"

"How could you ask for a better one?" said the girl eagerly. "That's his handwriting. What could he be talking about, besides, other than the last letter of poor dad to you?"

Mrs. Plank stood up, and remained trembling, but tall and determined, beside her chair.

"I have to see this Franchard," said she to Tom.

243

"Where is he now? If you got into the house in some wonderful way, is he here also?"

"I came in alone," said Tom, filled with wonder. "Franchard is outside. He's close to the house, watching the front door, and waiting for it to be opened."

"Kate, run——. No, I'll go myself. If—if this is true, then anything is possible. They might shoot you down, and Franchard both. But they—"

"And you, mother? I can't let you go—"

"Kate," said Mrs. Plank, "if what we've read here is true, they're willing to murder again; but if they're driven against the wall, still, they won't strike at me. I mean too many dollars!"

Her composure was extraordinary. Her eyes flashed with the excitement, to be sure, but otherwise she seemed to be thoroughly in command of herself.

"I'll go by myself," said she. "Mine is the only safe life in this house, perhaps. Kate, come with me if you will."

She went straight out of her room, and down the hall, with Kate supporting her beneath one arm and Tom behind her. So they came to the front door, which Mrs. Plank with her own hand opened, and as it sagged wide, the lamplight from the hall shone boldly out among the shrubbery of the garden.

She walked straight out in the bright column of the light, and out of the brush before her rose Franchard, and came to her quickly.

It seemed to Tom like black magic. For, exactly as Franchard had prophesied, the packet had proved to be a key, and it had opened the door with ease!

Neither Franchard nor Mrs. Plank said a word as they met, and turned hastily back toward the house. And as they went, a squad of four men came running, guns in hand. The sight of Mrs. Plank stopped them at a little distance, however. They stood with charmed hands, as it were, and gaped at Tom and the other three who went by them, and back through the door of the house, and down the hall to Mrs. Plank's room.

There, Kate helped her mother back into the invalid's

244

chair, and she sat up in it, her lips tightly compressed and her eyes eager.

"You have something more to say?" said she. "You are willing to talk, Mr. Franchard?"

"I'm willing to talk," said Franchard. "Of course, I am. I've come all this distance to talk to you. But there's no great hurry. Wait one moment, and we'll have another person in the room."

"Who do you mean?"

"I mean, your husband."

"My husband? You want Henry Plank here?"

"I want to see him. I want to look into his face," said Franchard with unspeakable malice. "I want to see what effect I can have on him when I give my testimony. Otherwise, he might be able to talk down my evidence later on. Let him come in. And he surely will."

"Do you know," said Mrs. Plank, "that he's a man of a bad temper, at times, and might—"

"I know him," said Franchard, "better than anybody in the world could know him. I tell you, he'll be here in another moment. He's desperate, and he's done for, and he knows it. He knows that he's a beaten man, but still he'll keep on fighting. The money in it is worth a last fight, and that's the fight that he'll be prepared to make. Sit down, be quiet. Tom, make me a cigarette, will you? I need only a little patience, and then we'll have the whole charming story out!"

He laughed a little, and as he laughed his teeth set and locked. Never had Tom seen a look expressive of more perfect malice than that which gleamed in the eyes of Franchard now. And he knew that this was the thing for which the man was willing to pour out his life. This was the blow which he was to strike, to ruin the great Henry Plank!

At that moment, there was a light tap at the door, which instantly was opened from without and exactly as Franchard had prophesied, Plank appeared before them.

42

TOM, IN THE CORNER of the room farthest from the door, could watch every face, and he saw enough to amaze him; it was like a scene out of a fairy tale. There was Kate Lane, alert, beautiful, fairly burning with suspicion; there was her mother, white and determined, in spite of fear and of pain; there was Franchard, with venom in his eyes; and finally, there was the man upon whom all this attention was focused.

But Henry Plank did not quail. He came into that room to fight for a fortune—to fight for his very life—but he came with a smile on his brown, healthy face. To see him, as it were, was to believe him; and suddenly all doubts against him became dim in the mind of Tom. He could hardly assure himself that this was the very man who had hunted him through the hills.

"Mr. Franchard said that you would come, Henry," said his wife. "And here you are!"

She was cold as ice, staring at him, but he maintained his smile with a perfect resolution.

He carried himself with a pleasant composure and bluntness.

He went, first of all, to Franchard, and extended his hand.

"Well, well, old fellow!" said he. "Here you are, after all, and I wonder what sort of a cargo of lies you have to tell!"

Franchard smiled at the hand, and at the face of him who offered it, and that was all his answer.

Plank went straight on to Tom and held out his hand again.

"And this is the boy who brought him here, through so many difficulties," said he.

Tom, not knowing what else to do, accepted the clasp of that hand, which instantly folded upon his with incredible power. He had to set his teeth and clutch back with all his might to endure the pressure; and at the same time he could see the face of Henry Plank contorted with fury such as he had never dreamed a human being could display. For his back was now to the others and he could risk allowing his soul to show for the moment. And it occurred to Tom that, if he were mastered, even then Henry Plank might strike!

Mastered he was not. His heart swelled; his head lowered a little; and the might of his hand gradually gained upon that of his host.

They stood for a brief instant before one another; then suddenly the pressure ceased, and Henry Plank turned away.

"I'm going to answer you," said Franchard, "because I want this to last a pleasant length of time. I want you to have an opportunity to taste the trouble that's coming to you, Henry. So we may as well talk at large."

"Of course we may as well," said Plank. "Unless this tires you, dear?"

His wife made a brief gesture, and Franchard said: "Tell them your story, Plank. Tell the yarn, and then I'll tell mine!"

"I don't know what story you mean," said Plank. "Of course I can't tell what's running in a beautifully imaginative and capacious brain like yours, Franchard."

Franchard smiled again.

"I'll put your story for you, then. You, Plank, met in New York a beautiful woman, and decided that you'd marry her. She was already married. Therefore, you'd get rid of her husband. Her name was Harriet Lane!"

He looked at Mrs. Plank. She said nothing. She had no eyes except for the face of Franchard.

"She had beauty. She had wealth, too," said Franchard. "She was worth while from any direction."

"Do you want to hear any more of this, Harriet?" asked the great Plank.

She raised her hand. It was a sufficient answer; and Tom saw the muscles bulge at the base of Plank's jaw.

"You made yourself a friend of poor young Lane. You went into the Orient with him. You finally went out sailing with him in a little sloop, manned by one Hindu, Lane, and yourself.

"You took that little sloop out from Bombay, and when you returned, there was only one aboard, and that one was you! That's the fact."

"Those are the facts," said Mrs. Plank grimly.

"You returned with a cut over your head—I see that there's a streak of white hair growing from the place. You had a good story to tell of how the Hindu had tried to murder both you and Jim Lane. That he slashed you first and left you for dead, whereas you were simply stunned, instead of having your head split to the chin as he had intended. You gathered yourself together, and got forward in time to see him strike down Lane in the same manner. Then you shot him. You took care of Lane. He lived for nearly a day. During that time, he wrote a letter to his wife, describing how Henry Plank heroically had come between him and his assassin, and had tried to save his life. A very glowing letter, that. And, in fact, when the little sloop returned to Bombay, Henry Plank was treated as a person of importance.

"There was a little talk, Plank, about the fact that you had not brought the body back on the ship with you, but you explained that the murder took place while you were still four days from land; and on the third hot day, you were compelled to throw the body overboard! Otherwise, your skirts were clean, and no one suspected you.

"You went to England, where Mrs. Lane had gone with her little girl. She was glad to see you. You were polite, respectful, and adoring from a distance. You did not press yourself upon her. But you were simply about, at all times. And she, eventually, began to consider you more favorably.

"However, you weren't entirely sure of her, and, in the meantime, you were running short of funds. You went hurriedly back to New York, and there you met Franchard, the man who had forged for you the 'last letter' of poor young Lane. You worked Franchard for the robbery of the Farmers' and Merchants' Bank in Buffalo, many years ago; and while you walked off with the loot, Franchard was stuck and held for the job. You were merely holding his share of the loot until he should get out of prison, you swore. And while he was in prison you kept sending him little supplies of money, et cetera. Franchard thought you were a grand fellow, even if you were able to do a little murdering now and then. He trusted you to play fair with him, and the result was that, when he managed to escape from prison, he went to see you to get what was due him. You were glad to see him. You were so very glad that you managed to tell your friends the police, and they came for him.

"But Franchard got away. He went on your trail. It was a long trail. It took Franchard around and around the world, trying to locate you. But he enjoyed the run so much that he's almost sorry that it has come to an end. He had a snapshot of a section of the country which, he remembered in the old days, you said you loved and that there you wanted to settle down and make your home. So, finally, the thread was followed. I found Rankin, who showed us the way to you. I found Tom Fuller, who was able to break through your line. And here I have arrived at last with enough information to hang you for the death of Lane. And all the millions of Lane's widow will be used to hang you, Henry Plank!"

43

THIS LONG speech rather staggered Tom, but he managed to struggle through to the obvious conclusion. He fixed his eyes upon Plank, and saw that master-criminal wince—then laugh.

"The man's undoubtedly unbalanced, Harriet," said he.

And she held it up. He recognized his own writing in the distance—seemed to know at once what the contents were—and he went back on his heel, as though he had been struck in the face.

"My handwriting?" said Plank through his teeth. "But this fellow is a forger, my dear. A famous penman. Don't you understand that he could manufacture any evidence in the world?"

"There is no forger," answered Franchard, "whose work can fool an expert. This is no forgery, Henry. The forgery was the copy of this letter which you were so glad to see me burn that day in Bombay! As for this one, it can be tested by all the experts. They could soon hang you with this, Henry, and I think you know it. You never should have written it. But you were young in those days, poor Henry."

The quiet, savage joy in the voice of Franchard seemed to eat like an acid into Plank. He whirled upon his wife with an outstretched arm, as though he were about to make an eloquent appeal, but her face was white and stern.

Instantly, the man's manner changed.

He chuckled, shrugged his shoulders, and walked across the room to the door.

"Well, Franchard," he called over his shoulder, "it appears, after all, that you've taken the bait out of my trap; but you've put yourself into it, instead. Harriet, my poor dear, I've worked these long years in the hope of getting your money into my hands, and if the confounded trust had terminated yesterday instead of next month, I should have had it! Kate, you see that you were right about me. But remember, all four of you, that you're still in the hollow of my hand."

He opened the door.

"No, no!" exclaimed the girl in a gasping whisper.

And Tom understood.

Henry Plank must not be allowed to walk out of that room or, undoubtedly, he would have them in the hollow of his hand.

"Plank!" Tom shouted suddenly.

Plank jerked his head around with the puckered face of a wild cat. Then he leaped through the door and slammed it behind him.

Tom was in full motion, then. And the running drove the fear of Plank out of his heart. His gun was in his hand, and as he crossed the floor, hearing the turning of the key in the lock from the outside, he put two .45-caliber slugs of lead through the lock, smashing it to bits. Then the impact of his shoulder knocked the door wide, and he lurched straight into the hall.

There stood Henry Plank, revolver poised like a man at a target range. His left hand was behind his back. He looked like a duelist sure of himself, for there was a cruel smile on his lips.

And, fair and true, he sent the bullet home. No, at the last moment Tom had dodged, leaping high into the air to disconcert the aim of the marksman. He felt the jar, the hot tearing and the numbness, as the bullet tore through his left thigh. Then, with outstretched left hand he reached the quarry, and struck with clubbed revolver at Plank's head.

Plank had raised his own gun to parry the stroke, and so truly did his hand move, and so fast, that the descending wrist of Tom struck his weapon; from his unnerved fingers the Colt flicked out and rattled upon the floor.

Other things were happening with wonderful speed.

From the room Tom had just left, he heard the voice of Franchard, shouting advice. He heard a swift pattering of feet from the same direction, and he knew that it was dauntless Kate Lane coming to him.

Other footfalls were sweeping in toward him. He saw three men, shoulder to shoulder, charging up the hall toward him. And whatever was done, must be done in an instant.

"You rat of a half-wit," said Plank, tearing to get his armed hand free, "if you've managed to make fools of some of my men, do you think that you're man enough to put yourself beside Henry Plank?"

And he succeeded in that instant in wrenching his armed hand free, and turning the muzzle down toward Tom's head. There the boy's life hung on the most meager balance, but he saw slender hands flash past his shoulder, and Kate Lane jerked the gun aside. The bullet merely crashed against the wall.

One gesture of the powerful arm of Plank was enough to cast off the girl, staggering; but that instant had been enough for Tom. On one leg he could not support himself. It was his grip on Henry Plank that steadied him as he reached inside his coat and jerked out his second revolver. He saw Plank turn his Colt again for a third shot, but that bullet never was fired. A half-inch slug had sunk above the heart of Plank, and that famous man, throwing up his hand, staggered, whirled toward his three gangsters, who were charging forward to his rescue, and then fell on his face at their feet.

Tom, tottering on his one leg, had fallen also, and they paid him no heed. They turned their leader on his back.

"Dead!" Tom heard them shout, suddenly. "Dead,

"by Heavens! Let's get out of here. Plank's dead! It ain't possible!"

They rushed off down the hall. In the distance, their voices could be heard, shouting. There was a noise of slamming doors. Then the beating of the hoofs of many horses. Plank was dead; and like the dark work of a magician, his armies were vanishing with his fall!

In that same house, some ten days later, Tom sat up in bed on heaps of cushions and pillows, and he saw, delicately framed against the blue square of the window, the face of Harriet Lane. She had been watching him while he slept. Now she smiled at him. And he looked into her clear, deep eyes and wondered at her.

"The sheriff?" he said.

"The sheriff came this morning. He seemed to lose interest in arresting you, Tom. And I don't think that interest will ever return."

Tom drew a great breath of joy.

"But Franchard?" he asked nervously.

"The sheriff saw Franchard, too. But he could not take him. Franchard already had been taken, Tom, and you never will see him again."

"Dead?" asked Tom.

"There was no will in him to live, after he knew that Henry Plank was dead."

Tom looked past her head, and saw a bird soar upward, swiftly through the blueness and the sunshine.

And watching it, he murmured: "What I was talking about to you the other day—I mean about the truth about myself—I mean, about opening Kate's eyes. I guess you've talked to her?"

He waited, hands gripped hard.

"Ah, yes," said Harriet Lane. "I've talked to her, but I might as well have talked to a bird in the air. You'll have to try yourself. And here she comes now!"

They heard her singing in the garden, her song broken a little, as though she were half running as she came.

"I—I'll try to be honest," said Tom. "You'd better stay and listen."

"I don't think I need stay," said she. "I trust in Kate—and I trust in you."

He looked at her in amazement, and then he saw that she was smiling down at him, like a mother. She left the room. In the hall he could hear Kate Lane, panting and laughing. And far off in the blue of the sky the songbird was dissolving in a flash of sun and of melody.